THE SHANGHAI STRAIN

JC RYAN

VINCI
BOOKS

By JC Ryan

Rex Dalton K9 Thrillers

Dedicated to my good friend Mitch Pender, a military dog trainer, for giving me the idea for this series and guiding me through the intricate and amazing capabilities and psychology of those majestic four-legged soldiers.

Mitch has a lifetime of experience and an exceptional depth of knowledge as a military dog handler and trainer.

I am deeply indebted to my friend, co-author, co-conspirator, and mentor, David Lee, who, with his in-depth understanding of Hong Kong and China, came up with the idea for this novel and tirelessly assisted me in developing the outline and advising and supporting me throughout the entire writing process.

Vinci Books

vinci-books.com

Published by Vinci Books Ltd in 2025

1

Copyright © JC Ryan 2020

Foreword

The idea for this novel was born in early October 2019, almost three months before WHO (World Health Organization) reported about a mysterious type of pneumonia from an unknown source, sickening dozens of people in Wuhan, China. On January 30, 2020, for the sixth time in history, WHO declared a "public health emergency of international concern," a designation reserved for extraordinary events that threaten to spread internationally. On February 11, 2020, WHO renamed it from the novel coronavirus to COVID-19. CO for corona, Vi for virus, and D for disease.

At that time, I had completed the detailed plot outline, and for the next week or two, wrestled with the question of whether to shelve the book and start another, which is what I did. However, what is a mind if you can't change it? As time progressed, I found myself drawn back to this story more often than I wanted to be. Finally, I decided to complete the story for two reasons: One, I hated the idea of leaving the story untold. Two, I realized I could finish the story as originally conceived. In other words, I could write it as if the tragic events of the COVID-19 pandemic had not happened in the fictional world where my characters reside.

Admittedly, with the pandemic raging across the planet while I was writing this story, my thoughts had unintentionally been influenced by the dreadful, unfolding events that are impacting so many, causing immeasurable emotional and financial stress to millions, already killed hundreds of thousands and still counting.

I only wish that the COVID-19 pandemic had never happened and that my heroes were real so they could have helped to prevent it from ever happening.

Everything under heaven is in utter chaos; the situation is excellent.

—Mao Tse Tung

Major Characters

Rex Dalton: Former black operations specialist working for CRC.

Catia: Married to Rex. Former Mossad mission support specialist.

Digger: A black Dutch Shepherd. Former military dog. Rex and Catia's companion.

Josh Farley: Black operations specialist working for CRC. Friend of Rex, Catia, and Digger.

Marissa: Married to Josh. Black operations specialist working for CRC. Friend of Rex, Catia, and Digger.

John Brandt: CEO of CRC (Crisis Response Consultancy), a private military contractor specializing in black operations on behalf of their clients such as the CIA and other US security agencies.

Chris McArdle: Second in command of CRC.

Declan Spencer: John Brandt's best friend. Former Navy SEAL commander, now captain of the luxury yacht, the *TOMATS.*

Greg Wade: Team leader of CRC's small but highly skilled group of IT specialists.

Rehka Gyan: Rex's technology expert, virtual assistant, researcher, and friend. Greg's love interest.

Yaron Aderet: The head of the Mossad's largest department, Collections, tasked with all the many aspects of conducting espionage overseas.

Li Lingxin: President of the PRC (People's Republic of China).

Jethro Matz: A Hong Kong Jew and CEO of Matz Enterprises, the largest electricity supplier in Hong Kong.

Tamara Matz: Jethro's sister and co-CEO of Matz Enterprises.

Tao Meng: Jethro's personal assistant.

Ramesh Ojha: Jethro's head of security. Nepalese, a former Gurkha.

David Sarlin: A Hong Kong Jew and CEO of HK Securities. A close friend of Jethro and Tamara.

Dora (Sarlin) Frankel: David's sister and close friend of

Tamara and Jethro. Married to Robert Frankel, living in California.

Benjamin Yatsir: A Hong Kong Jew, Dora, and Tamara's friend from school. A very successful medical microbiologist and virologist.

Howard Lawrence: Director of the CIA.

Martin Richardson: Deputy director in charge of CIA operations

Dr. Zheng Xuefeng: The CEO of Zexian Biomed, a biotech company located in Shanghai, China, Benjamin Yatsir's boss, and friend.

Dong Yan: Chinese industrialist and dissident.

General Dai Min: A senior general in the PLA (People's Liberation Army) in charge of China's nuclear arsenal. Board member of Matz Enterprises nuclear power station ninety miles northeast of Hong Kong sole supplier of electricity to several of South China's mega industrial plants.

Dr. Abiram Sharot: Chinese Jew and physician at East Shanghai Private Hospital, ESPH.

General Yuan Lee: A senior general in the PLA (People's Liberation Army) in charge of China's Bioweapons Program.

TOMATS: The luxury yacht the name derived from the first letters of Ernest Hemingway's classic short novel, The Old Man and the Sea.

SYO, Sun Yee On: Chinese triad (mafia) group operating out of Hong Kong.

About The Shanghai Strain

An idyllic holiday turns into a race against time to stop a diabolic plot.

Rex, Catia, Digger, and their friends, Josh and Marissa, are on holiday in Hong Kong. The nature scenes are breathtaking, the people enlivening, and the shopping exhilarating.

That is until Catia, Marissa, and Digger go shopping at Stanley Market. Two ladies are attacked by members of the triad group, Sun Yee On. Seeing it happen right before their eyes, without hesitation, Catia, Marissa, and Digger jump into action and rescue the women.

Thus, their blissful holiday comes to a violent end, and they become the targets of the Chinese government who wants them dead to prevent the uncovering of the diabolic scheme of the President of China to get control of the world.

Chapter One

A CHANCE MEETING

Shanghai, China

Day 1

It was Dora Frankel's chance meeting with her old school friend at Shanghai Pudong International Airport that unwittingly triggered the chain of the events that would rouse Rex Dalton, his wife, Catia, and their military dog, Digger, from their brief retirement from the world of covert operations.

Dora arrived at the airport on time to check in and had an hour or so spare for shopping before flying to her friends and family in Hong Kong where she grew up. She didn't live in Hong Kong anymore; she met her knight in shining armor, Robert Frankel, while doing modeling work in California and married him. That's where she lived now.

Dora was a head-turner; she had been all her life. She was a tall and elegant sixty-five-year-old, with beautiful, wrinkle-free skin and a toned body that was the envy of women forty years younger. Her face was one romance writers studied when they described their heroine. In her younger days, she was one of Hong Kong's top models, so popular that when she wore an outfit to a public event, the next day, top clothing stores would have the same outfit on their shelves and sell it out in hours.

She was about to enter a fashion store when she heard a man's voice behind her. "Dora? Is it you?" Turning, she smiled. "Benjamin! What a pleasant surprise . . ." She hesitated; there was no mistake. The man *was* Benjamin Yatsir, her old friend from school, but he looked disheveled, stressed, withered. "How are you?"

"I'm well. How about you?"

A few minutes later, when the pleasantries were out of the way, Benjamin told her he had just arrived on a flight from Beijing and that he had time for lunch before having to return to the lab where he worked. Benjamin grew up in Hong Kong and had attended the same school as Dora.

With their lunch orders in front of them and the server out of the way, Dora leaned forward toward Benjamin and said, "Ben, excuse me, but you don't look well. When I saw you a year ago you looked well, but now . . . you look troubled . . . anxious, and you've lost weight. What's going on?"

"Ah, just work stress, the usual. There's so much going on, and I'm struggling to keep up. Maybe it's the age thing sneaking up on me."

"Ben, you've never been a good liar. I know you better than your siblings. Out with it."

It took a few more rounds before Benjamin relented. "I didn't lie when I said it's about my work."

"What about your work, Ben?"

"As you know, it was your brother who got me appointed

as the lead researcher at Zexian Biomed, for which I'll be eternally grateful but . . . there is a problem. I suspect a big one."

"What is it, Ben? Is there something you want me to talk to David about?"

"Yes, there is, but let me tell you what it is first." Ben smiled wryly.

"Sorry, I'm worried about you."

"We study zoonotic viruses, viruses that are transmitted between animals and humans, and then human-to-human. And we have made significant progress and some major breakthroughs. In other words, on that front, things are, or rather, were going well. Then two months ago, three officials working for the MSS turned up at Zexian Biomed and called Dr. Zheng Xuefeng and me into a private meeting."

The MSS was the Ministry of State Security, China's intelligence, security, and secret police agency responsible for counterintelligence, foreign intelligence, and political security. They have been described as one of the most secretive and brutal intelligence organizations in the world.

Dora raised her eyebrows inquisitively when Ben paused.

"Well, they ordered us to stop all research projects we were working on to concentrate all our efforts on the study of a new pathogen, a virus, which they gave to us in vials. They didn't tell us where the pathogen came from, only that it was Zexian Biomed's job to sequence its genome. To find out how it would spread, through bodily fluids, through the air, physical contact, etcetera. Also, they wanted to know about the gestation period and what impact it would have on the human body. And most important of all, they want us to find a cure and vaccination for it."

"Without knowing where and how it originated? That sounds irrational."

"Totally. And add to that, we were given no access to humans who'd been infected by the virus. They told us that the virus was contained, no one had been infected. That was a big lie. But I'll get to that soon.

"The next thing they did was order us to call every staff member into the staffroom where officials told them that they were a 'privileged' group who had been selected to work on a very prestigious but very top-secret project for their country in the interests of national security. Everyone then had to fill out and sign a form pledging us to absolute secrecy. The document was very specific about the dire consequences of discussing any of what we were doing at the lab with anyone outside our workplace as I'm doing now.

"Dr. Zheng has been ordered to ensure that all our research is meticulously documented and uploaded to a secured server every day. We're not allowed to make copies of the data or any document created by us, neither are we allowed to print anything."

"Draconian," Dora murmured.

"Absolutely. Especially the fact that we've come to realize they've placed all of us under surveillance."

"You mean as in being followed?"

"I don't know about being followed, but our telephones and mobile phones, work, and personal are all tapped. Our internet activities are being monitored, work and personal."

"Why?"

"I think I know. You see, when we compared the genome of this virus with the known viruses that are harmful to humans, we found signs of gene splicing. In other words, gene sequences of other viruses have been inserted into this new virus, which we call the Shanghai Strain."

"What does that mean?"

"It means, Dora, that this virus is manmade. It's not something that happens naturally—it is a lab-engineered virus."

"Oh my God!"

"The thing is, China may be engaging in biological activities with the dual-use application. In other words, in this case, they've engineered a virus that can potentially be weaponized. And that is a violation of the terms of the international Biological Weapons Convention (BWC), of which China is a member."

"We've got to stop it, Ben."

"Yes, we have to . . . if it's not too late already."

"What do you mean?"

"Well, there are no restrictions on the staff to talk to each other, and that's how we became aware of a new virus that's causing havoc in parts of the city. At first, the staff was mentioning about people that they've heard of that contracted the flu and a week or so later died. Then the stories became closer to home as people they knew became ill and died. Within a few weeks, this small group of about thirty people knew about more than one hundred deaths from this new flu.

"Within a few more weeks, stories were doing the rounds in the lab that the funeral homes in some regions of Shanghai were working overtime; smoke spewing out of their chimneys nonstop, day in and day out.

"We believe this virus we've been given to study is the one that's causing this new flu."

"But there's nothing in the news."

Benjamin grinned. "Are you surprised?"

Dora shook her head. "No, I guess not. Over the ages, China has earned its moniker as the land of the lie."

Benjamin continued and told her that one morning when on his bicycle on his way to work, he passed by one of the larger funeral homes and saw hundreds of people waiting in line. So, he stopped and asked the people what they were in the queue for, and several answered that they were all waiting to collect the cremated remains of their loved ones. He saw a few walking away with a ceramic urn and also a few walking away without any urn. He then found out from the emptyhanded ones that the funeral home couldn't cremate the bodies fast enough; there was a waiting list of two to three days.

Back at the lab, a day or so later, one of his co-workers said she saw several delivery trucks waiting on a side street that led to the backside of this funeral home. Her curiosity took over, and she asked one of the truck drivers what they were doing. The answer was they were delivering ceramic urns, and for the past few days, they had delivered a thousand urns a day to funeral homes in Shanghai.

"Ben, why has David not been told about this? After all, he is one of the directors."

"I told you, we're under orders not to talk to anyone on the outside. Dr. Zheng is being forced to send false reports to the board of directors. For the last two months, every report to them was false."

"Oh my God!"

Just then, Dora's flight was called. For a moment, Dora contemplated ignoring it, but then Benjamin stood and said he would accompany her to the departure gate.

At the gate, she kissed him on the cheek and said, "I'll tell David the moment I set foot in Hong Kong. In the meantime, please take care of yourself and send my regards to Sally."

"I will. Have a safe trip."

Dora went through the check-in, and when she turned to wave at Benjamin, an ice-cold shiver ran down her spine when she saw two men in dark suits approaching him from behind. He couldn't see them, not yet. She waved, and he waved back.

She turned and proceeded to board the plane, and when she looked back for the last time, she saw Benjamin being led away by the men in dark suits. She had no way of knowing who they were, but, in the light of what Benjamin had just told her, she suspected they worked for the dreaded MSS and that her friend was in serious trouble.

Chapter Two

THE SEVEN SEAS

Rome, Italy

42 Days Ago

It all started one night over dinner at CiPASSO Vineria-Bistrot, a charming little bistro in Via dell'Orso on the bank of the Tiber in Rome, Italy. Rex, Catia, and Digger were with Declan Spencer and his girlfriend, Simona Bellucci, and Spencer was telling them about the origins of the phrase "the Seven Seas."

Declan Spencer was a retired Navy SEAL Commander living his dream of captaining his own yacht and sailing the world. The *TOMATS* was not his yacht, but he was her captain for life. The yacht's name derived from the first letters of Ernest Hemingway's short novel *The Old Man and the Sea—TOMATS*. She was a luxury superyacht. Two-hundred and seventy feet of it, three-quarters the length of a football field, and thirty-seven feet wide. A masterpiece, custom-designed and built by some of the world's leading exterior and interior designers.

"The phrase 'Seven Seas' goes back to ancient times. Different cultures at different times in history defined their own Seven Seas to refer to the bodies of water along their trade routes, regional bodies of water, or exotic and faraway bodies of water," Spencer explained. "The Greeks' Seven Seas were the Aegean, Adriatic, Mediterranean, Black, Red, and Caspian Seas, and the Persian Gulf. To the Medieval Europeans, it was the North Sea, Baltic, Atlantic, Mediterranean, Black, Red, and Arabian Seas. When North America was discovered, the mariners' started referring to the Seven Seas as the Arctic, the Atlantic, the Indian, the Pacific, the Mediterranean, the Caribbean, and the Gulf of Mexico."

Rex smiled. "Declan, I've often heard you talk about your desire to sail the Seven Seas. So far, since you became the captain of the *TOMATS*, you've only sailed the Aegean, Adriatic, and Mediterranean. You're four short. Which seas are we sailing next?"

Rex, Catia, and Digger had permanent residence on the *TOMATS* in terms of an agreement with her owner, John Brandt, of Crisis Response Consultancy, CRC, a private military contractor specializing in black operations on behalf of their clients, such as the CIA and other US Security Agencies. CRC was Rex's former employer. Their other residence, when not on the *TOMATS*, was Catia's apartment in Rome, close to the Piazza di Spagna at the bottom of the famous Spanish Steps.

"The Red Sea, Arabian Sea, Indian Ocean, and the South China Sea in that order."

Catia laughed and raised her glass in a toast. "Hong Kong, here we come!"

They all clinked their glasses and shouted, *"Buon viaggio!"* Italian for bon voyage.

The three-deck *TOMATS* was equipped for ocean travel with ultra-modern stabilization technology, advanced communications equipment, a helipad, and every nod to comfort that one could think of. It had a range of six thousand nautical miles, a top speed of seventeen knots, and a cruising speed of fifteen. It was powered by two Caterpillar diesel engines producing close to five thousand horsepower.

Apart from the comfortable lodgings for the crew members, there were accommodations for fourteen guests in seven plush staterooms. There was a hot tub, sauna, Turkish bath, infinity pool, gym, dining room, and several lounges. One of the lounges had been repurposed to house the sophisticated electronics gear and computer equipment that could be concealed when necessary. Another was turned into a secured communications room. Inside the latter was, among others, an impenetrable encrypted satellite video system and the latest communications technology.

From Rome to Hong Kong

36 Days Ago

A week later, the *TOMATS* was stocked, fueled up, and lifted anchor from the Port of Civitavecchia, Rome, Italy. Setting out on a journey of more than eight thousand nautical miles that took them through the Suez Canal, the Red Sea, the Gulf of Aden past the Horn of Africa, across the Bay of

Bengal, past the Andaman Islands, through the Malacca Strait, past Malaysia, on to Singapore.

In Singapore, Rex and Catia's best friends and former colleagues at CRC, Josh and Marissa Farley joined them before they set out on the last leg of their voyage to the South China Sea and Hong Kong 1,460 nautical miles, four days' sailing away.

It was the longest time Rex, Catia, and Digger had ever been on the *TOMATS* uninterrupted. And it was the same for the crew members. There were two chefs, six Navy SEALS, four of them with wives or girlfriends and two single, four Delta Force guys, two with wives and two single, plus Spencer and his first mate. Rex, Catia, and Digger, like Spencer, were permanent residents. The idea of having Special Forces operators as the crew was Spencer's. When John Brandt asked him to come up with an idea of how the yacht could be put to good use, he contacted a few US Special Forces commanding officers, former colleagues, and told them about the exceptional holiday deal for Special Forces operators where they could spend some of their R&R on a luxury yacht, free of charge, food and accommodations included.

It was a winner. Spencer had a long waiting list of very keen operatives who wanted to spend time on a luxury yacht, even if it meant they had to attend to menial chores. The fact that they could bring a wife or girlfriend with them as long as they performed crew duties made it even more appealing. Even the chefs were military personnel. Since the launch of the *TOMATS* more than two years ago, the yacht had served as CRC's mobile mission control center for two covert missions conducted on behalf of the CIA.

Thirty-one days after leaving Rome, the *TOMATS*

lowered her anchor at the Lantau Yacht Club in Discovery Bay, Hong Kong.

Discovery Bay was an upmarket residential area of six hundred forty-nine hectares located on Lantau Island, close to Hong Kong's Disneyland and International Airport. The area was comprised of garden houses, high-rise residential buildings, a twenty-seven-hole golf course, a two-hundred-sixty-two-berth marina, two clubhouses, the first private, manmade beach in Hong Kong, international schools, two shopping malls, and the largest oceanfront alfresco dining area in Hong Kong. The area had a little over twenty thousand residents, about fifty percent of whom were expatriates from more than fifty different countries.

Automobiles were not allowed on the island except by special permission. There was an electric bus system in operation every day from six a.m. to midnight. There were no bus stops; one simply waved down a bus driving by and never had to wait more than five minutes.

The island was very pet-friendly. Digger loved it there because of the pristine beaches where he could go swimming with his pack, Rex, Catia, Josh, and Marissa. And, of course, the adults and kids loved him. Maybe it was because he was so shrewd at begging for their ice cream, which they gave him, despite Rex's failing objections.

Language was not a problem; everyone spoke at least English and Cantonese. Rex spoke both.

Chapter Three

SHOPPING AT STANLEY MARKET

Stanley, Hong Kong

Day 5

On the fourth day after their arrival, Catia and Marissa told Rex and Josh they wanted to go shopping at Stanley Market the next day. It was a street market in Stanley on the south coast of Hong Kong Island. In the old days, Stanley used to be a tiny fishing village. Although it still had its piers for the fishermen to dock where they could sell each day's catch, the erstwhile village was now a bustling place covered with skyscrapers and luxurious condos.

The ads and brochures said Stanley Market was one of the must-go places when in Hong Kong, promising visitors to find an exciting array of shops selling silk garments, sportswear, art, Chinese costume jewelry, and souvenirs.

Some online commentators tactfully called it a "bit

touristy"; some were more forthright and called it a "tourist trap," but most called it a "shopper's paradise."

Catia and Marissa didn't care what it was called; they had been mesmerized by the ads and brochures and wanted to see and experience it for themselves and make up their own minds.

Rex and Josh looked at the ads presented by Catia and Marissa and paid particular attention to the part that said, "Set over just two streets, it doesn't take more than an hour or less than two to get around the market," and they sighed. Neither Catia nor Marissa was a prolific shopper, but they were inexhaustible browsers. They asked if their spouses would be terribly disappointed not to accompany them on this shopping mission. They said they would welcome the opportunity to do hassle-free shopping and not be pushed along from one shop to the other.

At nine a.m. the next morning, outside the entrance to the market, Rex told Digger, "Hey buddy, I want you to take good care of Catia and Marissa. Don't try and hurry them; they'll get upset." Digger looked excited. He had a big dog smile on his face, and his tail was wagging incessantly when Rex handed the leash to Catia.

Rex and Josh hugged and kissed their wives and told them to take their time and enjoy themselves while they went on a beer-tasting mission, trying out the local craft beers, highly publicized in ads and brochures Josh and Rex had been collecting. The beers were apparently produced by small breweries that had become very popular over the past few years. Online, there were only positive comments about the brews.

"Call us when you're done. We'll stop drinking immediately to come and help you carry the loot," Josh said with a grin on his face.

Stanley Market, Hong Kong

DAY 5

About an hour later, Catia and Marissa were in a linen shop browsing. It was crowded, like every shop in the market.

The buzz in the shop went quiet when two graceful ladies, probably in their early sixties, entered. They were dressed in traditional body-hugging cheongsam dresses, one of them in green and the other in red. By the reaction of the shopkeeper and clients, there could be no mistake; the two ladies were of eminence.

"Nothing like rubbing shoulders with royalty while out shopping." Marissa smiled as she whispered to Catia.

"You know who they are?"

"No, but the one in the red dress looks familiar."

They returned to their browsing.

A minute or so later, they noticed two men dressed in dark suits wearing sunglasses and white, open-neck shirts, displaying part of the tattoos covering their chests and necks, entering the shop. They were rudely pushing their way through the people; one of them brushed past Catia, Marissa, and Digger.

Digger growled when the man came too close. Fortunately, the man didn't do something stupid such as kicking at Digger. He kept on moving, pushing, and shoving people out of his way as he went.

Catia looked down and saw Digger's hair standing on end. She assumed Digger didn't like that the man got too close to them. She said, "It's okay, Digger," scratched his head a few times, turned back, and looked at the piece of cloth Marissa was interested in.

She and Marissa were about three steps away from the two ladies who caught their attention earlier and were now looking at a Chinese embroidered tablecloth.

Catia heard Digger growling again and looked down. Then, out of the corner of her eye, she saw the lady in red spin around. One of the men who came in earlier was pointing a gun with a silencer at her. The man said something to her while waving his gun, gesturing that he wanted her to move in the direction of the door.

Without hesitation, Catia moved toward them.

The woman in red was furious. She swiped her arm to brush the gun away, but in the tussle, the man pulled the trigger. The shot missed her and hit her companion, the woman in green, in the neck.

By now, Catia was within striking distance and kicked the gun out of the man's hand. He stumbled while trying to get away from her and fell on his back. The second man started moving in and drew his gun. Digger jumped, grabbed his gun hand, and pulled him to the ground. The man yelled out in pain, but he held onto his silenced pistol. A shot went off and struck one of the shoppers, a young woman, in the lower leg. The man kicked at Digger, but he deftly jumped out of the way, growling and barking.

People started screaming, and then everyone rushed to the door to get out.

In the chaos, both attackers jumped up and ran for the door, the first attacker leaving his gun behind. Marissa lurched forward, picked the gun up from the floor, and shouted at both men to stop. They didn't; they smashed into people, yelling and screaming at them to get out of their way. The second attacker spun around and started raising his gun toward Marissa. She knew if she shot at him at the current angle, she could hit innocent bystanders. She dropped to her knee and fired in an upward trajectory. The bullet hit the man between the eyes, exiting the back of his head and lodged high up in the wall without hitting anyone else. He dropped to the floor.

The other man made it through the door. Catia pulled the quick release strap on Digger's leash and shouted, "Get him!"

The man progressed about ten yards down the alley before Digger took him down. He was screaming and shouting in Cantonese, probably profanities. Catia arrived and kicked him in the face, and he went limp.

"You can stand down, Digger."

Digger let go and stood back immediately.

Before Catia could pay attention to the unconscious man, the first wave of what would eventually become a crowd arrived. Pushing her out of the way, they started kicking and punching the man.

She took a few steps back and decided it was better to get away from them. She said to Digger, "Let's check on Marissa," turned and ran back to the shop with Digger next to her.

As Catia entered the shop, which was now almost empty, she saw Marissa standing next to the man she had shot. She had her phone in her left hand talking to Josh while holding the gun in her right hand, ready to shoot anyone stupid enough to attack.

The young lady who got shot in the leg was sitting on the floor, holding her left lower leg and whining in pain. The shop owner was with her trying to comfort her.

The lady in green was resting on the lap of the one in red. The latter was quietly weeping, a panic-stricken look on her face. Her friend was alive but bleeding profusely. There was blood all over them and the floor.

Catia made a quick examination of the wound and saw that the bullet had nicked a carotid artery in her neck. It was a serious wound; this woman was going to bleed to death unless Catia did something to stop it and quickly if it were not too late already.

Catia apologized, pushed the lady in red away unceremoniously, and said, "She's going to die if I don't stop the bleeding right now." Catia knew both carotids supplied blood circulation to the brain, and if she blocked one of them, the brain would still get enough blood. She immediately applied direct pressure to the artery with her bare fingers and over her shoulder called for Marissa to get her a clean cloth.

Marissa ripped a tablecloth hanging off the hook on the wall and handed it to her. Catia pressed it onto the woman's neck. She would need to hold it in place until the paramedics arrived.

She dropped her head to the woman's neck and listened for a high-pitched, whistling sound as the woman breathed. Such a sound would've meant that her trachea was damaged. Catia was relieved to hear no such sound, and said, "She should be okay now. Hopefully, she hasn't lost too much blood already."

The wounded woman was quiet, her eyes were open, but she was too shocked and weak to say anything and probably on the verge of losing consciousness.

Catia looked at the lady in red and said, "Do you speak English?"

She was shaking and sobbing but nodded.

Marissa stepped closer and put her arm around the woman's shoulders for comfort.

Digger sat next to Catia, making soft consoling noises to calm them all.

Catia said, "We've stopped the bleeding. Your friend will be okay now. The paramedics will be able to help her much better than I can. I trust they'll be here soon."

The woman nodded and said, "Th—thank . . . thank you. You've . . . you . . . and your friend . . . and . . . and the dog . . . you've . . . you've saved our lives. We . . . how . . . how can we ever . . ."

"Shh, don't worry," Marissa said softly. "Everything is going to be fine."

The woman threw her arms around Marissa and started crying again.

When she stopped, Marissa introduced, "My name is Marissa Farley, and she is Catia Dalton. The dog is Digger."

Digger looked at the woman and smiled.

"I . . . ah . . . my . . . I am Dora Frankel. She . . . is . . . my friend . . . best friend . . . ah . . . she is Tamara Matz."

Marissa frowned; both looked distinctly Chinese, but their names were not.

"Dora, do you know who those men were?" Catia asked.

Dora started shaking her head, then stopped and said, "Triad, Chinese Mafia, I think . . . I'm almost sure. The tattoos . . ."

Tamara stirred. Catia told her to try and relax, that she was going to be okay and that the paramedics would be there soon.

Rex and Josh arrived with the sirens of the police vehicles and ambulances.

Chapter Four

Stanley Market, Hong Kong

Day 5

Within minutes, the police cordoned off the market, and the paramedics arrived at the shop with their foldable gurneys and equipment. In short order, they took charge of the two wounded shoppers, and in less than five minutes, they rolled Tamara Matz, and the young lady with the leg wound out on the gurneys to the waiting ambulances.

The man Digger and Catia took down was dead, beaten to a pulp by the crowd outside. Catia and Marissa were perplexed as to why the crowd had descended on the man and killed him in such a brutal fashion when he was already unconscious. All they had to do was to tie him up and hand him over to the police.

"Maybe they have a serious gripe with the triad types," Rex said.

More police arrived, and soon they started questioning and filtering the people into two groups — those who saw what happened and those who hadn't. The names and addresses of the latter were taken, and they were sent home. They took statements from the remaining group.

The senior officer and two of his men were in the shop where it started questioning Dora, Catia, and Marissa. Rex, Josh, and Digger remained in the shop but stood a few paces away, not interfering with the police while listening to what was said.

Dora was in such a state of shock it was impossible to get a coherent statement out of her. Eventually, the police had no choice but to ask the paramedics to give her a mild sedative. They helped her to a chair and turned their attention to Catia and Marissa.

Catia and Marissa were not exactly unperturbed, but they had much better control of their emotions and told the police what happened.

The officer questioning Marissa asked her, "Did he threaten you? Why did you shoot him? Was there another option? Why didn't you shoot him in the leg or arm? Why didn't you just fire a shot over his head?"

But Marissa was trained in interrogation techniques. She kept to her story and told him she had no time to think about it and no other choice; the man was going to shoot her. She acted in self-defense.

Josh and Rex were getting worried that Marissa might be in trouble. But soon, some of the eyewitnesses who were interviewed confirmed what she said—she had no choice, the man was raising his gun to shoot her, and she shot him in self-defense.

The one thing that was clear as daylight to Rex and Josh

was that the attack was aimed at Dora, not Tamara. But it was mystifying that no one mentioned it.

By the time they'd finished their statements, the Hong Kong Commissioner of Police had arrived on the scene.

"Those ladies must be of high prominence to warrant the personal attention of the Commissioner of Police," Rex remarked to Josh, who nodded his agreement.

The chief investigator onsite briefed the commissioner about what had happened and then introduced him to the Daltons and Farleys. The commissioner thanked them for what they did and assured them the police and people of Hong Kong would be eternally grateful to them.

He asked them, "Do you know who those women are?"

"Dora told us her surname is Frankel, and her friend is Tamara Matz," Catia replied. "We got the impression that they might be of some standing, but that's only a guess."

The commissioner smiled and agreed, "Indeed, of some standing as you've said. Let me give you a bit of background. Those ladies are members of two of the wealthiest and most influential families in Hong Kong. They're members of the Hong Kong elite, respected and loved by all. Their families are prominent philanthropists, helping not only people in Hong Kong but also in mainland China and other parts of Asia.

"Tamara is the sister of Jethro Matz, the richest man in Hong Kong, and one of the richest men in the world. They live on their own private island. It's called Matz Island. Matz Enterprises is the biggest player in the energy industry in these parts of the world. Tamara is the co-CEO of Matz Enterprises with her brother, Jethro. She never married.

"Dora Frankel, born Sarlin, is the sister of David Sarlin, CEO of HK Securities. He is big in the financial industry, banks, investments, insurance, and such. Not as rich as the

Matz family, but not too far behind. Dora lives in California."

"Ah, now I know why Dora looked familiar," Marissa said.

Rex asked, "Commissioner, do you or your officers have any idea who the assailants were and why they would want to attack the women?"

The commissioner shrugged and said, "It's too early to say for sure. The men were in all likelihood members of the Triad, Chinese Mafia. We suspect they were members of Sun Yee On, the most prominent Triad group in Hong Kong. As to why they wanted to harm the women, we don't know yet, but I intend to find out very soon."

Rex couldn't help but grin. The name Sun Yee On translated roughly to New Righteousness and Peace. What they did here today was neither righteous nor peaceful.

The commissioner then asked them where they were from and what they were doing in Hong Kong. Rex was the spokesman for them, and although he was friendly and respectful all the time, and the commissioner had been amicable, he kept his answers short and vague without being rude. He didn't trust the commissioner; Hong Kong was, after all, an administrative region of the People's Republic of China, and he was sure the man took his orders from Beijing.

When they were allowed to go, the commissioner said he would take Dora to her brother's home in his official vehicle and promised he would get in touch with them, wanting to take them out for dinner as a token of his appreciation.

On the way back to Discovery Bay, Josh couldn't let the opportunity pass to have a crack at Marissa and Catia as he looked at Rex and feigned a sigh. "Our women, we can't leave them alone for an hour and they go shooting and kicking people."

Rex laughed. "And I thought Digger would keep them calm and relaxed."

Digger let out a short yelp.

Catia looked at Digger and questioned, "And what exactly does that mean?"

Digger's tongue lolled out in a big smile, but he made no reply.

Rex said, "I think he said, 'I tried, but they wouldn't listen.'"

Catia and Marissa smiled but only a little.

It was after two p.m. when they were back on the *TOMATS* at Lantau Yacht Marina in Discovery Bay.

Chapter Five

Discovery Bay, Hong Kong

Day 5

At around four p.m., a black Mercedes Benz SUV pulled up on the pier next to the *TOMATS*. A man in a dark suit, white silk shirt, and red tie got out of the back and approached.

Declan Spencer went out to meet him. After a short conversation, Spencer invited him on board, introduced him to the Daltons and Farleys, and told them this man was the personal assistant of Jethro Matz, Tao Meng, and he was there to talk to them.

They took him to one of the lounges where he told them that his employer had sent him to invite them, the Daltons and Farleys, and Digger, of course, to join him and his wife and friends for dinner at his house on his private island at eight p.m. "It would be a great honor for Mr. Matz if you would be so kind as to accept. He would send his helicopter to pick you up from here and bring you back afterward."

"But we don't have clothes to wear for such a fancy occasion," Catia protested.

Tao laughed and said, "Nothing to worry about, Mrs. Dalton. It's going to be an informal occasion, just the five of you and the Matz and Sarlin families. Please don't give it another thought. You can come as you are now."

They accepted. After all, when would they ever get the chance again to see Hong Kong by night from a helicopter? Not to mention socializing with some of the wealthiest people in the world.

Matz Island, Hong Kong

Day 5

Matz Island was not big, maybe forty hectares, but it was spectacular. The house and outbuildings were palatial—high-security fences and guards, a runway for private jets, and a helicopter pad. Jethro's high-speed, eight-passenger Airbus H155 helicopter that they were traveling in could reach Hong Kong's financial district in less than thirty minutes, where Matz Enterprises headquarters was in the penthouse of the tallest building in Hong Kong. There was a helicopter landing pad on the rooftop.

Jethro Matz and his wife, Liu, were there to meet them, and so was David Sarlin and his wife, Ren, and his sister, Dora. They were all dressed informally in jeans, T-shirts, and matching jackets. The adage "first impressions last" would prove to be accurate. The Matz and Sarlin families were sociable people and genuinely grateful for what Catia and Marissa did.

It was immediately apparent that Dora was in much better shape than earlier in the day.

After the introductions and greetings, which included Digger's usual antics of extending his paw to be shaken when he was introduced to new people he liked, Dora told them Tamara was doing well. The surgeons had operated on her, given her a blood transfusion, and she was out of danger. There was no brain damage, and if there were no complications, she would be able to get out of the hospital in four to five days. She mentioned again that she and Tamara had their lives thanks to Catia and Marissa's selfless actions.

Over dinner, in which Digger was served a variety of meats and treats in a bowl placed on the floor next to Rex's chair, the conversation soon turned to the family history of the Matzs and Sarlins. They were Jews, and that answered Marissa's question about their names she had earlier in the day.

The hosts were delighted to hear that Catia was Jewish and immediately wanted to know more about her family history. She told them that her family had been living in Rome for more than four hundred years. And with a bit of prompting from Rex, she told them about her masters and PhD studies and the recovery of the Jewish libraries that the Nazis had stolen during the Second World War. They were listening to her with their mouths hanging open. Catia was careful not to divulge the exact information about the mission they had to launch to get the libraries back. Even so, they cheered her when she finished her telling.

It was the Matzs and Sarlins turn to tell about their history and the history of Jews in China and Hong Kong. It was fascinating.

Originally the Matz and Sarlin families migrated from Baghdad, Iraq to India. In the early 1800s, they settled in Shanghai, China, from where they moved to Hong Kong when it was ceded to Great Britain by China in 1842. They transferred their offices from Shanghai and helped to develop this new port.

These days, the Jewish community of Hong Kong numbered about five thousand. They were a close-knit and dynamic community and strongly tied to Israel. Although there were only a handful of Jewish families in Hong Kong in the mid-19th century, they enjoyed enormous success, and several became fabulously wealthy. Like the Matz and Sarlin families, Jethro told them without a hint of arrogance.

"The Jewish community in Hong Kong is diverse. We have Jews from Europe, the Americas, the Middle East, Asia, and Africa. There's also great diversity in how we practice Judaism. At the one end of the spectrum, some are entirely secular, and on the other end are those who adhere to Orthodox streams of Judaism. I know in America and other places, Jews from different denominations of Judaism tend not to mix. But here in Hong Kong, we all share one school and one community space, the Jewish Community Centre, adjacent to the Ohel Leah Synagogue. This type of pluralism is very unusual, and it makes us all proud to be part of this community," David said.

Dora and Tamara went to school together, and Jethro was smiling when he told them that in their young days, he had a crush on Dora.

Dora laughed and said, "Fortunately, Jethro came to his senses before it got serious."

David was proud to tell them about his beautiful sister. Apparently, Dora was quite a celebrity in her younger days, a model and actress. While doing modeling work in the USA, she met her husband, Robert Frankel, billionaire, owner of a major venture capital company, and a famous vineyard. She owned a successful modeling business, and they lived in Fresno, San Joachim Valley. Dora was visiting friends and family in China and Hong Kong and arrived from Shanghai only a few days ago to spend time with her best friend from her childhood days, Tamara, and of course, her brother, David.

That morning Tamara had commandeered one of Jethro's luxurious motor yachts to take her and Dora to Stanley for a shopping spree at the Stanley Market.

That's when Rex brought up the matter that had been bothering him since that morning. "No one has mentioned it, but it is obvious the attack this morning was aimed at Dora and not Tamara. Why would they want to attack her or Tamara?"

The furtive glances exchanged by their hosts didn't escape Rex and his companions' notice.

Eventually, Jethro spoke. "We don't know. Our families have many enemies who envy our money and possessions. The fiercest of them are the triads. Those men at the market this morning were members of the Sun Yee On triad. They're the most powerful of the triads in Hong Kong, with more than fifty-five thousand members world-wide. They hate it that we are not submitting to them. They can't control us, and they will not let an opportunity pass to do us and our businesses harm."

Rex was about to interject and ask what the SYO could

possibly gain by killing Dora, who didn't even live in Hong Kong. But he didn't because it was clear they didn't want to talk about it. They were hiding something, and they probably had some good reason for it. He was not going to offend their gracious hosts and new friends.

David deftly steered the conversation away from the topic and asked Rex, Josh, and Marissa to tell them about their family histories.

They glanced at each other as they didn't expect that question. They had to wing it.

Marissa said she used to be a secretary at one of the major Wall Street brokers, and she and Josh got married only a few months ago. They'd decided to start a family. Therefore, she was now a housewife. Josh told them he worked as a financial analyst for the same brokers Marissa worked for; that's where they met. Catia told them she was a research assistant for a professor at Sapienza, the University of Rome. Rex started telling them he was a former schoolteacher, that he had received a sizeable inheritance from his parents, but he couldn't finish his story before Jethro and David burst out in laughter.

David said, "Okay, we won't talk about it anymore. Safe to say that from what we've heard about what happened at Stanley Market today, and my observations, I'll eat my hat if all of you, including Digger, are not involved in some kind of military capacity. I'd also eat my jacket if it's not in the special forces."

Catia said without blinking an eye, "We cannot confirm or deny it."

With a big grin, Rex added, "But I can tell you this; we know nothing about it, we've done nothing wrong, and we promise it will never happen again."

"The politician's credo," Jethro said as they all exploded in laughter.

When the mirth subsided, Dora asked what their plans were for the next few days.

They told her they wanted to do more sightseeing.

Dora immediately insisted she wanted to be their tour guide. "We'll take one of the Mercedes minibusses and two guards, and we'll be safe."

They accepted.

It was after midnight when the helicopter took them back to the *TOMATS*, making a wide circle over a large part of the city for their entertainment.

Hong Kong

Day 6

The next day, Jethro's helicopter picked them all up from the *TOMATS* to accompany Dora, David, and Jethro to Hong Kong Sanatorium and Hospital, one of the best private hospitals in Hong Kong, to visit Tamara.

Tamara was doing very well and was very happy to see them. She kept on thanking Catia and Marissa for saving her life.

After the visit, Rex invited them all for drinks on the *TOMATS*, where Declan Spencer was proud to welcome them and show them the yacht.

Chapter Six

SIGHTSEEING IN HONG KONG

Hong Kong

Day 7

Dora with a driver and two bodyguards picked them up from the *TOMATS* shortly before eight a.m. in a luxury nine-seater Mercedes minibus. Their plan for the day was to visit a few museums first and the Tsz Shan Monastery in the afternoon.

It was late day when they arrived at the Tsz Shan Monastery, the brainchild of tycoon Li Ka-shing, the largest real estate developer in Hong Kong, who spent $1.5 billion and took twelve years to build the massive monastery, the world's leading religious compound of its kind.

The 46,451-square-meter, Tang dynasty-styled compound featuring, among others, a remarkable Bodhi tree, sweeping gardens, and a "brilliance pond" and was both state-of-the-art yet admiringly traditional in its composition. It was located in Tai Po's Ting Tsz hills near Tai Mei Tuk. The seventy-six-meter-tall, steel-framed, bronze-forged, white statue of Guan Yin (Goddess of Mercy, also known as Kwun Yum) was a breathtaking sight. It was the world's biggest Guan Yin bronze statue; the impressive lady was twice the size of Lantau Island's Big Buddha.

Finishing their visit to the monastery, they made their way to the minibus in the parking lot. They were all strapped in and ready for the trip back to the *TOMATS* when a white police sedan with a blue-and-red 3M retroreflective stripe around the sides with the word "Police" in Chinese and AM government, license plates pulled up behind them and blocked their way. Red-and-blue emergency lights were flashing, but no sirens sounded.

The officers in the police vehicle got out of their car and approached the van, one to the driver's side, one to the passenger side.

Digger started growling, and Rex said, "Stand down Digger."

He stopped growling, but his lips were still parted in a snarl, revealing his fangs, and the hair on his back and neck was standing on end. Rex knew Digger didn't like these guys, that much was clear, but he couldn't see the reason for Digger's dislike. Nevertheless, he knew better than to ignore Digger's warning.

"Lower all the windows," the lead officer said to the driver in Cantonese.

He complied.

Three more police vehicles, minivans, arrived with flashing lights but no sirens. Within seconds, the minibus was surrounded by six policemen. There were four more standing a few yards away with their hands on their holsters.

The two guards in the minibus were getting uneasy. The officer saw it, pulled his gun out, and pointed it at the two guards who were sitting in the row behind the driver. "My men have orders to shoot if you make any wrong moves."

In response, the rest of his men drew their guns and aimed through the open windows at the occupants.

"All of you put your hands on your head and keep them there. And keep that dog under control, or he'll get shot."

Rex translated for them, and they all complied. He spoke to Digger softly to calm him.

"What's going on?" Catia asked in Italian.

Rex replied in Italian, "I'm not sure. But I've got a gut feeling they're not the police. Digger doesn't like them at all."

He was about to translate for Josh and Marissa when the police officer shouted, "Quiet!" in English.

"Take the keys out and give them to me," the officer said to the driver.

He complied.

"What's the problem, officer?" Dora, sitting in the front passenger seat, asked in English.

He ignored her question and said, "I told you to be quiet. Now, all of you get out, slowly, and do exactly as my men tell you. Keep your hands on your heads."

"Officer, I have to insist. What's going on here? Why are you doing this?" Dora asked.

"Quiet, woman!" He pointed his gun at her. "Do as you've been told."

As they got out of the minibus, the policemen cuffed their hands behind their backs and made them lie on the ground next to the Mercedes.

While getting out, Rex caught a glimpse of parts of tattoos on the necks of two of the policemen not covered by their collars or sleeves. They weren't policemen. They were triad. Digger was right.

Digger was not happy at all, but he obeyed when Rex told him to be calm and to stay in the van. Rex was seriously worried that if Digger got aggressive, they would shoot him. Digger probably didn't understand the danger they were in, or maybe he did. Because it was his nature to protect his pack, he wouldn't care about his own safety. Fortunately, he did what Rex told him.

By now, a crowd was gathering. The officer told two of his men to disperse them. They did so quickly and efficiently.

Rex and Josh were next to each other on the ground; two guards were next to them.

"These guys are not the police. They're triad," Rex whispered to Josh.

"Yes. And they're after the women, not us," Josh said as the women were pulled to their feet and shoved toward one of the vans at gunpoint.

"Shit. I've never been so blindsided and so helpless," Rex said.

"That makes two of us."

"But one thing is certain. If they so much as harm a single hair on the head of any of our women, I'm going to feed them to the sharks," Rex whispered.

"Count me in. That's if they don't execute us here."

"I doubt they'd do it in full view of the public. But then again, they are triad. Like mafiosos across the world, they like nothing better than a public display of power."

Dora, Catia, and Marissa were shoved into the police van, their feet were tied, and they were gagged. Rex and Josh couldn't see what happened next; if they could, they would've seen that the women got injected with sedatives, which rendered them unconscious shortly after.

As soon as the van with the women drove away, the leader shouted in Cantonese, "Let's go!" They all got into their vehicles, drove away, and left Rex, Josh, Digger, and the two guards there without saying another word to them.

"We'll meet again, assholes! And it can't be too soon," Rex shouted in Cantonese in raging frustration.

Rex and Josh quickly got out of the handcuffs and helped their guards get their cuffs off as well. Rex asked one of the guards to give him Jethro's number, and he phoned him.

Jethro answered in person on the second ring. Rex told him what happened.

The keys to the minibus had gone with the "police," and the sophisticated lock mechanism of the Mercedes was near impossible to hotwire without special tools.

Jethro was furious; he told Rex they should stay there; he would come and pick them up in his helicopter.

Digger was not in a good space. He was constantly whining and yelping, looking accusatorily at Rex as if he wanted an explanation for why they were not going after the bad guys who took the women.

Rex felt guilty. He put his arm around Digger and said, "I know, buddy, it's terrible. But they'll be okay. We're going to find the bastards. And I promise I won't stop you."

Digger whined, then calming down, he nestled up with Rex as if trying to comfort him.

Twenty minutes later, at five p.m., Jethro's helicopter landed in the parking lot and picked them up to take them to Matz Island.

After hearing from Rex, Josh, and the guards what had

happened, Jethro's face was pale with shock and anger when he phoned the Commissioner of Police.

Rex and Josh were listening on their headphones as Jethro demanded to know from the commissioner what was going on.

Jethro was probably one of only a handful of civilians in Hong Kong who could speak to the commissioner in such a tone and get away with it. Jethro was also one of the very few who had the number of the commissioner's personal cellphone and direct telephone line. The commissioner knew that although he was a puppet of the communists in Beijing and under their protection, Mr. Matz had a lot of influence in high places in Beijing and Hong Kong. Therefore, he didn't get his nose out of joint with Mr. Matz.

The commissioner pled ignorance. "Mr. Matz, I'm giving you my personal assurance; there was no police action of that kind today. In fact, there hasn't been such a takedown in quite a few days. There was definitely no reason for action against Ms. Frankel or Mrs. Dalton or Mrs. Farley, or anyone of the Matz or Sarlin families."

Jethro didn't trust the man. The Hong Kong police had a longstanding reputation for corruption and scandals relating to the triads, taking bribes from them to turn a blind eye to drug deals and illegal gambling operations, brutality, torture, and falsifying evidence. "Well, then you better find out who the hell has been imitating your officers."

"That I'll attend to immediately, Mr. Matz. I'll order a manhunt for the abductors. At the same time, I'll initiate an investigation, which I will lead personally, to find out how it was possible that something like this could've happened in broad daylight and how the police vehicles and uniforms were obtained."

"You do that. In the meantime, I'll do my own investigation. It's the second time in two days that my family and friends have been attacked. I think it's time for you to do your job and see to the protection of the citizens living in your jurisdiction." Jethro ended the call.

Rex's and Josh's fury was at boiling point, and it was clear Digger could sense it. His ears were pitched forward as he stared at Rex and Josh in turn.

Most infuriating was how easily the SYO had blindsided them with that Hong Kong police routine and rendered them, highly trained special forces operators, powerless. It was galling to admit that although they were outnumbered and outgunned, they had been outwitted as well. As highly skilled operators, no strangers to violence and bad guys, they knew, in circumstances like that, surrounded and staring down the barrels of guns, it was better to play along and wait for an opportunity. But in this case, they never got that opportunity.

It was maddening that they had no idea where to start looking for the women. Although they were certain the SYO was responsible, they had no idea why they were so bent on getting the women. Some of it certainly had to do with Catia and Marissa ruining their plans two days ago when they wanted to abduct or kill Dora. But what was the reason for wanting to kill Dora? Jethro's explanation of mob activities at dinner two nights ago just didn't cut it. There was more to it than what he had said.

Most worrying was what the SYO's intentions were. Would they kill the women? Their actions two days ago indicated that they wouldn't hesitate to do so. But then why didn't they kill them all? Two days ago, they were happy to do it in full view of the public in broad daylight. Why didn't they do it today? Maybe that was a glimmer of hope—they didn't want to kill them, at least not right away.

Chapter Seven

THE REASON

Matz Island, Hong Kong

Day 7

In Jethro's spacious and opulent study on Matz Island were Rex, Josh, Digger, David, Jethro, and his personal assistant, Tao Meng, and his head of security, Ramesh Ojha. The latter was a fair-skinned man, obviously not of Chinese heritage. He was Nepalese.

Rex and Josh learned that Ojha was a former Gurkha officer. The Gurkhas had a storied history as superb soldiers, humble, respectful, and fearless, known for their exceptional bravery, ability, and heroism in the face of impossible odds. It was said that if there was a single reason no one goes to war with Nepal, it was because of the Gurkhas' reputation. They served in not only the Nepalese Army but also in the British and Indian armies as well, a tradition since the end of the Anglo-Nepalese War in 1816.

Standing a little over one-point-six meters tall, it would have been easy to overlook Ojha, let alone see him as a soldier. However, that mistaken belief may very well be your last thought if ever you were to encounter him as your enemy on the battlefield: The Gurkha's motto, "better to die than be a coward," suggests as much.

Rex couldn't help but remember Field Marshal Sam Manekshaw's words, "If a man says he is not afraid of dying, he is either lying or a Gurkha."

And Josh couldn't help but remember a bit of humor about the Gurkhas from his time in Afghanistan. Taliban commander to one of his officers: "Huh, you lost thirty men because of one Gurkha?"

"Yes sir, he ambushed us!"

After learning what happened at the Tsz Shan Monastery, Ojha had, even before Jethro's helicopter had landed, dispatched another helicopter with two of his men, also former Gurkhas, to the hospital to keep watch over Tamara because he didn't trust the police who were guarding her. If the SYO knew what was good for them, they would not come near that hospital.

Rex cleared his throat and said, "Jethro, David, I apologize in advance if what I'm about to say offends you; it's not my intention. But at dinner night before last, when we talked about the reason for the attack on Dora and Tamara, I got a distinct impression you were not exactly forthcoming."

Jethro glanced at David and Ojha, they nodded, and he said, "No offense taken. You're right. We didn't want to drag you into our family problems. Your wives had already put their lives at stake to save our sisters—"

"But now it's different," Rex interjected. "We're part of whatever it is you didn't tell us."

41

"Yes, indeed you are, and we apologize for that," David said. "But you can be sure we'll use every bit of influence we have to get them back."

Rex and Josh looked at each other and then at the rest in the room, and Josh said, "I certainly hope that doesn't mean we're going to sit around here and wait for the police to find them?"

"No, definitely not," David said. "So, let's give you the background, and together we can decide what the best course of action would be."

Rex said, "Before you do that, to be fair, we've also not been entirely forthright with you about our backgrounds. In other words, David, you don't have to eat your hat or your jacket; you've come to the right conclusion about our backgrounds. We, that's Josh, Marissa, Catia, and I, are indeed trained and experienced black ops operators. Digger is a trained military dog."

"Thanks for telling us," said Jethro. "Your skills are exactly what we need."

Between the four of them, they told Rex and Josh what they didn't want to tell them the night before.

Dora had been in Shanghai the week before to visit friends. She only arrived in Hong Kong three days before the incident at Stanley Market.

At the airport in Shanghai, on her way back to Hong Kong, she ran into an old friend from school days, Benjamin Yatsir. Benjamin was a Hong Kong Jew, Dora and Tamara's friend. A very successful medical microbiologist, he was heading a team of scientists at Zexian Biomed, specializing in human transgenic antibody technology, developing innovative therapeutics in the field of antibodies, immunotherapy, and inflammatory diseases.

David told them that his company, HK Securities, had

invested large sums of venture capital in some Chinese biotechnology startups over the last few years, including the promising Shanghai biotechnology company Zexian Biomed, where Benjamin worked. It was David who, as a condition of his substantial investment in Zexian Biomed, insisted Benjamin be appointed as the lead scientist.

The CEO of Zexian Biomed was Dr. Zheng Xuefeng, also a renowned scientist, but with the business acumen to manage a biotech company. He was Benjamin's boss, and the two of them got along very well. Indeed, they were good friends.

David was on the board of directors of Zexian Biomed. David knew Zheng; he did a thorough background check on him before investing in the company. David had regular contact with him and received regular progress reports from him, which he had learned from Dora upon her arrival from Shanghai were all false for the past two months.

"Dora told us she was shocked when she saw Benjamin. According to her, since she saw him about a year ago, he had lost weight, he had grayed, and he looked disheveled and uncharacteristically nervous. We all know Benjamin very well. He is a very clever man, always friendly, calm, and composed—a man not easily given to panic. But according to Dora, he was panicking," David said.

"She asked him about it, and he tried to brush it off as work pressure. But she knew him well enough and didn't buy it. She pushed him, and in the end, he told her that about two months ago, three officials from the MSS turned up at Zexian Biomed and called him and Dr. Zheng Xuefeng into a private meeting and told them to stop all research projects they were working on and concentrate all their effort on the study of a new virus.

"The staff members were made to sign a pledge of

secrecy, not to share their research with anyone outside their own group, and they were all placed under electronic and physical surveillance.

"The Zexian scientists quickly discovered that this virus was engineered in a lab. And, according to Benjamin, they've now got reason to believe that this virus has somehow escaped from a lab somewhere and is killing people in droves in some suburbs of Shanghai.

"Dora saw two men in dark suits, which she believes were MSS agents, leading Benjamin away a moment before she entered the plane for her trip to Hong Kong. She's been trying to get in touch with him and his wife and children since her arrival here but had no success."

Jethro took over the narrative. "We think Benjamin and his family have been 'disappeared.' He would've been inter-rogated and, no doubt, tortured if he didn't cooperate. He would've told them what he told Dora, and now they want to get rid of her to plug the leak."

"China is not called 'the land of the lie' for no reason. They've been lying and covering up for as long as the communists have been in charge. Remember the Tiananmen Square massacre? Several thousand students gathering in the square in June 1989, and government forces opened fire on them. Beijing says only a few people died, two hundred civilians and several dozen security personnel, insisting that troops were dispatched merely to disperse so-called 'hooligans' and maintain public safety. The truth is, more than ten thousand died.

"You must have heard about the Muslim Uighurs in western China? About one million Uighurs, one-tenth of the Uighur population, are held in 'education centers.' We don't know how many have died inside those barbed-wire camps while being educated in President Li Lingxin's school of thought.

"Think about Hong Kong. They lied to us and the world when they said they intended to honor their 1984 agreement with the British government about the transfer of authority of Hong Kong to China. Ever since, like a boa constrictor, they have steadily been invading the political affairs of our city."

"If what Benjamin told Dora were indeed true," David said, "and this virus escapes from China and reaches the rest of the world, don't be surprised if they blame the origins on someone else such as the USA, UK, or Taiwan. Anywhere but China."

Rex said, "Well, if it's true, then they're in panic mode over there. They're trying to smother it and keep it a secret within their borders. But they won't be able to keep it under wraps for much longer if people are already dying in large numbers. Somewhere, that's going to leak out."

"That might be so," Jethro said, "but by then, it could be irreversible. That's if they even have the desire to stop it..."

Chapter Eight

WE NEED INFORMATION

Matz Island, Hong Kong

Day 7

"In other words, we've to conclude that the kidnapping of the women is related to this virus thing?" Josh said.

He and Rex were raring to go out and find the women but had no idea where to start. They couldn't charge out there like Don Quixote tilting their lances at windmills as though they were dragons. They had to continually remind themselves that without the right information, they were powerless.

"Undoubtedly," Jethro said. "And that means the Chinese government, or a faction of them, is behind it."

"What's the SYO's role in this?" Rex said.

"It's no secret that some security agencies in China use the SYO from time to time as their muscle to solve intractable problems for them here in Hong Kong. Almost certainly, in exchange for the police turning a blind eye to the drug-dealing, money laundering, gambling, and other illicit activities of the SYO. To answer your question, we believe the SYO is acting on instructions from the MSS," David said.

"In the end, it doesn't matter who is behind the abduction," Rex said. "Nothing bodes well for the women. A few days ago, they were bent on killing Dora, but now they've gone to great lengths to abduct her and our wives. That means they want the women alive . . . for now. We need to start shaking trees to get information."

"Agreed," Jethro said. "And if we're right that the SYO is acting on behalf of someone in China, then I'd expect they're keeping the women somewhere here in Hong Kong, biding time until they can get them transferred to mainland China . . . and I hate to say it . . . to interrogate them . . . and then . . . kill them."

Rex glanced at his watch. "It's been a little over three hours since they took them. It's already dark. Could they still be in Hong Kong?"

"Yes, I'd think so," affirmed Jethro. "With the police out looking for them, they'll probably lie low for a day or so before they'll move them."

"That's if the police are indeed looking for them," Josh clarified.

Jethro nodded slowly. "Sad as it may be, that is a possibility. It's not inconceivable that the commissioner received instructions from the MSS not to interfere."

"What bugs me," Josh said, "is that they didn't take or kill Rex and me. I mean, if they're out to silence anyone who might know about the virus situation in China, then surely, they must be worried about anyone who had been in contact with Dora since her return? That would include all of us in this room, Tamara, your spouses, and others, wouldn't it?"

"Yes," Jethro agreed. "And by the looks of it, they have watchers out there who are tracking all our moves as we come and go from this island. As for why they have not taken you and Josh and the guards, it's puzzling. There might be a specific reason why they only wanted the women."

"Such as getting leverage over you?" Rex asked.

"Yes, or as a warning not to interfere in their business."

Josh mumbled, "Well, whatever their reasons, they're going to be the sorriest gangsters on this planet when Rex and I catch up with them."

Ramesh Ojha, who had been quietly listening all the time, smiled and added, "Please count me in."

"You're most welcome; the more of us, the more pain we can inflict," Josh said.

Digger was getting excited as he would have been sensing the familiar pre-mission tension building in Rex and Josh.

Rex said, "I think we should let Declan know that these SYO jackasses might get it into their heads to come looking for us on the *TOMATS*. That's assuming they know we live on the yacht and know where it's anchored. If they don't know already, they could torture it out of the women."

Everyone nodded wordlessly.

Jethro suggested, "Why don't you bring your yacht to Matz Island and anchor it here? We have guards and electronic security down at the marina. Or would you prefer to get her out of the territorial waters of Hong Kong and China?"

Rex's and Josh's "No!" came out at the same time.

Neither Rex nor Josh told them about the *TOMATS*'s

special crew, a contingent of ten special forces operators, six Navy SEALS, and four Delta Force, not counting Spencer, his first mate, Rex, Josh, and Digger.

If the SYO was going to be so stupid as to launch an attack on the *TOMATS*, they were in for a very nasty surprise.

Rex said, "I'll ask Declan to move the *TOMATS* here." He took his secured satellite phone out of his pocket and pressed the speed dial button for Spencer. When he had him on the line, Rex told him what happened, and they agreed it was best to move the *TOMATS* over to Matz Island. Spencer said he would recall everyone who was onshore to get back on board and then proceed to the island. On the way over, he would brief the crew about the potential threat and make the necessary preparations.

When Rex finished the call, Jethro said, "On the premise that the police are not our friends and that we're on our own, I'll send out some of my men to make contact with our network of informants among the various triad groups including the SYO.

"We know that Tian Song-li is the leader of the SYO. But he is a very slippery man. Always heavily guarded, he never publicizes his plans or his whereabouts. He has been arrested many times but has never been convicted. He would know where the women are and would know all about the instructions from China."

"That's the guy I'd very much like to have a chat with," Josh said, bringing wry smiles to the faces of everyone.

Maddening as it was, there was nothing more they could do until they could get information out of the SYO informants.

Ojha suggested that David and his wife move to Matz

Island, where they would be better protected than at their home, and David agreed.

Unknown location, Hong Kong

Day 7

Catia heard herself groan as she slowly exited the twilight zone from unconsciousness to awareness. Her head was throbbing, her mouth dry, and her tongue stuck to her pallet. The room was semi-dark; the only light in the room was seeping through the bottom and sides of the door. She had no idea where she was or how long she had been there. She tried to move but couldn't—her hands and feet were tied with duct tape to a chair, and the chair wasn't moving. It was bolted to the floor.

She became aware of muffled, monotonous drumming music emanating from somewhere below her.

Then she remembered what happened. "Rex!" she shouted, but only a soft moan came from her dry mouth. "Where . . .?" Then she became aware that she was not alone in the room. Someone or something had stirred to the right of her. She shook her head and tried to focus her eyes. It took a while before she could make out another person in a chair, three paces away, tied up like she was. She heard a few soft moans coming from the person. Then she recognized her. "Marissa!" The saliva glands in her mouth were functioning better now, and she could speak almost clearly. "Are you okay?"

"Huh . . . ah . . ." She shook her head but stopped abruptly. "Damn . . . it . . . hurts."

"Marissa, it's me, Catia. Can you hear me? Are you okay?"

"Argh . . . head . . . killing me. Thirsty . . . I'm tied to a damn chair. Oh my God. Josh!"

Just then, they heard a groan coming from the opposite side of the room.

Must be Dora, Catia thought. "Dora, is it you? It's Catia."

"Augh . . .."

"Dora, is it you?"

"Uh-uh."

"Are you okay?"

"I ... headache ... I ... I ..."

"Give it a minute. You'll feel better soon," Marissa said.

A few minutes later, still feeling very groggy, agitated, and seriously worried, they were able to converse much better and recalled what happened in the parking lot at Tsz Shan Monastery earlier. Soon, they realized they had no idea what happened after they were loaded into the police minivan. Frantically worried about Rex, Josh, Digger, and the guards, they had no idea where they were or if they were even alive. Nevertheless, it didn't take them long to figure out they were almost certainly not in a police station. No police station would be located above a bar, which is what they had agreed was where the pounding music originated from.

Catia and Marissa thought they were there because they had killed the two SYO members a few days before, and revenge was in the cards for them.

But then Dora started crying. "I'm so sorry. It's all my fault. I got you into this."

"Stop it, Dora," Catia said. "You didn't get us into it. Those thugs who attacked you and Tamara got us into it."

"You don't understand. They were after me."

"We already know that. Jethro told us over dinner the other night. Remember?"

"I remember, but Jethro didn't tell you the truth."

A long silence followed before Marissa said, "Then tell us the truth, Dora."

Dora nodded and started, "I'm almost sure the men who abducted us are SYO, and they are doing it on behalf of the MSS, the Ministry of State Security, China's secret police."

"What are you . . .?" Catia started then stopped and said, "No, don't answer that; they could be listening to us. But please stop blaming yourself."

"But . . . I . . ."

"No buts, Dora," Marissa said. "You didn't kidnap us. Beating yourself up over it is not going to change anything."

Dora was still the only one in the room who knew why they were in custody and had a good idea of how it was going to end, and she wanted to tell them. "Okay, but let me tell you—"

Before she could complete her sentence, the lights in the room went on, and the door opened.

Chapter Nine

IT WILL BE DONE

Yuen Long, Hong Kong

Day 7

The triads used numeric codes, inspired by Chinese numerology, to distinguish ranks and positions within their various gangs. The top person usually referred to as The Mountain or Dragon Master or Dragon Head, got the number 489. The number 438 was assigned to the second level, 432 to the third level, and 49 to lowest level members. Blue Lanterns were uninitiated members, equivalent to Mafia associates, and not given a number. Undercover law-enforcement agents or spies from another triad got the number 25, which had become popular Hong Kong slang for an informant.

Tian Song-li was number 489, Dragon Master of the SYO. In a Mafia hierarchy, he would have been known as the Don. Being a Bruce Lee devotee, Tian always dressed the part in Chinese tunics, sunglasses, and bowl haircut.

He was a controversial, self-made businessman, a big player in the Hong Kong underworld. But where he came from, where and how he grew up, was all shrouded in mystery. Some say he came from humble beginnings, started working as a hotel doorman at the age of twelve and worked his way up from there. There were rumors that he was once a high-up in one of the major triad groups in mainland China. No one knew who his parents or siblings were or if he had any that were alive.

He had been in and out of police custody and before the courts more times than he would care to count, but he had always managed to walk away a free man. He was ruthless, and after so many failed attempts at putting him behind bars, he firmly believed he was invincible, that he could operate with impunity.

In his spacious study at one of his nightclubs in the SYO-controlled Hong Kong suburb of Yuen Long, he was pacing back and forth behind his desk, yelling at two withering men. Sweat was dripping from their pale faces.

"You idiots! You didn't follow my instructions. I told you to kill them, their guards, and the damn dog."

"We couldn't, sir. There were too many bystanders. In our police uniforms, the crowd believed we were on official police business. If . . . if we killed them execution-style, we . . . well . . . our cover would've been blown. They might have called the real police or, worse, attacked us . . . Please, sir, we had no choice."

"Do you have any idea where to find them now?"

"No, sir. We don't, but we can—"

"Then I don't need your services anymore." Tian picked his gun up from his desk and, in quick succession, shot each man in the face. He put the gun down, picked up his glass, and swallowed the rest of the whiskey in one big gulp. Then he pushed a button on the intercom on his desk, and in a calm voice said to his personal assistant, "Please step into my study."

The assistant entered, glanced around the room, caught his breath, and said, "Want me to take care of this, sir?" nodding toward the bodies in the growing puddle of blood on the floor in front of the desk.

"Yes. Don't bury them. Cut them up in very small pieces. Take that out in the harbor and feed the fish."

He walked out of the study and turned down the hallway, mumbling to himself, "Morons surround me. I'll do it myself."

Yuen Long, Hong Kong

Day 7

The women squinted against the bright light and saw they were in an unfurnished room unless one wanted to regard the six chairs bolted to the bare cement floor as furniture.

Two men with guns in their hands entered. One was short and stocky. Every part of his body not covered by clothes was covered in colorful tattoos. The other was a muscled man, tall by Asian standards. His most noticeable feature was a big, ugly scar that crossed his face from his forehead over his empty left eye socket. Scary.

Following them was a man who Dora immediately recognized as the leader of the SYO, Tian Song-li. "Mr.

Tian, what's going on here? What's the SYO's business with my friends and me?"

"Quiet," he said in a soft voice, speaking English.

"You're not going to get away with this. My family and the Matz family will pursue you to the ends of the earth. You've got nowhere to hide where they can't find you."

Tian said, "I'm not going to tell you again to be quiet, Ms. Frankel."

Dora closed her mouth and stared at Tian with hate-filled eyes.

"I have one question for you, ladies. It's simple. Answer me, and nothing will happen to you. Refuse, and you'll find out how eager my men are to get a piece of you."

The women made no reply.

"Where are the men you were with at Tsz Shan Monastery earlier today?"

He looked at Marissa first. She shook her head and said, "No idea. They could be anywhere. They could be at the front door right now. Maybe you should check?"

"Okay, have it your way," Tian said with a grin on his face.

He turned to Dora and repeated the question.

She said, "I wouldn't tell you even if I knew."

"Another brave soul who prefers to be raped rather than save herself," he said.

He looked at Catia. "How about you? Will you tell me and save them, or do you feel it's better that you all go through the same ordeal?"

Catia feigned fear. She swallowed, stuttered, and nodded, then dropped her head. She had decided she *wanted* them to go to the *TOMATS*. These guys had no idea that they'd be walking through the gates of hell the moment they set foot on that yacht. She had placed all her hope in Rex,

Josh, and Digger, and the crew. It was a gamble, but one she was prepared to take. Between Rex, Josh, Digger, and the crew, there was no way these thugs would get on the yacht without them knowing. They would be captured, some of them questioned, and Rex and Josh would find out where they were being held.

When she spoke, her voice was soft and wavering, "They're . . . they're on a yacht . . . in . . . it's called the *TOMATS*. It's . . . at the Lantau Yacht Club . . . Discovery Bay . . . Please, sir," — tears were streaming down her face — "please don't hurt us. Please . . . can we go now? We won't tell anyone. Please just let us go."

Tian smiled and said, "Thanks. I knew at least one of you would have enough brains." He looked at Marissa and Dora and said, "She's saved your lives. You should thank her."

Marissa and Dora were staring at Catia, undoubtedly wondering why Catia gave up the information so easily.

It took a little while for Marissa to figure it out, and she grinned. But Dora didn't. She couldn't be blamed for not knowing about the unique skills of the people and the dog on the *TOMATS*.

She was, however, for now, relieved that she had not been asked any questions about her meeting with Benjamin at Shanghai airport. That meant the gangsters presumably knew nothing about it. But it was not much consolation as she would be asked those questions once the SYO handed them over to the MSS.

Closing the door behind them, Tian told his number 438, his deputy Dragon Master, Xing Ruogang, the big man with the ugly scar across his face, to follow him to another room where they could talk in private. Tian's assistant and helpers were still cleaning out the mess in his study.

"You've got the address now," he told Xing. "Here are the photos of the men and the dog. Assemble a team, go there later tonight, find them, kill *them*, and anyone who tries to stop you.

"Don't screw this up, Xing. Make sure you get all of them."

Xing nodded and said, "It will be done."

Chapter Ten

WELCOME ABOARD

Matz Island, Hong Kong

Day 7

By ten p.m. the *TOMATS* was in the private marina at Matz Island. On the way over from Discovery Bay, Spencer had called the crew together and told them what had happened the past two days, about Catia and Marissa's kidnapping, and that the SYO might launch an attack against the *TOMATS*.

Spencer said, "I'm sorry to spoil your peaceful holiday like this."

Although everyone in the briefing immediately understood the danger and the seriousness of the situation, the nervous excitement among the battle-hardened special forces members was noticeable.

"What do you mean, spoil?" one of the SEALS

mumbled. "How can one have a good holiday without *some* excitement?"

By the time the *TOMATS* anchored at Matz Island, they had their security plan and guard-duty roster in place.

Rex, Josh, and Digger joined them on the *TOMATS* shortly after and gave Spencer and the crew a more detailed version of the events of the past few days. Rex told them that the kidnappers were probably still holding the women at an unknown location in Hong Kong, but that they would soon hand them over to the Chinese Secret Police, the MSS.

"Therefore, if they attack, try and capture as many of them as possible, but if you can't, then shoot the bastards."

Spencer took the ten combat-trained crewmen down to the armory and handed them their weapons. If the SYO had a soft target in mind, they were going to be terribly disappointed.

Matz Island, Hong Kong

Day 8

Spencer and Rex were on the bridge searching the sea around them through night vision equipment for signs of anyone approaching. It was a quarter past midnight when Spencer said, "I think your friends have arrived." He pointed out a medium-sized double-deck motor yacht, according to the range finder, one-point-four kilometers away.

As a specialist black ops operator, Rex knew all about fighting boredom while waiting for a target to arrive, leave, or make a move. During their training at CRC, John Brandt —the Old Man, as they called him—drilled it into them: "A CRC agent's life consists of waiting, soul-destroying tedium and boredom, punctuated by sudden bursts of terrifying violence, followed by more waiting." And Rex was good at it, but this time, the waiting was driving him to distraction, and he knew it was no different for his best friend, Josh.

Rex studied the yacht through his night vision binoculars for a while, and said, "I sincerely hope it's them. This waiting and uncertainty are going to turn me into a mass murderer."

"Looks like they've heard you," Spencer said. "They're lowering inflatable dinghies. They have electric motors to move quietly."

Rex focused his binoculars on the dinghies, and a few seconds later, he said, "Three dinghies, two men each."

"Yep," Spencer confirmed.

"Welcome to the *TOMATS* boys," Rex said. "We've been looking forward to your visit. Please don't be shy, come over and step aboard. We'll make you feel right at home."

Spencer spoke into his throat mic to the men on guard elsewhere on the yacht. "Okay, guys, we have six men in three dinghies on their way over for their early morning cuppa joe. Wake the others and take up your positions. I'll keep you posted. They're about ten minutes out."

Within minutes, everyone was in place. The wives and girlfriends and two chefs were assembled in the dining room.

Rex, Josh, and Digger were responsible for anyone stepping onto the lower deck stern-side. The ten SEALS and Deltas were spread around the bow, port, and starboard sides to welcome the visitors if they decided to board over the side rails.

Spencer and his first mate kept them posted with the progress of the approaching assailants. When the dinghies were about a hundred meters out, they parted ways; two went for the starboard and port sides, the third went around to the stern.

Rex and Digger were on one side of the entry and Josh on the other, hidden from sight to anyone coming on board.

The dinghy approached almost noiselessly. Digger growled softly. Rex looked at Digger and put his finger on his own mouth. Digger stopped. Rex whispered into his ear, "Good boy. Thanks for letting me know they're here. Be very quiet now."

The men tied their dinghy to the railing, got out quietly, and stepped abreast through the opening onto the *TOMATS*. They crouched and reached for their guns in holsters under their arms. At the moment their hands touched the butts of their guns, their heads exploded in unbearable pain, and everything went black for them as they lost consciousness.

"Two down, tying them up now," Josh whispered into his throat mic.

Rex ziptied and gagged the men but had a hard time keeping Digger from ripping them apart. He was unusually aggressive. Normally when Rex took a target down, Digger would stand aside and let him get on with it. But now Digger seemed to have his mind set on sinking his teeth into these guys even though they were unconscious.

The rest of the takedown of the SYO hitmen was equally uneventful. The thugs were uninformed and unprepared. Even if they *were* better prepared, they were outnumbered, not to mention the fact that they would never in their lives attain the combat skills of the men who awaited them on the *TOMATS*.

Within two minutes after the first two set foot on the yacht at the stern, it was all over. Not a single shot was fired. There were, however, a few thuds, followed by brief grunts and groans as the assailants were neutralized. Six SYO goons were rendered unconscious, tied up, gagged, and would wake up with stupendous headaches in the next half hour or so.

Five minutes later, they were all laid out in a neat row on the gym floor on the lower deck.

As soon as Ramesh Ojha got the message from Spencer that the six hitmen were secured, he and four of his men got into Jethro's helicopter and headed for the SYO yacht.

As the chopper approached the yacht, a man with an automatic rifle ran out onto the upper deck and fired a volley at them. The pilot flipped the switch on the landing lights, which blinded the shooter momentarily. A single shot rang out from the chopper. The man's chest exploded, and the force of the bullet body-slammed him into the rails.

One of Ojha's men pumped a fusillade of bullets into the upper deck with his HK 416 automatic rifle. The next moment two more men ran out onto the deck into the light with their empty hands held high above their heads in surrender.

Ojha told the pilot to drop him and his men on the deck. Two of them tied the men up while the rest quickly searched the yacht and found no one else. A few minutes later, Ojha gave the chopper pilot the signal that he could return to base. He started the yacht's engines and steered it to the Matz Island marina.

Chapter Eleven

EVER THOUGHT OF TAKING UP BASEBALL?

Matz Island, Hong Kong

Day 8

While they were waiting for the gangsters to regain consciousness, Rex was mulling over the reason for Digger's strange behavior earlier when he and Josh took their charges down. *Is it possible that he could somehow have made a connection between these men and the abduction of the women? Only if he could pick up their scents from those men . . .*

Josh was staring at him inquisitively. "You look, pensive buddy. What's up?"

"I think Digger is picking up the scents of our women from these men."

"Huh? You reckon? Well, I've learned when it comes to Digger's smelling prowess, I'll believe anything. But how will you—?"

"Let's each go and get a piece of clothing worn by

them, let Digger smell it, and ask him to point out the ones who match that scent."

They ran to their respective staterooms, got pieces of clothing, and returned to the gym.

Rex kneeled next to Digger, rubbed his ears and back, and said, "Buddy, I suspect you might be able to help us out here very quickly. What do you say?"

Digger smiled, licked Rex's face once, and stood. He was ready.

Rex held Catia's T-shirt under Digger's nose for a second or two, pointed at the captives on the floor, and said, "Seek."

Digger jogged to the row of men on the floor and started sniffing at them. He spent only a second or two with each when he reached the fourth man in the row. He stopped and started growling, his ears pitching, and his hair raised.

Rex turned the man around to see his face; it was one of the two he and Josh took down. He was a tall and muscled man with a big, ugly scar that crossed his face from his forehead over his empty left eye socket.

Rex pointed to the rest of the men on the floor and said, "Only one of them?"

Digger quickly sniffed the rest and returned to Scarface. Rex gave Digger a scarf worn by Marissa to smell, pointed to the men on the floor, and said, "Seek."

Within less than thirty seconds, Digger was back at Scarface.

"Good boy. You're such a clever boy. Thanks, buddy."

The Navy SEALS and Deltas, who were watching it all, started cheering Digger. They'd all seen a lot of action in their lives, and they knew what a tremendous force multiplier these military dogs were.

It was General David Petraeus who described the role of the military dog best when he said, "The capability they (Military Working Dogs) bring to the fight cannot be replicated by man or machine. By all measures of performance, their yield outperforms any asset we have in our inventory. Our Army (and military) would be remiss if we failed to invest more in this incredibly valuable resource."

Digger was basking in the praise. He worked for praise, not for food and treats, and he had done a great job.

Just when Rex and Josh picked Scarface up off the floor, Ojha and his men arrived with the two captured SYO thugs. He told them he and his men had secured the SYO vessel, killed one, and captured two. The yacht was now anchored in the marina. His men dropped the captives on the floor.

Ojha came closer, had one look at Scarface, and said to Rex and Josh, "Tian Song-li must be very serious about having you two captured or killed. This man is Xing Ruogang, Tian's second-in-command, a ruthless, violent, and cruel man."

"Well, Digger is saying Xing is carrying the scents of both Catia and Marissa on him," Rex said. "We didn't have anything with Dora's scent on it readily available, but I can't think of any reason why she would not be with Catia and Marissa. We'll question this scumbag first."

Ojha nodded and said, "Agreed. If anyone other than Tian knows where the women are, it will be this man."

A few minutes later, Xing was tied up in a chair in the engine room. Rex held a bottle with smelling salts under Xing's nose, and he stirred. A minute or so later, he was awake and fully aware.

Ojha had joined the party as a silent observer.

Rex spoke to Xing in English, but he didn't respond.

Rex tried Cantonese and got almost the same result, Xing raised his head and stared at Rex with his one eye, grinned, and spat on the floor in defiance.

Josh had enough. He tapped Rex on the shoulder with the wooden baseball bat, and without saying a word, indicated he wanted Rex to step aside.

Rex turned to Xing and said, "Now you've screwed the pooch. It would've been much less painful if you talked to me when you had the chance. He's going to beat you to a pulp." Rex stepped aside.

Unfortunately for Xing, Josh was in a nasty mood. And when he was in such a mood, he never talked much. Without a word, by way of introducing himself, he smashed Xing's knees, one after the other.

He was lining up to go to work on Xing's ankles when he started begging Josh to please ask him any questions he had. He was now fluent in English.

Josh stopped, spent a few seconds in thought, shook his head in silence, and smashed Xing's right ankle. Xing was howling in pain.

Wordlessly, Josh walked to the other side of the chair and lined up to do the left ankle. Xing was screaming and yelling; tears were streaming down his face. He begged Josh to say something, anything.

Josh ignored him and smashed his left ankle.

That was when Xing must have realized that he was expected to do the talking, with or without being asked questions or this big man with hate in his blue eyes was indeed going to beat him to a pulp.

He started with his title, deputy Dragon Master, second-in-command of the SYO. His Dragon Master was Tian Song-li, the man who sent him, Xing Ruogang, and his team to kill them.

Josh was aiming at Xing's right elbow when he got around to telling them where the women were. They were held at a nightclub, the Voco, owned by Tian Song-li, in the Yuen Long district. The plan was to move them out of Hong Kong within the next twenty-four hours.

He saved the rest of his limbs and, in all likelihood, his life when he told them where the women were and assured them they were not hurt. The SYO's brief was to kidnap them, treat them well, and deliver them to a ship off the coast of China when told to do so. He reiterated that they had received strict orders from their Chinese client not to hurt the women in any manner. The client was the Chinese MSS. But he had never dealt with them directly; only Tian knew the names and faces.

Ojha activated his throat mic and told Jethro and David that they had a location for the women.

Rex, Digger, and Ojha remained with Xing to question him in more detail while Josh went back to the gym to question the rest of the captives.

The first few tried to put up some heroic resistance, but they were no match for Josh and his baseball bat. Within an hour, it was clear that none of the hoodlums were involved in the kidnapping, had any idea where Tian or the women were, or even that any women were held captive by their Dragon Master. All they had to do was to get onto the *TOMATS*, kill the man with the dog and his friend, and anyone trying to stop them.

And, of course, they were very sorry about it and promised they'd never do it again.

When Josh left the gym, he looked at the men moaning and groaning and squirming in pain on the floor in their own urine and feces, and said to Spencer, "I guess we'll have to water blast and sanitize the gym before anyone can use it again?"

"Yeah, I guess we'll have to." Spencer smiled wryly. "By the way, you've got a mighty swing with the bat. Ever thought of taking up baseball?"

Josh snorted. "Nah. I'd rather stick to beating up gangsters; they don't come at me at ninety miles an hour."

Chapter Twelve

WE'RE HERE FOR OUR WOMEN

Matz Island, Hong Kong

Day 8

Josh's baseball bat had done wonders for Xing's language skills and attitude. He gave them a detailed description of the nightclub where the women were held. He told them everything about how many armed guards they could expect to find onsite, their weapons, and their positions.

Fortunately, Josh didn't get around to smashing his hands, and he was able to draw a detailed floorplan for them. It was a five-story building. The bottom floor was a bar and dance floor. The second was for gambling. The third and fourth were used as a whorehouse. The fifth was Tian's den, his office, a bedroom for his trysts, and the holding room where they were keeping Catia, Marissa, and Dora. There was a helipad on the roof.

The Navy SEALS and Deltas were upset and very

disappointed when told they were not allowed to be part of the rescue team. But as active members of the US military, they were not allowed to operate without the authority of their commanders or the President of the United States.

"But we've just taken part in military action," one of them said to Spencer. "Getting our friends back is phase two of the same operation."

Spencer smiled and said, "Guys, believe me, I'd like nothing better than letting you loose on those sons of bitches, but it can't be done. You'll be dishonorably discharged from the military. I can defend you with your commanding officers for acting in self-defense, but I'd have no leg to stand on if you go out and attack a civilian target, even if it is to rescue our friends. That's what the police are supposed to do."

Only after making sure Spencer and Rex understood how disgruntled they were, they relented but insisted on helping Rex and the others plan the mission. With Google Maps and Xing's help, they quickly constructed a scale model of the target building and surroundings and took it to Jethro's study to plan the rest of the rescue mission.

The task force who would enter Tian's nightclub consisted of Rex, Josh, Digger, Ojha, and one of his men. Four more of Ojha's ex-Gurkhas formed a second team, responsible for creating a diversion before Rex and his team would enter the Voco nightclub.

Jethro had called in one of his utility helicopters, an Airbus H225 Super Puma, a heavy lifter, frequently used by offshore drilling companies, and search-and-rescue crews. His company used it to move service crews around to inspect and service powerlines and stations. This one had seating for twenty people.

Jethro and David were also part of the team but would

not be onsite; they'd be based in the helicopter throughout the operation. Not that they didn't want to be involved, but Rex and Ojha told them in no uncertain terms to stay out of it as they, with no military training, would get in the way and endanger not only their own lives but also those of the team members.

According to Xing, they were to expect sixteen armed guardsmen on the premises. Three on the top floor, protecting Tian, five on the ground floor, keeping the peace in the bar and on the dance floor, and the rest roaming the remaining floors.

Rex's teams were outnumbered, but it didn't bother them. They were highly skilled and experienced warriors. Speed, surprise, and violence of action were the tactics to use to change the odds. They'd all used it in the past and knew it worked.

Usually, nightlife in the nightclubs of Hong Kong kicks into gear at around nine p.m. and carried on until just before sunrise.

Yuen Long, Hong Kong

Day 8

The four-man diversion team arrived at ground zero by way of four different taxis. The helicopter with the rest of the mission team was circling a few kilometers away.

At precisely three a.m., the attack commenced when three men of the diversion team simultaneously lobbed flashbangs into the nightclubs next to and across the street from the Voco. The fourth man was on the roof of the building across the street from the Voco. As soon as the first patrons stormed out of the premises where the explosions happened, he started firing smoke grenades into the street below. His comrades started firing their assault rifles on automatic, using blanks. They each emptied their magazines, slipped away from the street, and climbed up the fire escape ladders to the top of the roofs of the surrounding buildings from where they would exacerbate the chaos by throwing more flashbangs and smoke grenades and a few tear gas canisters into the street below.

Within minutes, there was total and utter pandemonium on the streets and in the nightclubs. The earsplitting noises of the fire alarms, the burning sensation caused by the tear gas and smoke, and the gunshots were driving people into a frenzy. Some of them pulled out guns and started shooting at anything and nothing in the belief that they were under attack from a rival triad gang.

All of Tian's guards, except the three on the top floor, abandoned their positions and rushed out of the Voco to fend off the attackers. None of them, including Tian and his guards, one in his study with him and two outside in the hallway, heard the sound of the helicopter above.

Tian and his guard in the study were staring at the door, expecting someone to come through there momentarily when the window behind them shattered. They spun around just in time to see a big man, clad in black from head to toe with a black balaclava covering his face, landing on the carpet.

Tian had no gun, having left it on his desk. His guard raised his gun but was too late. Two bullets entered his face, one through the bridge of his nose and the other through his left eye. It made a complete mess of the back of his head upon exit.

Tian started moving to his desk, but the big man said, "One more step and you're dead."

He stopped and turned to face the intruder. The next moment, another man in black with his face covered by a black balaclava accompanied by a snarling big, black dog also came through the window.

"Good evening, Mr. Tian," the man said. "Sorry to drop in on you like this. We won't be long. We're only here to collect our women and have a quick chat with you."

Tian's face was white as paper, and he was trembling with rage. Slowly, while staring at the two masked men and the dog, he raised his hands, moved his legs apart, and took some kind of kungfu stance.

The man with the snarling dog started laughing and said to the big one, "Josh, will you take care of Mister Bruce Lee here, while Digger and I go get the women?"

"It'll be my pleasure," he said.

Before Rex and Digger reached the door, they all heard glass shattering followed by two rapid double taps, and then everything went quiet. Rex tapped the switch on his throat mic and said, "Great. Digger and I are coming out of the study in a sec. Please come over here." He looked at Josh and said, "Floor cleared and secured."

Josh nodded and took a step closer to Tian as Rex and Digger headed for the door.

Ojha was waiting for Rex outside the study and told him there were two guards on the floor, both dead. His companion was watching the hallway, escalator, and fire escape stairs.

Rex thanked him, and said, "Keep an eye on Josh and Tian inside. They're about to get into the ring."

Rex missed the askance look from Ojha as he was talking to Digger, saying, "Hey buddy, take me to Catia."

Digger yelped, got up, and sprinted down the hallway straight to the fourth door, sat down, and started barking excitedly.

Rex caught up. Trying the door handle, it was locked. He pulled out his Glock 17 and shot the lock to pieces in two rapid blasts and kicked the door open.

Digger shouldered Rex out of his way as he rushed past him into the room and went straight for Catia, where she was sitting tied to a chair.

Rex quickly scanned the room. There was no danger. Catia, Marissa, and Dora were there, tied to chairs bolted to the floor. They looked unharmed, though all three of them were laughing and crying.

In the meantime, Ojha had entered the study just in time to witness Tian's quick but brutal lesson in hand-to-hand combat from Josh. Tian got a few harmless punches across, but by the time Ojha heard Rex's shots that destroyed the door lock, Tian already had a broken nose and jaw. Seconds later, he screamed like a baby when Josh broke his left elbow. He dropped to the floor, yelling and swearing. Josh's kick to the side of his head silenced him.

Josh pulled him to his feet by his hair, threw him into one of the chairs, and gave him a piece of his mind. Then with the help of Ojha, ziptied, and gagged the gang leader.

Rex couldn't cut the restraints off Catia quick enough for Digger's liking; he was whining and yelping nonstop. When Rex cut the final pieces of duct tape off her legs, Digger was on his hind legs pinning Catia to the chair and licking her face. Rex let him be and moved on to free Marissa and Dora.

Catia threw her arms around Digger, talking, laughing, and crying.

It was only after Rex had freed Marissa and Dora that he was able to get a chance to hug and kiss his wife while Digger doted on Marissa and Dora, still very excited but not as much as with Catia.

A little less than fifteen minutes after the first flashbang went off, Jethro's helicopter lifted from the helipad atop Tian's Voco nightclub and headed to Matz Island.

Inside the chopper were Rex's assault team, his diversion team, Jethro, and David. Apart from a few small bruises that Josh sustained during his encounter with Bruce Lee's disciple, they were unscathed. The same could not be said of their guest, Tian. He was in excruciating pain, moaning and swearing continuously until Josh hit him over the head with his Glock 17.

They left behind three bodies that they had produced. They also left behind an unknown number of dead, which they did not produce directly, and scores more wounded and injured in the chaos that ensued in the wake of the diversion attack.

Chapter Thirteen

NEW RIGHTEOUSNESS AND PEACE

Matz Island, Hong Kong

Day 8

Back on Matz Island, Rex, Josh, and Ojha took Tian down to the marina and onto the captured SYO yacht. They made a point of showing him the body of his dead employee on the upper deck.

Spencer and one of the crew members who had the technical knowledge had set up a video camera to record the conversation they were about to have with Song-li. The camera would also stream the event to Jethro's study and the communications room on the *TOMATS*.

Rex led the interrogation. Despite his injuries and pain, Tian was defiant. Rex was tired and irritated, and so was Josh. They wanted to be with their wives and not with this arrogant lowlife. When he refused to answer their questions and instead let loose a barrage of profanities, Rex contemplated handing him over to Josh for a bit of baseball practice. But in the end, he decided Tian was the right candidate for waterboarding—Rex's version of it.

They tied him up good, attached a few heavy metal weights to his feet, tied the end of a long rope around his body, and threw him overboard. They left him underwater for a full minute, pulled him up, had a look at him, listened to him beg for his life, ignored him, and let him drop again. This time, Rex left him there for a minute and a half. When Tian came up gulping for air, he screamed and begged them to take him out, promising he would answer any question they had.

Rex looked at Digger, Josh, and Ojha in turn and asked, "Do you believe him?" Josh and Ojha shook their heads, and Digger growled.

Tian went down for the third time and stayed there for two minutes.

When he came up, he vomited water and seaweed, and when he got his voice back, he started begging profusely again.

Rex said, "Okay, against the advice of my comrades, I'm prepared to give you a chance. But you're not coming out of the water until I have all the answers I want."

Tian nodded vigorously and said he would cooperate.

The cameraman moved the camera to the side of the yacht, checked that he could capture everything adequately, and nodded for Rex to start.

"Was it your men who attacked the two ladies at Stanley Market three days ago?"

"Yes."

"Why?"

"I had orders to kill Ms. Frankel."

"Whose orders?"

Tian hesitated. "I . . . I can't . . . They'll kill me."

Rex let the rope slip, and Tian disappeared below the water. He left him there for a minute, pulled him back out, and said, "You don't have to worry about that. You can only die once. I'm going to drown you before they can lay a hand on you." With that, Rex let go of the rope again, and Tian slipped back below the waterline screaming. Rex pulled him back up just far enough so that his head was above the water and said, "Did you say something?"

"Yes! A man by the name of Qian Lim. He's an agent of the Chinese Ministry of State Security, the MSS."

"Were you also acting on his orders when your men kidnapped the women yesterday afternoon?"

"Yes."

"Where can I find this Mr. Qian?"

"I don't know . . . I . . ."

Rex let the rope slip again and left Tian down for a minute while he asked Josh and Ojha if they thought their prisoner was truthful. They thought he was.

"Why did you do that?" Tian shouted when he got his breath back. "I'm telling you the truth. I honestly don't know where to find him. He lives in China; he works for the MSS, and that's all I know. I met him a few years ago."

"And no doubt since then, you've done numerous jobs of this nature for him?"

"Yes, I have."

"In exchange for?"

"They make sure that the Hong Kong police don't interfere with our business activities."

"You call kidnapping, killing, drug dealing, and human trafficking business activities?"

Tian didn't reply, and he went underwater for another ninety seconds.

When he came back up, after throwing up more seawater and seaweed, he shouted, "Yes! Among the triads, we call it business."

"Shitty business you're in. It's been your undoing. We can chat about that later. What were you supposed to do with the women?"

"We were supposed to deliver them to a ship off the coast of China tomorrow night."

"Name of the ship and the coordinates of the rendezvous?"

"Qian Lim was going to provide that information to me only tomorrow night when we were on our way."

Rex shook his head and let the rope slip through his fingers. When Tian's head disappeared underwater, Rex said into his throat mic, "Anything else anyone wants to ask?" There were no questions. "I've got a good mind to leave him down there."

Jethro's voice came over Rex's earphones, "I feel the same, but let's keep him alive. You never know; we might be able to use him and Xing to persuade the SYO members to do a bit of work for us in exchange for releasing their leaders."

"Good point," Rex said, bringing Tian up from the water.

Ten minutes later, the ringing of the Commissioner of the Hong Kong police's private cellphone woke him from his peaceful sleep. He was an early riser. By his definition, early in his books meant between six-thirty a.m. and seven a.m., not 5:20 a.m.

"What the hell? This better be very important," he growled with his eyes still closed.

"My apologies for waking you so early, Commissioner,

but we have a bit of a crisis," Jethro started without announcing who he was.

It wasn't necessary; the Commissioner immediately recognized his voice.

"Mr. Matz, what's the crisis? Are you and your family okay?"

"Thank God, we are. But if not for my guards, we would all have been dead now."

"What happened? I'll send a SWAT team out immediately."

"Not necessary, Commissioner. My men took care of it. But it's a mess. You better send your men to come and sort it out."

"What happened, Mr. Matz?"

Jethro managed to keep the smile that was on his face out of his voice as he told the Commissioner how a group of SYO hooligans got it into their heads to launch an attack on the yacht of friends in the marina at Matz Island. Fortunately, his guards saw them when they were boarding the yacht and tried to stop them. A fight broke out, shots were fired, one of the attackers was killed, and their yacht took a few bullets in the upper deck. Thank God, no one else was killed. But in the ensuing fight, most of the attackers sustained injuries.

"They're all alive, tied up, and on their yacht in my marina, waiting for your men to come and take them into custody," Jethro ended the account.

Just then, the Commissioner's landline started ringing. He apologized and answered the phone. Jethro could hear him talk.

"What the hell! When? Almost two hours ago, and you only phone me now? How many? Hang on; I'm talking to someone very important on my other phone. Another damn crisis. Stay on the line."

"Mr. Matz, I am very sorry I've got another crisis to deal with. Apparently, the gangs in Yeun Long have gone to war with each other. I'll dispatch a contingent of my men to Matz Island immediately. We're still looking for the kidnappers. My men are working on some leads, and I believe we'll find them soon, maybe even today."

Jethro thanked him and ended the call without telling him not to bother looking for the kidnappers anymore.

The police arrived in two powerful motor yachts on Matz Island within an hour. They questioned Ojha as head of Matz Enterprises security first, and he confirmed what Jethro told their boss. They questioned a few guards, and they only reiterated what their boss told the police.

They retrieved the body of the dead gangster from the SYO yacht, arrested the remaining seven suspects, confiscated their yacht, and transferred them all to the Hong Kong main police station.

It was only later that they would find out that the SYO's second-in-command, Xing Ruogang, was with them during the attack, but when they woke up, he was gone. He must have managed to escape.

By eight a.m., the story of the gang war that erupted in the early hours of the morning in Yeun Long broke in the media. The reports were confusing, to say the least. No two eyewitnesses saw the same thing. Some said there was a helicopter involved in the attack, but others said those who saw a helicopter were hallucinating. No one knew who started it, but everyone agreed it was triggered when three enormous bombs exploded. Whatever happened and who saw what didn't matter much, in the end, there were close to seventy people injured, some seriously, and ten were dead, killed by the bullets from the guns of the enemies of SYO.

None of them seemed to notice that the only dead and injured were SYO members. None of them were ever privy to the whereabouts of their revered leader, Mr. Tian Song-li, so they didn't know he had gone missing. However, they fully expected him to make an appearance and issue a statement about the cowardly attack on the peace-loving people of the Sun Yee On in Yeun Long. After all, as their name suggested, they were all about New Righteousness and Peace.

Chapter Fourteen

TIME FOR YOU TO LEAVE OUR SHORES

Matz Island, Hong Kong

Day 8

After questioning Tian, Rex and Josh spent a few hours with their wives. Understandably, both women were still perturbed by their ordeal. However, the tender loving care of their husbands and the *TOMATS*'s crew helped a lot to stabilize their emotional seesawing.

Rex and Josh told them the real reason for the SYO's interest in Dora. They also shared the information provided by Tian. By midday, Catia and Marissa had regained enough composure to tell their husbands to stop worrying about them, and the four of them went up to Jethro's residence to meet with him, Dora, David, Ojha, and Tao.

Dora was in one of the bedrooms with her brother by her side. His personal physician had been there earlier and had given her a mild sedative. But to her visitors, it was clear that she was still very much shaken by the nightmare. She told them that her husband, Robert, was on his way to Hong Kong to accompany her back home to California.

Dora fell asleep soon after, and they all went to Jethro's study. He started the discussion by addressing the Daltons and Farleys. "We are eternally grateful for what you've done for our families over the past few days. There are no words that can describe our appreciation and gratitude. It is a great honor to have met you and to count you among our friends . . ."

"But?" Catia said.

Jethro smiled. "But we think it's time for you to leave our shores and get as far away from the Chinese government as quickly as possible."

The indignation of the four was unanimous, and Rex verbalized it. "And let the Chinese communists have their way? Let them blindside everyone while they lie and cover up the potential threat this virus poses to the people across the globe?"

"No, Jethro, we're not leaving. Not until we have a solid understanding of what exactly is going on. But I'll talk to Spencer and recommend that he gets the *TOMATS* and the crew out of here."

David said, "That's what we thought you'd say. But you must know that we're now high on their hit lists. We expect them to spare no effort to silence us."

Rex said, "We understand that. But as far as we're concerned, it would be tantamount to desertion if we pack up and leave you to deal with the potentially serious international threat brewing in China. Of course, we don't have the capabilities to stop the Chinese. But we could be instrumental in stopping them by collecting the information and hand it to those who *can* stop them."

Rex's companions nodded their agreement.

"How do you want to approach it?" Jethro said.

"Well, as I've said before, we need to find out what is happening over there. We already know that China is adamant about obscuring it. We have to collect the information and pass it on to world leaders to take action."

"We have Dora's account of what her friend Benjamin told her," Josh said. "But that's secondhand information, not enough to get world leaders to circle the wagons. With Benjamin, our only source of information thus far, dead or in a Chinese jail, we need another reliable source of information . . . such as one or more scientists working at that lab you told us about."

"I might have one," David said excitedly. "It could be a risk, but one I'm prepared to take."

For Catia and Marissa's sake, David repeated some of the information about Zexian Biomed that he gave to Rex and Josh the day before. The CEO of Zexian Biomed was Dr. Zheng Xuefeng, Benjamin's boss and friend. He knew Zheng's background because he did a thorough check on him before investing in the company. He had regular contact with Zheng, and although they've never discussed politics, he suspected the sixty-odd-year-old Zheng was a potential dissident.

"You think he would be willing to cooperate with us?" Catia said.

"The issue is that Benjamin told Dora that the staff at Zexian Biomed were all under tight surveillance," Rex said.

"Yes, that's correct," David said. "But I'm thinking of luring him out of Shanghai to Hong Kong for a face-to-face meeting at my office."

"That would be ideal," Marissa said. "But how're you

going to get him to come over here when he's under such strict surveillance?"

"We don't know if travel restrictions have been imposed on him. But let's not speculate," David said, taking his cellphone out and dialing Dr. Zheng's direct line in Shanghai.

When Zheng answered, David activated the speaker on his phone. They exchanged greetings and pleasantries, and then David said, "Doctor, the reason for my call is that I've come across a very promising business opportunity, and I'd like to get your opinion about it. It's a small biotech company in Switzerland doing research in the same field as Zexian Biomed."

David's audience in the study was quiet, but all had big grins on their faces. David was a consummate actor.

"As you know, I'm no scientist, but the little I understand of their work has me quite excited. I was wondering if I could persuade you to make a quick one-day trip to Hong Kong the day after tomorrow?

"The CEO and lead scientist from this company are in Hong Kong for a few days. They're flying out in the evening the day after tomorrow. I'd like you to meet with them and assess their technology with the view of a possible merger."

"That sounds interesting, Mr. Sarlin. I'd certainly like to meet them. I'll have to delegate a few tasks and reschedule a few meetings."

"Tell you what. How about you bring your lovely wife with you for a bit of shopping in Hong Kong? My wife will be more than happy to accompany her. I'll make a car and chauffeur available to take them around, and of course, her airline ticket will be paid by us."

Zheng laughed. "You have just made me my wife's hero, Mr. Sarlin. I'm looking forward to the trip."

"Thanks. I'll get my secretary to arrange your flights

and for you to pick up your tickets at the airport. See you the day after tomorrow. Have a safe trip."

When the call ended, David said, "Fortunately, the Zhengs have no children and no siblings." He noticed Jethro's frown and explained, "I'm thinking of recruiting him, Jethro. If I'm able to convince him to cooperate with us, we can't send him back to China. We'll have to make arrangements to immediately move him and his wife to a place of safety; another country maybe."

"Good thinking," Jethro said. "I might have some options."

"Okay," Rex said, "now let's talk about how we're going to collect information from the people in Shanghai who are affected by this virus. We need to act on that as quickly as possible. If Benjamin's information is accurate, they're already in a crisis over there. They're likely to cordon off parts of the city, put everyone in quarantine, and use their military to enforce it soon."

Jethro nodded. "Yes, they won't hesitate to use heavy-handed tactics, especially if they think they'd be able to contain it in that manner."

Over the next half an hour, they worked out a strategy.

Tao Meng and one more senior staff member from Matz Enterprises and two from David's HK Securities would travel to Shanghai and work in different areas of the city, collecting information from the populace.

Tao was in charge of the mission. They agreed that it would be beneficial to have this information available when they meet with Dr. Zheng. "A tall order," Tao noted, "but not impossible."

The four of them would travel to Shanghai on two different flights. They would collect information and photos and videos of the funeral homes and the urn factory. They would talk to the people who had lost loved ones, tape the conversations—secretly, of course—discreetly asking about the symptoms and any other relevant information.

Jethro was wondering out loud if it wouldn't be a good opportunity to get a few blood samples from infected people but interrupted himself and said, "No wait, ignore that. Pretend I never said it."

Catia laughed and said, "I was just starting to wonder why you would want to be known as the man who brought the virus to Hong Kong. However, not a bad idea, Jethro. If we can get someone with the expertise to collect blood samples and secure them, we should definitely try and do it. But I don't think we have time for that now."

Everyone agreed.

Chapter Fifteen

TAO MENG'S SCOUTS

Matz Island, Hong Kong

Day 8

Tao Meng, although entirely supportive of the plan to go and collect information from the streets of Shanghai, pointed out that none of his "spies" had any street craft skills other than what they'd read in books and saw in movies. "I've booked flights for us; we're flying out tonight. The first flight is at eight fifteen and the second at nine." He looked at the Daltons and Farleys and said, "How much street craft skills can you impart to us from now until we leave?"

Rex glanced at his watch. It was two p.m. Tao's team would be there in half an hour. They had to be briefed, they had to pack, and they had to be at the airport two hours before their flights would leave.

He could've told Tao that intelligence agencies take

years to train their agents. Streetcraft was a significant part of that training. Besides that, professional field agents were a rare and unique breed; they had distinctive personalities and aptitudes; they went through extensive physical and psychological selection processes. But that would have taken almost as much time to explain than what Rex had in mind for their training. So, he said, "Get your cadets together, and I'll make double-O-sevens out of them in no more than a quarter of an hour."

Tao smiled dumbfounded. The rest of them stared at Rex, though they were wondering if he had lost his marbles. Jethro broke the silence. "Ah, Rex, would you mind if I attend your training session?"

Before Rex could answer, David, Catia, Marissa, even Ojha and Josh lodged similar requests. Digger was asleep on the floor next to Catia.

Thirty-five minutes later, they were all looking at Rex to start what would become known among them as Rex Dalton's "How to become a superspy in fifteen minutes or less."

Catia made a scene of activating the stopwatch on her phone, hovered her finger over the start button, looked at Rex, and said, "Ready when you are."

Rex smiled at her, nodded, and started talking. "Lesson one. You're not spies. Spies betray their own by giving or selling secrets to their enemies. You are scouts. You're going to observe the enemy and talk to the enemy, discreetly, of course.

"Lesson two. China has the most comprehensive camera surveillance system on the planet, one CCTV camera for every four people. They have the most sophisticated facial recognition, artificial intelligence, and digital technologies to augment their vast network of monitoring systems. Eight of the top ten most surveilled cities in the world are in China, and that includes Shanghai. In short, the Chinese will know who you are even before you land in their country. They will follow your every move from the moment you step off the plane.

"Lesson three. It's all about deception. Therefore, you're not going to act as scouts do. You're not going to wear a cloak and a dagger because that's what scouts do. You'll be unarmed, and you'll dress to impress. You're not going to hide, and you're not even going to try to blend in, because that's what scouts do. You're not going to act as most people do; that's what scouts do. You're going to make sure people remember you because scouts don't want to be remembered. You're going to complain loudly about the food in the restaurant. You're going to offend the waiters. You're going to insult the manager at your hotel tonight and tomorrow. You're not going to sit in a public place or on public transport with your face behind a newspaper; scouts do that. You're going to look around, be inquisitive, bump into people, and talk to them. You'll speak loudly; you want to be noticed. You'll be annoyingly rude, and you'll be overly friendly.

"You're going to do all of that because a scout would never do it.

"Lesson four. You won't be caught because only scouts get caught." Rex looked at Catia and said, "You can push stop."

There was a protracted silence in the room as if everyone were replaying Rex's words. For the uninitiated among them, it must've sounded like the rantings of a madman, but on replay, the brilliant logic of it became crystal clear.

Jethro slowly rose to his feet and started clapping his

hands, and soon everyone else followed suit. And to Catia's great enjoyment, for the first time in her life, she saw Rex blushing.

Shanghai, China

Day 8 and 9

With Rex's voice playing in their minds, Tao's team was working quickly and efficiently. Through the contacts they had prior to their arrival, and through casual conversations with total strangers, they gathered information. What they saw and heard during the exploits, they recorded, video-taped, and photographed as indiscreetly as possible.

By the afternoon of the day after their arrival, they had collected tons of pictures and videos of the funeral homes, urn factories, doctors' surgeries, and a few hospitals. They had audio recordings of conversations with the families of people who had died and with people on the streets and in restaurants.

They encrypted it all and uploaded it to Jethro's secured servers via a secured satellite data link owned and operated by Matz Enterprises. Then they cleaned out their phones and computers and cameras to make sure there was no trace left of the data they had collected and headed to the airport to catch their flights back to Hong Kong.

Chapter Sixteen

THE RECRUIT

Sarlin Tower, Hong Kong

Day 10

Dr. Zheng Xuefeng and his wife arrived in Hong Kong early in the morning. An HK Securities company car, a white Mercedes-Benz GLE 450 SUV, and chauffeur were waiting for them. Mrs. Sarlin was already in the car. They didn't notice the two vehicles following them from the airport to the Sarlin Tower, the headquarters of HK Securities in West Kowloon.

When the chauffeur pulled into the reserved parking at the Sarlin Tower, David got a call from the countersurveillance team that no one from the airport had followed Dr. Zheng Xuefeng. They also reported that there was no one hanging around the building watching. His office had been swept for bugs, and it was clear.

After seeing Dr. Zheng to the entrance of the building,

the chauffeur returned to his vehicle. Madames Sarlin and Zheng were talking excitedly and nonstop in the back. He took off and headed for the shopping malls of SOGO, Times Square, and Island Beverley, the best shopping districts in Hong Kong for clothing, jewelry, cosmetics, toys, and electrical goods.

When Zheng stepped out of the elevator on the twenty-fifth floor, David was there to meet him. He took Zheng to his spacious office, where he was introduced to two men, Rex Dalton and Josh Farley. Although David didn't say so when he introduced them, Zheng must have assumed they were the CEO and lead scientist of the Swiss biotech company.

Zheng's English was fluent, albeit with a heavy Chinese accent. Dalton and Farley only spoke English. Zheng must have noted that both spoke English with an American accent, but he didn't mention it.

David's secretary appeared and took their drink orders — coffee, tea, and fruit juice. While waiting for her to return with their orders, they spent the time exchanging pleasantries about the weather, Hong Kong, and the Zhengs' flight that morning.

A few minutes later, the secretary rolled in a trolley with their drinks and a variety of snacks.

When the door closed behind her, David asked everyone to take out their cellphones, switch them off, and remove the batteries before he went straight to the heart of the matter. His strategy was to unnerve Zheng as quickly as possible and get him to the point where he would show his loyalties. It was also part of the plan to let David do all the talking until they could establish where they stood with Dr. Zheng.

"Let's begin with Benjamin Yatsir. Where is he?"

The blood had drained from Zheng's face. "He took ill a

few days ago, and it looks like he won't be able to return to work for a while."

"Do you know what's wrong with him?"

"No, I don't."

"You know he's a friend of mine?"

Zheng nodded.

"The problem is, I can't get hold of either his wife or children."

Zheng shrugged, but his hand holding the teacup was shaking.

"Dr. Zheng, I'm afraid I've brought you here under pretense. This meeting is not going to be about a merger with a Swiss biotech company. I apologize for that, but we believe the circumstances call for drastic and rapid action."

Zheng's demeanor had changed from composed to very tense. "What circumstances?"

"It seems there is another virus on the loose in China. Well, at least in Shanghai."

Zheng shook his head slowly. "I . . . I . . . don't know anything about that."

"Dr. Zheng, this room is secure. What you tell us here will be treated with the utmost discretion, and you will not be put in any danger."

Zheng dropped his head into his hands and sighed deeply. It took him the best part of a minute before he spoke. "I . . . I . . . don't know what to do. If I talk about it . . . they'll arrest me, they'll . . . disappear me. You know what that means."

"Yes, I know. Who are *they*?"

"The MSS."

"Why would they do that? Why are they involved? What's going on there?"

Zheng went silent for quite a while, then he started in a

soft voice, almost a whisper. "Mr. Sarlin, I'm scared to death. If I tell you what I know, I've signed my death warrant and my wife's."

"Dr. Zheng, I can make arrangements for your safety and security."

"From the MSS? How? I don't think so . . . Nobody is safe from them."

"You see, doctor, we already know something big and bad is going on over there. Benjamin told us."

"Wha— what . . . Did you speak to Benjamin? When?"

"My sister did about a week or so ago when she was in Shanghai. He told her what was going on at Zexian Biomed. After that, he and his wife and children disappeared. That's what raised the red flags for us and why we brought you here."

For now, he did not need to know about the attempt on Dora's life and the kidnapping.

"I think I've said too much already."

"What do you mean?"

"Mr. Sarlin, this room is not secured." Zheng took a black and gold ballpoint pen out of his jacket pocket and placed it in front of him on the table. "I'm under orders to record everything in this meeting. Tonight, when I arrive back in Shanghai, they'll want to interview me and want the pen recorder back. There is already enough damning evidence on that recorder to get me in deep trouble."

"That means you can't go back. Can you?"

Zheng nodded. "No, I can't, unless I'm prepared to be tortured and disappear, and the same will happen to my wife. I had to get permission from the MSS to make this trip. They authorized it on condition that I carry this pen recorder on me all the time and record every conversation."

"Okay, doctor, I want you to relax now. Cooperate with

us, and everything will work out. We'll see to the safety of you and your wife."

"I don't know how you're planning to do that. I don't need to remind you how powerful and capable the MSS is. But it seems I don't have much of a choice now, do I?"

"You have a choice, doctor. I won't ask you to do anything you don't want to do. That recorder is not a problem. We'll be able to overcome that if necessary, and you can go back to China if that's what you prefer. The question you've got to answer for yourself is, are you happy to keep on working under the Communist government of China or not? In other words, are you really a communist supporter?"

"No, I'm not. And I haven't been for a long time. Lately, I've become totally embittered and disillusioned. I've been looking for a way out of China for some time now."

"That's what we hoped you would say. Don't worry about your wife; she's safe. My wife will take her to our house and keep her there until we've finished this meeting, and we've decided where we would take you."

Zheng had tears in his eyes when he said, "Thank you, Mr. Sarlin. I guess now you want me to tell you what's going on at Zexian Biomed?"

"That's the entire purpose of this meeting and, of course, to decide how you could help us and how we could best safeguard you and your wife."

Zheng nodded and took a deep breath.

"Before you continue," David said, "I've got a few more people who are very much interested in what you have to say."

Zheng nodded.

Chapter Seventeen

THE REPORT

Sarlin Tower, Hong Kong

Day 10

A few minutes later, they were all seated around the boardroom table: Dr. Zheng, David, Rex, Catia, and Digger, Josh and Marissa, Jethro, Tao Meng, and Ramesh Ojha. Dora and her husband, Robert, were en route to California.

David told Dr. Zheng that everything was being recorded on video and audio. He also told him that he was going to repeat some of the questions from the previous meeting for the sake of newcomers and to get it recorded.

Zheng indicated he had no problem with that and started by telling them about the day, about two months ago, when the MSS had turned up at Zexian Biomed's building.

"The MSS made us, all of us at Zexian Biomed, sign an

agreement that we would not divulge any information about what we're working on. The MSS has stopped all our research and ordered us to work on this new top-secret government project. They said it was in the interest of national security."

"So, this has been going on for two months already?"

"Yes."

"In other words, you've been working on a top-secret government assignment exclusively for the past two months, and you haven't reported any of that to the board of directors. That means the reports of the last two months are all fake. Correct?"

"Yes." Zheng nodded slowly.

"How do you feel about all of it? Are you happy with the government's interference in your operations?"

"Not at all, sir. But what could I do? I had to follow their instructions or face disappearing . . . like Benjamin."

"Please tell us what you know about Benjamin."

"I don't know the exact details, but an MSS agent turned up at my office a week or so ago and told me that Benjamin would not be returning to work. When I asked why, he told me that Benjamin was a traitor, that they had caught him red-handed disclosing information about the project to someone on the outside. They had an audio recording of the conversation. He ordered me to talk to my staff and reiterate the secrecy of the project and the penalty for disobedience. I take it that the outside person he referred to is your sister?"

"Yes, it is. Now tell us about this project."

Zheng took a deep breath and let it out slowly.

None of the audience were scientists, and some of what Zheng told them was technobabble to them, but he tried his best to keep it simple. And what he told them scared the living daylights out of everyone in the room.

He told them that viruses were, in a certain way, at the molecular and genetic level very simple, much simpler than bacteria. Yet, at another level, they were mindbogglingly complex. Unlike bacteria or fungi, a virus was not considered a living thing—it has no cells, no brain, no nervous system. But they mutated so easily; they were exceedingly difficult to understand and hard, if not impossible, to kill once inside the body of a living creature. And they had the uncanny ability, once they lodged themselves in the cells of a living being, to block the immune system from kicking into action.

There was something terrifying about an invisible inanimate entity that would come to life when it invaded the cells of a living creature and kill it.

About this specific virus, he told them that his scientists had mapped its genome and discovered the following:

"One, the virus is zoonotic, which means it's transmitted between animals and humans, and it also transmits from human-to-human.

"Two, although it's a corona-type virus, almost half of its genome showed a new lineage with no close genetic relationships to other known viruses—"

"What does that mean?" Jethro interjected.

"It means the virus didn't originate from random, natural mutations. We're dealing with a brand-new type of virus—made by humans in a laboratory."

A shocked silence descended in the room.

Zheng looked around the table, let the silence reign for a while, and then continued. "Corona in Latin means halo or crown. And that's what it looks like under a microscope, like a crown that surrounds the core of the virus. There are many different types of coronaviruses. A strain of the coronavirus causes the common flu or seasonal flu. This group of viruses causes respiratory tract infections in humans, and people who have existing health conditions or compromised immune systems are most at risk of severe complications.

"As you know, Benjamin has been researching how and why bats can be carriers of some of the most nightmarish viruses in the world, such as Ebola, SARS, and Coronavirus, and not get killed by them. However, during his research, he came across mutant Coronavirus strains that defeated the natural immunity of some bats—so-called superbug-Coronavirus strains. In other words, it would kill its host, the bat.

"This virus we've been studying the past two months is one of those, a type of bat Coronavirus—the superbug variety that Benjamin had discovered. We call it the Shanghai Strain."

"And by all indications so far, it seems the virus has escaped from the lab where it was engineered and is now creating havoc in some parts of Shanghai?" Rex said.

"Yes, that's what we believe has happened."

"Apologies for interrupting, please continue."

"Three, we know that Coronaviruses of any type spread very easily, like the flu; from human-to-human contact by touch, bodily fluids, etcetera."

"What will it take to develop a cure or a vaccine?" David asked.

"To develop either a cure or a vaccine won't be an easy feat. It will take time, a year to eighteen months, and the outcome will be dubious at best.

"You see, to develop a vaccine, we'll have to alter the genetic composition of the virus to make it weaker, then inject it into an animal such as a monkey. There could be three responses: the monkey contracts the disease and dies; it doesn't contract the disease, and it produces no antibodies; it doesn't contract the disease, and it does produce antibodies. The last one is what we're looking for. That means we can now develop a vaccine from the antibodies.

"But, unfortunately, that doesn't mean it's an effective vaccine yet. We must inject a healthy monkey with the vaccine and then expose it to the full-strength virus, and then two things can happen: the vaccine might not be effective, the monkey will not be able to overcome the disease and die. Or the immune response could be strong enough to fend off the virus, and the monkey will survive. Only when we have conquered all those obstacles can we start human trials.

"And then we still wouldn't know if the vaccine would provide long-term immunity to the virus. In other words, one could be vaccinated, and it might prevent them from becoming ill when contracting the virus, but the immunity might only last for a limited time. The next flu season might have a mutated virus to which the person might have no natural immune response. The vaccine that could be developed now won't be guaranteed to defend you against a second infection.

"We've developed a test for it, but it's expensive, invasive, and takes days to get a result. Not to mention that we've got no idea how accurate it could be because we couldn't test humans."

When Dr. Zheng paused, the facial expressions of his audience could not have been mistaken for anything other than trepidation.

He drew a deep breath and continued. "To make a vaccine against bacteria is possible, and it has been done successfully, such as the vaccines for tuberculosis, diphtheria, tetanus, cholera, typhoid, and others. But to develop an effective one against a virus has proved to be near impossible. After decades of flu vaccinations, we still can't stop it, between three hundred thousand to six hundred thousand people die worldwide annually from the complications caused by seasonal influenza. Remember the big deal about HIV? Well, after all the decades, there's still no vaccine that works for HIV, and the same goes for SARS, despite the time and the billions spent on it."

"So, what you're saying is scientists can't even cure or prevent the common cold?" Josh said.

"Yes, sir, that's exactly what I'm saying."

David was shaking his head. "Please continue."

"Four, we have no idea where this virus originated. We're not allowed to talk to any scientists outside our group. We know humans deliberately engineered it, and we've speculated that humans either accidentally or deliberately released it. However, we were not given access to any of the data that we know is being collected by the government. We have no access to any of the infected or surviving patients. But, from the streets, we hear that the symptoms are fever, coughing, a sore throat, and shortness of breath—very much like the flu.

"The thing is, the virus got out of wherever it was produced, and its killing people, at least in Shanghai as far as we know. All bodies are cremated; the funeral houses can't keep up. But there is nothing about it in the news or the internet. The government has blocked it out completely."

"I think we all have an idea why they're covering it up. But what's your opinion, Dr. Zheng?" Catia asked.

"We've been speculating about it. We suspect that we're not the only lab given the order to study this virus and find a cure and a vaccine. They, the government, would have all the data, they would know where this came from and how lethal it is or not. The fact that they're hiding it is troublesome. It's an indication that it could be lethal, not just another variety of the virus that causes seasonal influenza. Our worst-case scenario is that the virus had been weaponized. Need I say more?"

No one needed more explanation.

Zheng had dropped his head into his hands, and a long, uncomfortable quiet followed. Everyone was staring at him.

"Are you okay?" Jethro asked.

He nodded, took his handkerchief out of his pocket, and wiped tears from his eyes. "My apologies . . . This . . . virus. It . . . killed my mother a little over a week ago. We couldn't even have a proper funeral for her."

"Oh my God! We had no idea," David said. "Please accept our deepest condolences and sympathy."

"Thank you. Now you also know why I had become embittered with the communist government. I've never been a supporter; I kept my sentiments about them to myself for many years, but now I'm finally done with them. They're evil . . . Not that I've not known that for most of my life, but you know what it's like—you never really bother much about it until it arrives on your own doorstep and hurts or kills your loved ones."

The audience looked at each other. Their hearts went out to Zheng, and they had more than enough reason to be extremely concerned. They didn't have to say it; they knew if this threat was not stopped without delay, the images going through their minds of catastrophic pandemics, including the 1918 flu, that wiped out millions throughout human history, could soon, in a matter of weeks, become a reality.

Zheng clearing his throat, signaling that he had more to say, interrupted their thoughts. "I'm aware that I've scared you with what I told you so far, but I'm sorry to say, there's one more point I have to make."

Slowly, all eyes turned to him.

"As I said before, one of the troubling aspects of viruses is their ability to mutate into strains that are resistant to vaccines and medication, thus guaranteeing their own survival. But the most troublesome is that scientists can engineer viruses that would target cells with a specific genetic makeup."

"What . . . genetic, as in targeting people based on their DNA, such as race?" David said.

"Yes, sir. That's what it means."

"I thought that was just science fiction."

"Not anymore, sir. I know scientists in China, and I suspect there are in other parts of the world, have been working on that for more than a decade already."

"Scientists? I'd be more inclined to call them mass murderers," Marissa said.

"I agree," Zheng said and continued. "We don't know if that's the case with this virus, but playing devil's advocate for a moment, let's assume this strain we've been working on has been engineered for the Chinese or Asian DNA. Then it's also possible to engineer strains that would prosper in the DNA of say Europeans, Middle Easterners, Africans, etcetera."

"The viral version of a bullet from a sniper rifle . . .," Rex said in a whispered tone.

"Exactly."

"The erotic fantasy of psychopaths bent on ruling the world," Josh said.

Rex added, "When it comes to the threat of nuclear

annihilation, people usually have two viewpoints: Fatalistic —if it must be it must be, there's nothing I can do about it. Or ignorance—it will never happen.

"With biological warfare, people will probably have the same attitude except that it won't happen in an instant bright flash. It's going to spread slowly through the population at an ever-increasing rate, eventually overwhelming the health systems to the point that there are not enough healthy people to attend to the sick, and the dead lay rotting where they fell."

"That may be so," Josh said. "But the drill is the same for both. "Sit down, open your legs wide, bend down, and kiss your ass goodbye because it's the last time you'll see it."

Josh's gallows humor was a welcome reprieve from the ominous conversation they had so far.

Chapter Eighteen

WHO TO REPORT TO

Matz Island, Hong Kong

Day 10

The first order of business was to get Dr. Zheng and his wife to safety, immediately. The MSS would not start looking for him before that evening when their flight landed in Shanghai, and they did not deplane. By then, Zheng and his wife must be out of their reach.

Matz Enterprises had vast business interests in Singapore and therefore had offices as well as corporate apartments. From Hong Kong to Singapore was 2,585 kilometers, less than four hours flying in Jethro's luxury private jet, a Gulfstream G550 with a cruise speed of 705 kilometers per hour, and a range of 12,500 kilometers.

Ojha would send two of his men with them for protection.

Everyone around that table in David's office knew it

could not have been the easiest decision Zheng Xuefeng had to make in his life. When he and his wife said goodbye to each other a few hours before, one was looking forward to an exciting and fruitful business meeting, the other an exhilarating day in some of the best shopping destinations on the globe. Zheng Xuefeng's expectations had been ruined within the first half-hour. His wife was still wholly unaware of how dramatically their lives were about to change.

Apart from that, there was the emotional quagmire of abandoning their friends and acquaintances in China without so much as a goodbye or the prospect of contacting them soon.

With their Chinese passports, they could enter Singapore and stay for fifteen days without visas. After that, new arrangements had to be made for another country where they could stay. Everyone in the room expressed the hope that the United States would give them refuge, but no one could guarantee it.

Notwithstanding the personal and emotional issues facing them, Dr. Zheng had no illusions about what awaited him if he returned to China. For him and his wife to stay alive and free, they had to get on Jethro's private jet and say farewell to the country of their birth and the land of their forefathers. But his wife was a pragmatist, and they shared their loathing of the communist regime. However, she had no idea about the real state of affairs at her husband's workplace.

David had phoned his wife and asked her to take Mrs. Zheng to Matz Island and stay with her until her husband arrived. He would explain to her what was happening.

Shortly after the phone call, Ojha's second-in-command drove out of the basement of Sarlin Tower in a black

Mercedes SUV with tinted windows. Dr. Zheng Xuefeng was in the passenger seat. He had gotten rid of his suit and tie and was dressed in jeans, a T-shirt, sunglasses, and a baseball cap, all donated by some of David's staff.

Once on Matz Island, it was going to be much easier to get him and his wife on Jethro's jet unnoticed and take off for Singapore from the private airstrip on the island.

Matz Island, Hong Kong

Day 10

As soon as everyone said goodbye and wished Dr. Zheng a safe trip and he had left David's office, the thinking and planning started in earnest.

Admittedly, Zheng's report was terrifying, but they agreed that much of what he told them was the worst-case scenario. His narrative about what was going on in the streets of Shanghai was corroborated by the information Tao's scouts had collected. However, they still had no concrete evidence to prove that the virus that was killing people was the same virus Zheng's scientists were studying. Though, with the information they had, it was a logical conclusion.

Until the nexus could be proven, the most prudent approach was as Rex suggested, "Prepare for the worst, and hope for the best."

They had no problem agreeing that they would be remiss if they didn't bring what they had learned so far to the attention of world leaders immediately. This had the potential to become a severe global catastrophe. If it were indeed a Chinese-engineered, weapons-grade virus and not stopped presently, the rest of the planet might as well start enrolling in Cantonese or Mandarin language classes and learn the Chinese "straight march," better known as the goosestep.

That brought them to the juncture where they had to decide who had to report what, to whom, and when.

Jethro, more so than David, was on a first-name basis with many political leaders throughout Asia and other parts of the world, and he undertook to contact those they were sure were not under the influence of, bullied or bribed by the Chinese government. There were not many of those. The leaders of Japan, India, Taiwan, and Singapore were the ones they decided to approach.

They considered the Secretary-General of the United Nations but decided it would be best if the world leaders whom they intended to contact take the matter up with them.

Next, they considered WHO, the World Health Organization, a specialized agency of the United Nations. But the idea went down like a lead balloon when Jethro and David told them what they thought of the organization.

"WHO has been plagued by incompetence and internal corruption," David said. "With an annual budget of two billion US dollars, they're hopelessly underfunded. Even though they have one-hundred and ninety-odd member countries, the United States contributes a disproportionate twenty percent of their budget. China, with the biggest population on earth, contributes only a fraction of that."

"Despite continuous international requests that WHO should step in and demand that China shutdown the wetmarkets where they sell the most bizarre animal products, causing many health issues including viruses that jump from animals to humans, neither WHO nor China are doing anything about it. Besides the health risks, illegal wildlife trade is an international crime. But it's as if China keeps these markets going so that they can breed new viruses," Jethro said.

"Remember SARS, Severe Acute Respiratory Syndrome? It was sparked by the meat from wild civet cats sold in those wetmarkets. It killed more than eight thousand people between 2002 and 2003.

"Remember the outbreak of H1N1, swine flu? It was discovered in Mexico in March 2009, and by June, when WHO declared a pandemic, there were already more than 28,000 cases in 74 countries. More than 18,000 people died from it.

"When Ebola struck West Africa in 2014, WHO's inaction resulted in a disaster as they lost control of the situation. In the end, it was America and several other nations who stopped it when they stepped in and deployed more than five thousand military personnel to contain the disease. More than eleven thousand people died, most of them from just three countries—Guinea, Liberia, and Sierra Leone. The outbreak paralyzed their health systems and caused panic across the world, an egregious failure by WHO.

"There is no doubt that WHO is very much China-centric, often only echoing the communists' propaganda. They're more interested in the appeasement of China than doing their job in an unbiased and effective manner to stop these epidemics at their origin in the no man's land between legal and illegal trade, where those exotic animal products are transported on commercial routes with the help of bribes and legal loopholes.

"And last but not least, maybe WHO's love-affair with

the communists can be explained by the fact that in his young days, the current Director-General of WHO was a member of a Marxist revolutionary group fighting to overthrow his own government," David said.

"He is nothing but a third-rate international bureaucrat that lives in the pockets of the Chinese president and his cronies. We will get no help from them. The further we stay away from them for now, the better," Jethro said in conclusion.

It brought smiles to their wary faces when Rex ended the discussion with, "The WHO has just been found guilty of aiding and abetting the enemy."

Continuing the conversation about world leaders to contact, Jethro said, "I know the Prime Minister of Israel personally. I'll contact him."

Whether it was Jethro's intonation or the micro-expressions on his face that gave it away, Rex wouldn't know, but he was certain Jethro, and more than likely David as well, were *sayanim*.

The Mossad, a small intelligence agency compared to those of the USA, the UK, and other western European countries, had devised a brilliant plan to overcome their limitations, by recruiting helpers, *sayanim*, Jewish volunteers across the world.

The *sayanim* were bankers, restauranteurs, homeowners, hoteliers, owners and managers of guest houses, rental car companies, travel agents, lawyers, doctors, nurses, journalists, large corporates, and many others. It was estimated that across the globe, they numbered more than ten thousand, and whenever needed, provided mission support to Mossad's covert operations—free of charge. One of the benefits of the Jewish diaspora was what the chief of the Mossad called it.

Rex thought, with Jethro and David's means and influence, they would have been the ideal *sayanim* to keep Israel in the know about political and economic developments in this part of the world and to support Mossad covert operations. He was wondering how he could broach the subject with them without putting them in an awkward situation when he realized the answer was sitting right next to him, Catia. She was a *sayan*, a mission support specialist.

The Mossad often used her Airbnb in Rome as a safe house, and she also used to be one of their agent trainers. She was skilled in hand-to-hand combat and use of weapons, in street-craft, surveillance and counter-surveillance, how to set up weapons caches, and providing false identity documents when required by operatives. She was also trained to lead surveillance teams to collect information about targets. But she had scaled down her activities as a *sayan* during her PhD studies and when she and Rex got married.

He leaned closer to her and whispered in Italian, "Jethro and David are *sayanim*. I'm almost a hundred percent sure."

Catia smiled and said, "So am I. You want me to ask them?"

Before Rex could reply, he became aware everyone had stopped talking and was staring at him and Catia. He apologized and said, "Please excuse us for a minute; we'll be right back." He took Catia's hand and led her out into the hallway.

Digger lazily opened one eye, must have figured out they were not going far, no need for him to get up and follow them. He sighed softly, closed his eye, and went back to sleep.

Outside in the hallway, Rex told Catia what he had in mind; she agreed, and they went back.

Catia said, "David, do you have a private room where I can have a quick word with you and Jethro?"

Both had perplexed looks on their faces when David led them out of his office to an adjacent small room.

Catia got straight to the point. "I'm a *sayan*; I'm sure you know what that means?" She didn't wait for an answer. "Rex and I are sure both of you are too."

Jethro and David looked at each other then back at Catia, and David started laughing. "In your words of the other night, we cannot confirm or deny it. So, there's your answer.

"Just to put your minds at ease, my *katsa* is Yaron Aderet."

Katsa was the acronym for the Hebrew words *Ktsin Issuf*, meaning Collections Officer; in this context, it meant handler.

"Yaron! What a small world it is," Jethro said. "Well, he's also our *katsa*."

Yaron Aderet was the head of the Mossad's largest department, Collections, tasked with all the many aspects of conducting espionage overseas.

"But why is that important now?" David asked.

"We know there is a Jewish community in Shanghai, not big, but they are there. Do you know some of them? Are there *sayanim* among them that you know of?"

Jethro and David nodded in unison.

"Well, then the three of us should get on the phone to Yaron and ask him to contact the Shanghai *sayanim* and ask them to help us get more information out of Shanghai. What do you think?"

"Brilliant idea," Jethro said, and David concurred.

"Just to let you know, Josh and Marissa know all about the *sayan* system. They know about me, and they've both worked on joint missions with the Mossad. I take it Ojha and Tao don't know about you?"

"Correct," David said, "and let's keep it like that until there is a need for them to know."

"Agreed."

Back in David's office, they continued as if there was no interruption. Rex, Josh, and Marissa knew Catia would fill them in, in due time.

Rex told them that the only influential people he knew were the French president, Prime Minister, and a deputy minister, Margot Lemaire.

He didn't tell them how he and Digger had rescued Margot Lemaire a few years ago from a Russian government plot to embarrass the French president. Rex's timely actions helped to stop the Russians from blackmailing the president into signing a deal, which would have allowed the Russians to build a gas pipeline to France, making them totally dependent on Russian gas.

They all agreed that those were useful contacts, and Rex would take on the responsibility to talk to them when it became necessary.

Other than that, the most influential person the Daltons and Farleys knew was the CEO of CRC, John Brandt.

Josh and Marissa were in CRC's employment. Rex was a former employee. According to Brandt, "Rex Dalton is the best damn agent I ever had." But regardless of his official resignation a few years ago, Rex had since been called back for duty on two major missions.

Although for outsiders who didn't know better, it might have seemed that the relationship between Rex and Brandt was strained at best. The truth was, they loved and respected each other as a father and son would.

During the last mission, Brandt, who was almost seventy,

tried to persuade Rex to take over as CEO of CRC. It came as a total surprise to both Rex and Catia. At the time, Rex didn't accept or decline the offer, and they agreed to postpone the discussion until after Catia's PhD graduation ceremony. After the ceremony, they indeed had another conversation about it, but Rex had kicked the can down the road, telling Brandt he needed more time to think about it.

Via Brandt and his contacts, several directors and deputy directors of US security agencies, the information they had at hand would be passed up the ladder to the President of the United States within hours.

It was decided it was best to get the message to the President of the United States, as the so-called leader of the free world, and let him and his advisors decide what this group could do to help.

By the time Jethro's helicopter landed on Matz Island, the Zhengs were already halfway to Singapore and the start of a new life, free from communist rule.

On their way down to the *TOMATS* to make the call to John Brandt from the secured communications room, Catia told them about the discussion she had with Jethro and David about contacting Yaron Aderet to recruit the help of *sayanim* in Shanghai.

Chapter Nineteen

THE PHONE CALLS

Matz Island, Hong Kong

Day 10

It was two fifteen p.m. Hong Kong time when Rex, Catia, Digger, Josh, Marissa, and Declan Spencer were all seated in the *TOMATS* communications room and called John Brandt at CRC headquarters in Arizona where it was eleven fifteen p.m.

When the phone started ringing, a grin broke across Rex's face. He flipped the off switch on the video feed and held his hand up for everyone to be quiet.

"What's up, Declan?" Brandt answered. He was not a man known for embellishing his words. People who didn't know him well thought him to be rudely abrupt. He didn't care.

Rex replied in Cantonese.

The line went quiet for a beat. "What the hell . . .?

Who's this . . .? Dalton! You asshat, I'm going to wring your neck the next time I see you."

"Are you awake, Old Timer?"

"Take a guess."

"With you, it's always difficult to tell."

"Dalton, I'm going to put a contract out on you. My life will be much less complicated if you're not in it anymore. Switch the damn video on."

Rex switched it on and said, "Now listen, Old Man, I didn't phone you to have a crapshoot. We've got a situation—"

"Why am I not surprised? Wherever you go, *situations* are sure to arise. How many?"

"How many what?"

"Dead and wounded."

"Negligible compared to how many will be if you don't stop and listen to me."

Their trademark bantering was over, and they both got serious.

"I'm listening," Brandt said.

"Okay, John, I suggest you get yourself an extra-large, extra-strong coffee and pour an extra-stiff shot of that French cognac into it. You're going to need it."

"Damn. Okay, hang on, let me get myself fortified over here."

A few minutes later, Brandt appeared back on screen and said, "I took a few shots of cognac straight from the bottle while I waited for the water to boil. I'm ready. Shoot."

Catia and Marissa told him about the incident at Stanley Market and their abduction.

Spencer told him about the SYO attack on the *TOMATS*.

Rex and Josh told him about the rescue mission, and the meeting with Dr. Zheng that morning while Marissa uploaded all the information they had collected over the past few days to CRC's secured servers.

Brandt's face was ashen by the time they finished their reports. "When I was young, it was the Russians trying to kill me. When I was middle-aged, the Muslim crazies got their turn. Now that I'm old, the Chinese are thinking they can do it. Okay, stay sharp over there. I'm calling Martin right now and will get back to you."

Martin Richardson was the deputy director in charge of CIA operations. Richardson was a few years younger than Brandt, and they were good friends.

Secured telephone call

Day 10

It was 3:20 a.m. in Washington, D.C., when Brandt's call stirred Richardson from his peaceful sleep.

"You were asleep?" Brandt said.

"Of course, that's what humans do at this hour."

"Great. Exactly what I had in mind. Payback for waking me at four in the morning when I was on holiday last year to send me on an errand to find a couple of ancient Jewish Libraries."

Brandt was referring to a joint CIA-Mossad operation the year before, where CRC was tasked by the CIA to lead a mission to find two lost Jewish libraries that were removed from the Jewish Ghetto in Rome by the Nazis in October

1943. Catia had been working on a PhD about those libraries at the University of Rome when she discovered that the libraries were not destroyed during the war as everyone believed but still existed. The Israelis were worried that it could fall into the hands of radical Muslim groups and asked the President of the United States to help.

"Okay, you've had your revenge. May I go back to sleep now?"

"Yes, if you want to, after hearing what I have to say."

"Then say it, John."

It took Brandt a little more than an hour and a half to impart the information he got from Hong Kong and ruin Richardson's day while he was at it.

Richardson was quiet for a while when Brandt finished talking, then said quietly, "Okay, I'll get back to you as soon as I've shared this sensational news with the director. Get your IT guys to talk to ours and get that information transferred to our servers."

"Will do."

Langley, Virginia / Washington, D.C.

Day 10

Richardson's call at five a.m. caught Howard Lawrence, the Director of the CIA, while he was shaving and getting ready for the day in the office at Langley.

Forty-five minutes later, Richardson was in Director Lawrence's office, and an hour later, the two men were in the backseat of the Director's official vehicle on their way to the White House to meet the president.

They didn't have to wake him; the president was an early riser. The first part of the president's morning was devoted to what he called "executive time," which included getting his daily security briefing, watching or reading the news, making calls, checking in with members of Congress, friends, administration officials, and informal advisers.

Today, Lawrence and Richardson were going to upset the president's daily routine and saddle him with what could very soon be another international crisis.

Chapter Twenty

MEETINGS AND BRIEFINGS

En route to the White House, Washington, D.C.

Day 11

Lawrence and Richardson didn't talk much on the way to the White House, both were ruminating on the information about the potential new threat lurking just below the horizon.

Over the past two decades, American politics had slowly deteriorated into what some called a warzone. There was a vast and expanding gap between Republicans and Democrats, which at times seemed to be unbridgeable.

A hyper-partisan atmosphere reigned in Washington. The parties have taken up positions in the trenches and were facing each other over "gun barrels" about issues such as climate change, immigration, abortion, religious freedom, same-sex marriages, minimum wages, free healthcare, free education, economic matters, redistribution of wealth, and many others. Those were not new issues; they had been debated over and legislated for decades, but for the past two decades, it had become more and more difficult for Congress to do their job because of the toxic partisanship that existed between the parties.

And, of course, the ruling party, no matter who they were, got the blame for the state of disrepair.

It was therefore not surprising that some commentators said that the current president was a bit like the jokes of some standup comedians—you either liked the joke, or you didn't.

The president had been accused of many misdeeds, but his unforgivable transgression, in the eyes of his critics, was that he won the race for the White House. There were very few scorns that the media spared him. Notwithstanding, the president seemed to be impervious to the vicious rants of his denigrators.

Even though Lawrence had a good working relationship with the president, he was more than a little nervous because he expected an ass-chewing was in the cards for him. Not because he had neglected his duties, but because intel on the Chinese was at a low point since the Chinese laid waste to the US's intelligence networks a year or so before. It had been a slow and tedious process to rebuild the networks, but it was nowhere near the levels it should be.

Oval Office, White House, Washington, D.C.

Day 11

Lawrence had briefed the president on security matters many times. Richardson had been in meetings with the president before but had never been called upon to brief him. He was going to remain quiet and speak only when asked to do so.

Lawrence started with a condensed version covering the essential aspects of the full brief. Sometimes referred to as an elevator pitch—from the idea of having to impress a senior executive during a brief ride in an elevator.

"Mr. President, it's about China. We have received what we believe to be reliable information that they have another virus problem. Our information is that people in Shanghai are dying in droves from this virus. But the Chinese government is concealing it. Aggressively."

"Why haven't I seen that in my daily briefing yet?"

"We only got the information an hour or so ago, sir."

"How did you come by this intel?"

"Mr. President, I'm more than a little embarrassed to admit that it was by chance. Not through our own intelligence network."

"Explain what you mean by chance?"

"Mr. President, as you are aware, the Chinese decimated our spy networks a few years ago. We don't have many informants left, and what we do have left don't operate in this space. Moreover, our SIGINT and ELINT gathering efforts are mostly blocked by their draconian internet policing and cyber counterespionage measures."

SIGINT was the acronym for Signal Intelligence and

ELINT, the acronym for Electronic Intelligence. Their focus was on the monitoring, collecting, and processing of communications and other electronic information as well as the cracking of secret codes.

Lawrence continued and told the president about Dora Frankel's unexpected meeting with her old school friend at Shanghai airport and what he told her.

Before he could continue, the president said, "We have the most sophisticated equipment and technology in the world. We have eyes and ears on close to, if not more than, ninety percent of all intelligence gathered on the planet by overt and covert means. Yet, you're telling me, on this, we got caught with our pants down?"

"Unfortunately, I can't deny that Mr. President. There may be some intel about this in our systems already, but we haven't connected the dots as yet."

'Why not?"

"Mr. President, the immensity of data collected by the NSA and others is mind-bending. And once the data has been collected, it has to be analyzed, categorized, and prioritized. Only then can we collate the relevant pieces of intelligence and put together the pieces of the jigsaw puzzle that make up the picture. It's an operation of industrial magnitude."

The president nodded. "I understand. Let's move on. Give me the details."

Lawrence was about ten minutes into his report when the president stopped him and said, "Give me a second." He called his chief of staff and asked him to reschedule his meetings for the next hour and to set up an urgent meeting with the White House National Security Council, NSC. A forum consisting of senior national security advisors and Cabinet officials to advise the president on matters of national security, military, and foreign policy.

"Please continue," the president said.

It took Lawrence another forty-five minutes to complete the briefing.

At the end of it, the president said, "You'll have to give this same information to the NSC in about half an hour. Until we can get a better understanding of what's going on in China, I'd like you to leave out the names and details of those rich people in Hong Kong and their family members and also that scientist and his wife in Singapore. The fewer people who know their details and whereabouts, the better. We might have to move the scientist and his wife to the US in the future. I think it'll be good if you could look into how we should go about doing it in case it becomes necessary."

"Will do, Mr. President."

Richardson asked to be excused and went back to Langley to give CRC their orders and assemble an internal task force to start work immediately.

Situation Room, White House, Washington, D.C.

Day 11

The core members of the NSC were the president, who was the chairman, five statutory members, who were the Vice President, Secretary of State, Secretary of Defense, Secretary of Energy, and Secretary of the Treasury. The rest of the group were made up of the White House Chief of Staff, the Chairman of the Joint Chiefs of Staff, the Director of

National Intelligence, the National Security Advisor, the Homeland Security Advisor, the Director of the Central Intelligence Agency, Howard Lawrence, and others. Not all of them always attended all meetings; some were invited to attend only when appropriate.

The president started. "I've called the meeting to discuss a matter concerning China that was brought to my attention by the Director of the CIA this morning. I'll ask him to brief you about it now."

Lawrence took a sip of water, thanked the president, and started. It took him a little over half an hour to impart the information to them without going into as much detail as he had with the president.

When he finished, the president said, "As you can see, we've got a serious lack of intel. Not enough to confront the Chinese government with yet. We will, however, be negligent if we don't take note of it and do everything in our power to get the information we need and act upon it. The floor is open."

"I understand that we have a lack of intel and the reasons for it. But do we have any assets in the area at the moment? Or could we get some in place without delay?" the Chairman of the Joint Chiefs of Staff asked.

"We have assets throughout China, but not nearly as many as we should have. Martin Richardson, my deputy director of operations, is in the process of contacting their handlers and briefing them. However, our best option right now is the people who brought this to our attention. They work for one of our private military contractors. My understanding is that there are four of them, highly skilled in covert operations, among the best we have."

"Where are they right now?"

"Vacationing on a luxury yacht in Hong Kong. Martin

Richardson is in contact with their CEO. They're ready and waiting for the word from us to activate them. On that yacht are also ten special forces operators, six Navy SEALS, and four Delta Force."

"What are they doing there? It sounds as if we're preparing to invade China." The concern was evident in the Secretary of State's voice.

Lawrence grinned. "No, Mr. Secretary, nothing of the kind. They're also on vacation, a little R-and-R."

"And if I understood you correctly, they happened to be in the right place at the right time, got wind of this virus in Shanghai, and reported it to you?" the vice president asked.

"Yes, sir."

"Howard, I won't call it good luck, I believe everything happens for a purpose, but what you're describing sounds like a frightening lot of coincidences without which we would've had no clue of what is going on behind the Bamboo Curtain."

"Yes, Mr. Vice President, that's true. That's the result of the Chinese rolling up our intel networks and the difficulty we have in rebuilding them. It took years to build them, and it's going to take years to get them back to the levels we had them before."

"Ladies and gentlemen," the Director of National Intelligence said, "I think it's important to understand that China's espionage and counterespionage efforts against us are massive, extensive, aggressive, and highly creative."

Everyone got the message; stop battering Howard Lawrence.

The president said, "We're digressing. The bottom line is, we don't have intel. We need to get it yesterday. I suggest we focus on that for now. Any questions?"

There were none.

He continued, "I don't know about all of you. Maybe it's just me; maybe I'm paranoid; maybe I'm overreacting; call it what you want, but the fact that they have their secret police running around making people disappear, killing, and abducting them to silence them makes me nervous."

"I agree with you, Mr. President," the Director of National Intelligence said. "It makes me uneasy too."

"Over to you, Howard. Shake the trees, rattle the cages, pull out all the stops, and if you need help, let me know. If you find any resistance or reluctance, let me know.

"I'd also like us to review our epidemic response readiness," the president said to the Homeland Security Advisor. "Do it quietly; we don't want to raise suspicions and send people into a panic. And for God's sake, make sure it stays out of the media."

"Yes, Mr. President. I'll get onto it immediately."

"Thank you for your time, ladies and gentlemen. I will keep you posted with progress. Let's hope and pray the next time we meet, it's to hear that we have nothing to worry about." The president ended the meeting.

Chapter Twenty-One

ASSEMBLE THE TEAMS

CIA Headquarters, Langley, Virginia | CRC Headquarters, Arizona

Day 11

As soon as Richardson was back behind his desk at Langley, he made a video call to John Brandt. "John, I just got back from a meeting with Howard and the president. Howard and I still have our jobs, but it might not be for much longer . . ."

"Okay, tell me what it'll take to keep you and your boss gainfully employed." Brandt chuckled.

"Put those agents of yours in Hong Kong, and any others you have to work, and get me the information the president needs as quickly as humanly possible. For now, you can't use the SEALS or Delta Force guys, but they'll be put on standby right away.

"Your team is responsible for the HUMINT. Bryan

Shafer will head the SIGINT and ELINT efforts here, and I'll instruct them to work with your IT team. Questions?" HUMINT was the acronym for Human Intelligence.

"Nope."

"Good. I expect to hear from you at least once a day."

"No problem."

When the call ended, Brandt called Declan Spencer. When Spencer answered, he said, "Vacation's over. Henceforth, the *TOMATS* is the Hong Kong base for the Shanghai mission. The special forces members onboard have just become operational on the orders of the president; their commanders will let them know about it shortly.

"Rex will be the mission team lead over there. You and the spec ops guys will support their mission. Chris and I will coordinate from here."

"No problem, we've expected something like this, and we're ready."

"Good. Get Rex and the others, and let's meet again in an hour. I need to brief Chris and Greg first."

"Man, I love this retirement thing, vacationing all over the world while captaining a luxury yacht and kicking bad guys' asses every now and then for a bit of excitement. What more can a Navy SEAL want? See you in an hour."

When the call ended, Brandt called his second-in-command, Chris McArdle and his lead IT specialist, Greg Wade, to his office and briefed them.

Greg Wade was the team leader of CRC's small but highly skilled group of IT specialists. Essentially, they were computer hackers, among the best in the business. With a few keystrokes, they could create havoc, blackout a city, take control of its traffic lights, enter government and corporate databases, access the bank records of any individual and organization, break through firewalls, break encryption, and much more.

"I'd like to have Rehka join my team over here," Greg said.

Brandt smiled. "Of course, you do. Make it so."

Rehka Gyan was Rex's technology expert, virtual assistant, researcher, and friend, the daughter of a friend from Bilaspur, India. Rex and Rehka had met when he and Digger liberated her and six other women from a Saudi Arabian prince (Mutaib bin Faisal bin Saud, an international black-market arms dealer and human trafficker), a scumbag whom Rex had killed a few years before.

With a master's degree in computer sciences, Rehka had exceptional skills in programming and online research. If anyone anywhere left a digital footprint, be it on social media, email, or online searches, she could track that person down. She had enough black hat and gray hat skills to operate anonymously on the Darknet and get unfettered access to some of the most secure private, government, and law enforcement databases across the globe without leaving so much as a hint that she had been there. And since she had met CRC's IT guru and had worked with him and his team on missions, her knowledge and skills had gone from strength to strength. And everyone knew about the blossoming romance between her and Greg.

When Richardson ended the call with Brandt, he had called Bryan Shafer, the person in charge of the Directorate of Analysis, and his sidekick, Stacie Barrett. He quickly brought them into the picture and instructed them to assemble a team of specialists and start work on the intel gathering and to cooperate closely with CRC's IT team. "I want you to go back three months, more if necessary, in the NSA and our own data, pull out every bit of data related to

Shanghai, and analyze it. Somewhere, this virus must have been mentioned, and we've missed it. The president wants it, I want it, and Director Lawrence wants it. Get it."

By the time Howard Lawrence walked back into his office after the NSC meeting and asked Richardson to join him in his office, the Shanghai mission was well and truly on the way.

The TOMATS, Matz Island, Hong Kong

Day 12

One of the *TOMATS* lounges had been repurposed to house the sophisticated electronics gear and computer equipment that could be concealed when necessary. Another was turned into a secured communications room. Inside was, among others, an impenetrable encrypted satellite video system, the latest technology in communications. That was the room where Spencer was sitting at a V-shaped table facing the big TV screen on the wall, sipping on a large espresso, reflecting on the Shanghai mission team members while waiting for them to arrive for the video call with Brandt.

Spencer and John Brandt were bosom friends, born in the same year, in the same hospital, lived in the same neighborhood, grew up together, went to the same school, same university, and joined the Navy SEALS at the same time. John was recruited into the CIA, and Spencer retired as a Commander in the SEALS at the age of sixty-five. Both had lost their wives. John's wife, a fellow CIA field agent, had been killed in an operation gone wrong. A heart attack took Spencer's wife. Both had been widowed for more than seven years. Both had new love interests—Brandt was engaged to be married to Christelle Proll, a deputy director of the French intelligence service, DGSE, and Spencer was in a relationship with an Italian lady eighteen years his junior, Simona Bellucci.

Soon after taking on the captaincy of the *TOMATS* on behalf of CRC, Spencer had met Rex, Digger, Catia, Josh, and Marissa and had since worked with them on several missions and had learned about their backgrounds.

A terrorist attack on a Spanish railway station in 2004 killed Rex's parents and two younger siblings. The peaceful young man who'd looked forward to a career in the US Foreign Service was emotionally damaged in that attack, and he'd transformed into a brooding, angry man who'd joined the Marines to avenge his losses. From there, he was recruited into Delta Force and trained as a Special Forces operator. Then he was recruited into John Brandt's black ops outfit, CRC, where he was trained as one of the world's most lethal assassins—a capacity in which he rained terror, destruction, and death on the enemies of the US.

Brandt showed him his file once. Rex was trained as a sniper who could take a target out at eight hundred yards to a mile. He could kill with a long gun, short gun, or no gun. He was lethal with edged weapons, explosives, poisons, or no weapon at all. Targets could be taken out from a mile away or die with Dalton's breath in their face.

Onto this was added intensive spycraft training. He learned how to develop legends, his covers when he was on the move in other countries. He learned about infiltration, explosives, and sabotage. He had been drilled in finding and using safe houses, transmitting secured messages, recruitment of informants, disguises, digital communications, signals, and caches.

And to crown it all, Rex was a polyglot. Spencer had lost count of how many languages he spoke—seven? It could be more. The latest one he mastered was Hebrew. He had an almost supernatural ability to learn new languages, and a mysterious quirk was he adopted the accents of his language instructors. The only language he spoke with a strange accent was Hebrew because Catia spoke it with an Italian accent.

Rex and Catia met in 2010 when she provided him with part of his European tradecraft training. At the end of Rex's training in Rome, he and Catia, although they didn't say so, both knew much more than a tutor-student relationship had developed between them. But they also knew the rules. No fraternizing between agents and handlers. It could get both killed.

They saw each other again in 2011 when she provided him with support for a mission in Naples. After that, it took four years before they again saw each other and realized the spark was still there. They got married in May 2016.

Catia was an only child. Terrorists had also killed her parents. In their case, it was a lone assassin, working for the Jihad Council, the military wing of Hezbollah, who had poisoned them while they were on holiday in the Caribbean, though the official version was they drowned while on a boat trip. It had happened in 2005, the year after Rex's family was killed.

Catia was twenty-two years old at the time, and she knew what her father had been. The first thing she did after getting over the initial shock of her parents' deaths was to contact her father's chief of station in the Rome office. She'd told him coolly that she knew who and what her dad was, and she wanted to take her father's place. She wanted to stop terrorists—any terrorists. It took a lot of talking from her and a lot of dissuasion by the COS, but she got it her way in the end.

Rather than placing her in the embassy, the Mossad trained her as a mission support specialist—a *sayan*.

Josh Farley was a pleasant-faced, All-American type. Not movie-star handsome, and he looked slightly older than he was. Brandt always told Spencer that Farley was one of his agents whom he judged to be nearly as good as Rex Dalton. Rex had trained Josh himself in hand-to-hand combat and street craft and, in Rex's words, was "one tough, lean, mean bastard."

Marissa, on the other hand, looked quite a bit younger than she was, making it appear as if she and Josh were of the same age.

Brandt described Marissa as the best of CRC's handful of female agents. And she was beautiful—shoulder-length, raven hair and azure eyes suggested French heritage, and her forty-something years gave her an alluring mantle of maturity. She was almost ten years older than Josh, but one would have to have seen her birth certificate to know that.

She was an expert social media analyst and spy and, if necessary, could handle herself in a fight. She also spoke two languages besides English, Arabic, and French. The latter she had spoken along with English since her childhood thanks to her French father. She and Josh got married in December 2016.

Spencer's thoughts had turned to Digger when he heard the footsteps on the stairs, presumably the Daltons and Farleys. Whenever Rex and Catia were out in public, Digger had a "Service Dog" sticker attached to his harness. But the big black Dutch Shepherd wasn't a service dog. It was the ruse Rex had used ever since inheriting the dog from his friend, Trevor Madigan, a former SAS operative from Australia, who'd been killed in an ambush in Afghanistan. Digger, an Australian military dog, had been his companion since Trevor asked Rex to take care of him with his dying breath. Rex, mortally scared of dogs since he'd been attacked by one as a small child, had agreed.

The two of them, Rex and Digger, at best had what could be called a strained relationship while Trevor was still alive. That was mainly due to Rex's fear of dogs, which he never told anyone about but was sensed by Digger, who badgered him about it.

And since Rex was a man of his word, he and Digger worked through their issues, and they'd become inseparable mates. Digger had acknowledged him as his alpha in their pack and accepted Catia into his pack from the moment he met her. Digger was Rex's "best man" at their wedding; he brought the wedding rings in on a dainty white satin cushion balanced on his nose.

As for his name, Trevor had explained; in Australia, the troops were called "diggers," and although way back, it could have been a derogatory term, it wasn't anymore. The Aussies loved and respected their diggers just as much as the Americans loved and respected their soldiers. Even the Australian Prime Minister and other politicians used the term diggers when they referred to the Australian troops. This name came from WWI with the trench warfare – the Aussies, because of their skills as miners, were the ones who designed and dug those trenches.

Although Rex never learned to give Digger proper commands, like military dog handlers do, working as a team on many missions over the years, they had worked out a communications system between them which left some of

Rex's colleagues with the notion that the two of them spoke some kind of "language" only they understood. The reality was Rex had learned to be very attentive to Digger's behavior at all times.

Dutch Shepherds were known for their affectionate, obedient, reliable, loyal, alert, and trainable temperaments. They were great guard- and watchdogs. They were also smart, energetic, loyal, and protective, loved children, and got along with other animals.

It was five minutes before the start of the video conference when the four of them, with Digger in tow, walked into the communications room. They poured themselves large espressos and took their seats. Digger stood close to Rex and Catia, looking at them in turn, wagging his tail and licking his lips. It was his way of saying, "Hey, what about me?" Catia laughed, ruffled his ears, and took out a few pieces of beef jerky she always kept with her from a plastic bag she had in the side pocket of her cargo pants. She held it out in the palm of her hand for him. It earned her a nice, big dog-smile.

Chapter Twenty-Two

A FOUR-PART PLAN

Secured video conference

Day 12

From CRC headquarters in Arizona, Brandt, McArdle, and Wade were looking at their big screen at Spencer, Rex, Catia, Digger, Josh, and Marissa seventy-five hundred miles away in Hong Kong. Brandt started with an update of the meeting Lawrence and Richardson had with the president and the president's orders to get him intel he could act on.

"I'd like Rehka to join our team here on the *TOMATS*," Rex said after Brandt finished.

Greg was smiling from ear-to-ear. "You can't have her. She's spoken for. I've already booked her on a flight from Mumbai to Arizona."

"No worries. As long as she's on the team, I'm happy." Rex chuckled and said, "But the moment I hear that you're a distraction to her, she's on the first plane out of there to Hong Kong."

Greg smiled and ignored him.

"Now," Brandt said, "the five of you over there, ah . . . six with Digger—I'm still getting used to the idea that one of my agents is a dog—you've been closest to the fire. I'm sure you've got ideas ready about how to approach the mission. Tell us about it."

Everyone was looking at Rex. "We have indeed. But before we get into that, we need to give you a bit more background information about our new friends, the Matzs and Sarlins. They're more than likely going to play a consequential role in the mission."

"Go for it," Brandt said.

During the first briefing earlier in the day, Rex told Brandt about their new friends but didn't elaborate on their backgrounds and heritage. Now he and Catia told them that they were Hong Kong Jews, about their massive business empires, their social status, and widespread influence not only in Hong Kong but throughout Asia and other parts of the world.

"Jews, you said . . . hmm . . .," Brandt murmured. "Catia, you wouldn't perhaps know if they perchance would be acquainted with our mutual friend, Yaron?"

She smiled. "They are. It's part of the plan we have."

"Excellent. Who is going to contact Yaron?"

"Rex and I are thinking it would save time if we setup one video conference with all of us, that includes you and Chris, and get it all done in one go."

"Perfect. Let me know when."

"As soon as we finish this meeting."

Rex started, "Okay, here are the broad-brush strokes of our plan. It's got four parts.

"One, HUMINT. We need to get collaborators in Shanghai, people who can collect information not only from the people who are afflicted and their families, but also from physicians, surgeries, hospitals, clinics, morgues, funeral homes, and such."

"Agreed," Brandt said.

"Two, SIGINT and ELINT. Greg, Rehka, and the rest of the CRC IT team have to get into the computer systems of those surgeries, clinics, hospitals, morgues, etcetera. If we can recruit staff who work in those places, it might be easier to get into their computer systems than trying to hack into them remotely, especially in the light of the communist regime's megalomaniac obsession to control all internet traffic. We also need to get the Zexian Biomed lab's research data. Of course, the CIA and every security agency that can do so must dedicate teams to collect and analyze every scrap of signal and electronic information that comes out of and goes into Shanghai."

Brandt nodded. "Martin Richardson has already instructed Bryan Shafer to assemble a task force of analysts to do exactly that. Shafer and his sidekick, Stacie Barrett, were responsible for that breakthrough during Operation Badr, which helped you and Josh stop those lunatics from starting World War Three."

"Excellent," Spencer said. "Shafer's team did an outstanding job there. It's good to know we'll have them in our corner again."

Rex continued. "Three, MEDINT . . ."

Chris McArdle frowned.

"Medical Intelligence," Rex said.

McArdle laughed. "Of course."

Rex continued, "Okay, so, one of our highest priorities must be to get samples of this virus from people who were infected. Jethro and David know some Chinese Jews in Shanghai; there are physicians among them. We're hoping that at least one of them is a *sayan* who will be able to collect virus specimens for us. That's where Yaron's influence would be of tremendous help. However, we must think about how we're going to smuggle the specimens out once we've collected them. For that, we'll need the help and advice of a virologist lest we let the virus escape and become the ones who spread it beyond the borders of China."

"Agreed," Brandt said.

"Four, more HUMINT. We must make a serious effort to identify one or more individuals high up in the regime that would have the necessary inside information. Then get the person to defect."

"Just like that, you reckon?" Brandt said incredulously. He was a veteran of the Cold War; he knew what was involved in a recruitment and defection.

Rex nodded. "Just like that."

"Catia, what's that boy been smoking lately?"

Everyone burst into laughter.

"Tell you what, Dalton. You identify the potential defectors and let me know so I can fill that gap in your training for you."

"Deal," Rex said.

"Okay, let's take a break. I want to give Yaron a heads-up. In the meantime, you can contact Matz and Sarlin and let them know we'd like to meet in half an hour."

Chapter Twenty-Three

AVERT A VIRAL HOLOCAUST

Secured video conference

Day 12

Catia was waiting for Jethro and David on the gangplank when they arrived and told them that the people in the meeting were all aware of the *sayan* system, and they knew about her relationship with the Mossad and now also about theirs.

They smiled, and Catia asked about it. To which David replied, "We just got off the phone with Yaron, and he told us all about him and Mr. Brandt. He speaks very highly of Mr. Brandt and all of you. We're looking forward to meeting him and the others."

"Perfect. One less thing to worry about then. Let's go in; they're waiting for us." Catia escorted them to the communications room and offered them espresso or tea. Both opted for the coffee.

Spencer connected the video call to Brandt and McArdle in Arizona. Greg had left to brief his team and start working. Spencer made the necessary introductions, after which Jethro and David thanked Brandt for the work his agents had done to rescue their sisters, and of course, rescuing Dora after being kidnapped.

Brandt acknowledged and thanked them for taking care of his "boys and girls" and "his" canine agent and providing a safe haven for the *TOMATS*.

Rex couldn't help but smile at Brandt's claim that Digger was his agent. Things had come a long way since the first time Brandt and Digger met, and he kept on calling Digger the "damn dog" and chided Rex for how stupid it was for a CRC agent to go around with a dog.

Jethro told them that Tamara was out of the hospital and back on Matz Island, in her own home, under the care of a private nurse. Dora and her husband were back home in California and had hired a private security company to protect them.

Brandt told Jethro and David that Rex et al had filled him and McArdle in about their background information. He also told them that he and Yaron Aderet were old friends and worked together on many joint CIA-Mossad missions in the past. The latest mission being the one to salvage the lost libraries from the Jewish Quarters in Rome.

That put Jethro and David at ease as it corroborated with what Aderet told them on the phone.

"Okay," Brandt said. "With that out of the way, let's get Yaron on the line. He's expecting our call."

Aderet was in his office in Tel Aviv when he appeared on screen. He waved, looked at everyone on his screen, and said, "No need for introductions, I know all of you." He smiled and added, "Whether that's a good or a bad thing, I guess I'm about to find out. So, what's the PRC up to now? John didn't have time to give me all the details earlier but mentioned there is a potential virus problem."

"Yes," Jethro said, "that's what it is. And the Chinese government seems to be deathly serious about secreting it, so much so they'll kill for it."

"SOP for them, is it not?" Aderet said.

"SOP?" Jethro asked.

"Standard operating procedure. Burying problems before they're embarrassed by them."

"Precisely."

For the next two hours, they gave Yaron the full picture, told him about the request or rather demand for more information from the president, and shared Rex's four-part mission plan with him.

"So, Yaron, my friend, there you have it, soup to nuts. The question is, what can you and your *sayanim* in this part of the world do to help us?" Brandt said.

"Well, you've already got Catia, Jethro, and David," Aderet said. "Now, Shanghai. A Jewish community has existed there since the late nineteenth century. During the 1920s and '30s, thousands of Russian Jews fled the Bolshevik Revolution, and many of them settled in Shanghai. During the 1940s, tens of thousands of Jews escaped from the Nazis, and again many of them settled in Shanghai. By the end of the Second World War, there were more than twenty thousand of them in the city. Over the years, many migrated to Hong Kong, the USA, and other countries. Today, there are less than two thousand left in the city.

"As you can see, in a city of more than twenty-four million, the Jewish influence has dwindled to the point of insignificance. Among those left, we have less than a handful of *sayanim*. However, the few we have will help us, and the good news is that there are two physicians among them. I will instruct their *katsas* to get in touch with them and put them to work.

"As for the SIGINT and ELINT part of Rex's plan, I'm afraid there's nothing we can contribute that would even remotely compare with what your CIA, NSA, and others can do with their unrivaled technological capabilities.

"As for identifying and recruiting potential defectors, Jethro and David are in the best position to tell us if they have ideas."

Slowly, all eyes turned to David and Jethro.

Jethro nodded and started, "Matz Enterprises owns the biggest power company in Hong Kong and a nuclear power plant ninety miles northeast of Hong Kong. That nuclear plant is the sole supplier of electricity to several of South China's mega industrial plants. It's a situation that doesn't sit very well with the communist government who, as you know, always wants to have all control over everything and everybody. Under Li Lingxin, it became worse.

"The long and short of it is, a few years ago we were given a choice. A general from the military had to be given a permanent seat on the board of directors, or the government would nationalize the power plant. The choice was easy.

"The general's name is Dai Min. He's in charge of China's nuclear arsenal, and he is part of a group known as 'the Marshals'. They're the most powerful people in China, but not many people know that, especially outsiders. David has made an in-depth study of them and their history. It's best that he tells you."

All eyes shifted to David.

"It's a bit of a long story, so please bear with me because

we, Jethro and I, think it's important to understand the background."

Everyone nodded.

"In theory, under China's constitution, the president of the People's Republic of China is mostly a ceremonial office with limited power. I say in theory because since Li became president in 2013, that went out the window. Not only has he managed to remove the term limits to his presidency, which was always two terms for his predecessors, he has also centralized much of the institutional power around himself. He took personal charge of economic and social reforms, military restructuring and modernization, and the Internet.

"The sycophants in Beijing have lent him demigod status, to the point where his political dogma has been written into the party and state constitutions. On his watch, we have seen a dramatic increase in censorship, mass surveillance, and deterioration of human rights.

"The president is supposed to serve at the pleasure of the National People's Congress. He's not supposed to take executive action on his own, but Li managed to change all that.

"However, despite the guy's apparent unlimited power, what very few people outside the Communist Party's inner circles know is that the president is actually beholden to the marshals. There are currently eighteen of them. They are generals of the People's Liberation Army, PLA. Now, it's important to know that the PLA is not controlled by, nor is it a part of the PRC government. They are part of the CCP, Chinese Communist Party.

"I'm not going to bore you with the history, suffice it to say that this group of marshals originated during the civil war in the late 1940s when the Kuomintang were ousted and the ascension of Mao Tse Tung to Chairman. Back then, there were twelve marshals, seven backed Mao, then the third-ranking member of the CCP, against Liao Xiao Chi and Zhou En Lai, and that's how he became Chairman Mao.

"Over the years, the marshals had maintained their hold on the presidency. When Deng Xiao Peng came to power, he tried to dilute the marshals' power by increasing their numbers to eighteen. The marshals saw through his plan, banded together, and thwarted his scheme. They're every bit as powerful today as they were in the time of Mao Tse Tung.

"Li Lingxin came to power with the support of eleven of the eighteen marshals. Not a big margin; if two generals change allegiance, Li is in trouble. And that's exactly what the seven who oppose him are trying to do, persuade two, preferably more, of their colleagues to cross the aisle. That's the history," David concluded and looked at Jethro to continue.

"General Dai Min is one of the seven dissident marshals. Ex officio, he and I often meet for business, and we have lunch or dinner at least once a month. During these excursions, General Dai never hides his antagonism towards President Li; he's quite outspoken. I've always been wary about his rantings and never participate. It could have been a trap to get me in a compromising situation which he could exploit.

"So, after all that babbling, what I'm trying to say is that I might have to throw caution to the wind and see if I can dangle a carrot in front of the general's nose to see if he would go for it and help us get the information we want."

"Jethro," Brandt said, "it's too high-risk. I can't ask you in good conscience—"

Jethro held his hand up to stop Brandt. "I've considered

the risks. There are three possible outcomes. One, General Dai reports me, I get in trouble, and in the worst-case scenario, we lose the nuclear power plant. The financial loss to Matz Enterprises will be enormous, but it won't wipe us out. Two, the general can't or won't help, don't report me but gets leverage over me to use for blackmailing whenever it suits him. Three, the general does indeed come to the party and help us get that critical information. Anyone of those outcomes beats facing the virus."

A protracted silence followed as everyone mulled over Jethro's proposal.

Aderet broke the silence. "Jethro, if you're sure you are willing to take the plunge, I support you. It's a courageous step and might, in the end, prove to be the step that helps us avert a viral holocaust."

Slowly, everyone added their support for Jethro's plan.

Chapter Twenty-Four

FIND ME VIRUS DATA

CIA Headquarters, Langley, Virginia

Day 12

Eighteen analysts of the CIA's Analysis Division and their head, Bryan Shafer, were staring at the large corkboard on the wall. In the middle of the otherwise empty board was a glossy picture of a vibrantly colored object, a spherical particle with spikes, resembling an alien invader, floating in an opaque background.

Although the team had the best computers, software, and technology available to do their job, and Stacie was well versed in computer use, she still liked to also have an old-fashioned link chart or investigation board, as some called it, on the wall. For this operation, she and her team had been allocated a fully equipped operations room with two big TV screens, secured telephones, computers, water cooler, fridge, microwave oven, and espresso machine.

Stacie said, "I take it you all know that thingamabob on the board is a virus. Despite its nice looks, it's a killer. We are the CIA's virus-hunting posse. Bryan will brief us now, and then we'll go to work."

She nodded for him to take over.

At fifty-six, with all her working life after university spent at the CIA, it was not Stacie's first rodeo. She had a reputation as a meticulous worker, near anal retentive, an uncanny ability to see connections between seemingly unrelated pieces of information to reveal the whole picture, and a remarkable ability to recollect. Her human relations skills sometimes left a bit to be desired, but her colleagues knew her and didn't even notice it anymore. Most of them liked her. She was a straight shooter, not a single bone of political correctness in her body, and she got results. She never claimed the accolades following success for herself; neither did she blame failure on her underlings.

Bryan Shafer had been Stacie's manager for the past five years. There was no one else in the CIA he would have picked to assign this job to. She and her teams had delivered exceptional results in the past to help thwart terrorist plots that could have killed thousands of innocents. Shafer admired and respected her—she made him look good at his job.

Forty-five minutes and a few questions later, Shafer finished his briefing and headed for his office, thinking that Stacie Barrett was well deserving of her title as the Battle Tank of the Analysis Directorate. She was also known as M1 or Abrams, a reference to the US M1 Abrams battle tank. Her nickname had nothing to do with her looks—tall, in good shape, with curly, dark brown hair and sparkling brown eyes—she was quite attractive.

"Okay," Stacie started when the door closed behind

Shafer. "We have nothing except for the knowledge that a virus is killing people in Shanghai, and the Chinese government is trying to hide it. We're going to sift through NSA and other data going back three to four months.

"We want to know if anyone mentioned the virus. We want to know if someone sneezed, coughed, or blew their noses and talked about it. There are more than twenty-four million people in Shanghai. As you've heard, many thousands have become ill and are dying from this virus. People would have mentioned it in emails, text messages, chat programs, blogs, and over telephones before the government clampdown on information started. They would still be mentioning it. We need that information, all of it. Nothing is unimportant.

"As for timelines, we're at least three months behind right now. Therefore, we're on twenty-four seven from here on in. Eight-hour shifts, six to a shift."

No one even bothered to ask her if someone would relieve her. They already knew, from previous experience, that when an operation reached a critical stage, she survived on catnaps, in her chair, at her desk.

"If you need anything, let me know. We have the authority of the president behind us. So, if anyone anywhere gives you any grief at any time, you let me know.

"Any questions?"

There were none.

"Good. Go and find me virus data from Shanghai and China. And when you feel like giving up, have another look at that alien creature on the board and imagine millions of them coursing through your own body and the bodies of your loved ones, slowly killing you all. Eventually wiping out all human life on the planet." She knew she was perhaps a little melodramatic, but it was a good motivator.

Chapter Twenty-Five

SETTING UP TWO MEETINGS

Matz Island, Hong Kong

Day 12

Upon their return from the *TOMATS*, Jethro and David went directly to the study to start planning how they were going to approach General Dai Min.

David had never met the General nor dealt with him in any manner. He knew about him from the little Jethro had told him, which was not much.

Jethro now gave him more details. "You see, Dai carries an air of authority, patriotism, and moral superiority about him. The latter is fake."

David raised an eyebrow.

"I know from personal experience, he's not immune to money and the good life. He likes to take his wife and mistresses, of which there are quite a few, on shopping trips and holidays to Hong Kong and other places under the pretense of official business.

"I know this because, on occasion, I had been footing the bill."

David frowned again. "He's not holding sway over you that you haven't told me about, is he?"

Jethro shook his head. "No, he doesn't, not in that manner. But then you must keep in mind that I have to keep him happy to assure his support and cooperation in the board meetings. Although he doesn't have the majority vote, he does have a kind of veto power in a sense. If he doesn't like an idea, he could dig in his heels and make life difficult for me. So, although he has never demanded money and favors directly, he always offers shrewd hints when he is planning one of his trips."

"And let me guess. He never refused the money or the favors nor returned any of it?"

"Exactly."

"So, your friend, the general, is definitely not an incorruptible man," David murmured. "Are you thinking of using that to extract information from him?"

"I won't even try that. His indiscretions would not be regarded as serious by anyone in the upper echelons of either the CCP or PRC, for the simple reason that most of them are doing it themselves. Being allowed to do it with impunity is part of the perks of their jobs. No, what I'm thinking is to create an opportunity where we can meet and have an open discussion about our political views without fear of repercussions."

"I suspect that such a discussion would be accompanied by a lot of comradely backslapping and palm greasing?"

"Undoubtedly."

David went quiet for a while before he said, "You know

it's ironic that we're thinking of conscribing the help of a man who opposes Li not because of his opposition to communism but because he and his co-dissident friends want to put their man in the presidency to implement *their* version of communism. I mean, it's not as if they'd abolish communism and adopt capitalism and democracy."

"You're right about that."

"So, what do you have in mind for this opportunity you want to create?"

"One of his favorite hangouts is Macao. He likes gambling but not nearly as much as his wife likes it. I'm thinking of inviting him and the missus for an all-expenses-paid weekend on Macao."

Jethro looked at his watch, made a quick calculation, and dialed General Dai Min's number.

When Jethro's call with General Dai ended, David said, "Do you remember about six weeks ago there was a story in the news about a Chinese industrialist that fell from grace with the communist government?"

"Yes, I remember. Dong Yan, if I'm not mistaken. He defected to Singapore. Why do you ask?"

"I know him. He's one of my clients. But I haven't spoken to him since he fled to Singapore. The thing is, he was a close friend of Li Lingxin for most of his life and very much in with the ruling elite in Beijing. I don't know the reasons for his fallout with them. I suspect it's not because he was caught spying for the Americans as the Chinese government wants us to believe. The viciousness of their disinformation campaign against him speaks volumes."

"Are you thinking of contacting him?"

"Yes. I think it might be worthwhile hearing the true story from the horse's mouth, especially since he defected fairly recently when the virus problem in Shanghai was already reaching epidemic levels. Maybe he heard something."

Jethro nodded. "Excellent idea."

David took his smartphone out and searched through his emails for the email from Dong Yan containing his new contact details.

A few minutes later, he was talking to Dong, making arrangements to meet him in Singapore in two days.

"Maybe you can check in on the Zhengs while you're in Singapore?"

"Yep, that's the plan."

Chapter Twenty-Six

THE DOCTOR OF SHANGHAI

Shanghai, China

Day 12

Back in 1949, health care was free to everyone in China. The communist state operated all clinics and hospitals, and it employed all doctors, nurses, and health workers. In 1984, the government started making free-market reforms, and people lost their access to free medical care. That opened the market for the influx of multinational health-related companies such as AstraZeneca, GlaxoSmithKline, Eli Lilly, and Merck to get a slice of the explosive growth in the Chinese healthcare market.

All major cities had state-run hospitals, equipped with some modern facilities providing free medical care. But the best medical care in China was available in foreign-run or joint-venture, Western-style medical facilities with international staff in cities such as Beijing, Shanghai,

Guangzhou, Shenzhen, and a few other large cities. But they were up to ten times more expensive than state hospitals.

East Shanghai Private Hospital, ESPH, a medical insurance hospital, as they called it, was established in 2001. It was the first private hospital in Shanghai and serviced the entire East China region. It was a modern hospital with more than twenty departments, equipped with modern clinical laboratories, pharmacy, infusion rooms, wards, and operating theaters.

Dr. Abiram Sharot was the third generation of the Sharot family, Jews who fled from Austria on the eve of the Second World War in 1939, to find refuge in Shanghai. He was a general practitioner; he loved his job at ESPH, where he had been working for the past fifteen years. He was passionate about the health of his fellow human beings and had never gone into private practice. Though, the past few weeks, he had been giving it some serious thought.

Four weeks ago, ESPH had been commandeered by the government. Their patients had been transferred to other hospitals, and they were told they were now the primary specimen collection facility for a new virus. They were effectively turned into what Sharot thought of as factory workers on an assembly line. They were not allowed to treat anyone. Dr. Sharot kept his own counsel about that, believing it was probably because it would have required them to know what type of virus this was, and with the cloud of secrecy surrounding it, he couldn't help but conclude it was the kind of knowledge that the government would not want a private hospital to have.

Whether the hospital staff wanted to do it or liked to do it was not asked of them. And they knew, in China, it was not a good idea to vent your spleen, not in public, and definitely not in the presence of government mandarins. In any event, they were under strict orders, affirmed by their signatures on official documents to signify their pledge to keep everything a secret. The few who had not kept their vow had disappeared.

The new virus had no scientific name; it was merely referred to as "The Virus." Though Dr. Sharot had seen one of his coworkers scribble it down as Virus Li. The Li could have been the Roman numeral 51, or it could have referred to the President of China. If the latter, it was better not to make any mention of it. In a country where images of one of the world's most popular children's fiction heroes, Winnie-the-Pooh, was banned because of its striking resemblance to the president, naming a virus after him would have been detrimental to one's health and well-being.

To say Dr. Sharot was bone-weary would have been a gross understatement. No sleep for thirty-seven hours would do that to any human. Spending thirty-four of those hours in protective gear comprising of gloves, gowns, eye protection, and a surgical mask, taking it off only to take a shower and have a meal, of which he'd had only three so far, was enough to take anyone to the brink of total collapse.

The most common symptoms were fever, dry cough, and fatigue. Less common but more serious were aches and pains, sore throat, diarrhea, conjunctivitis, headache, loss of taste or smell, a skin rash, or discoloration of fingers or toes. The severe symptoms were difficulty breathing or shortness of breath, chest pain or pressure, and loss of speech or movement. One thing Sharot did not doubt was that this was not "an aggressive strain of the common flu" as they were ordered to call it.

He had lost count of how many specimens he had taken over the past six weeks. The procedure was tediously repetitious. Call the patient in. Explain the process. "Please sit down on the chair." Open the swab package and take out the swab. Tilt the patient's head back to straighten the nasal passage. "Now close your eyes." Insert the swab along the nasal septum until resistance was felt. Rotate the swab for ten to fifteen seconds. Withdraw the swab. "Thank you; it's all done. You can open your eyes." Insert the swab into the collection vial. Fill in the label. "Thank you. Next, please."

For twenty-four hours a day, seven days a week, nonstop for the last four weeks, and no end in sight, as the number of patients was increasing by the day, the hospital staff had been collecting swabs like a production line in a factory. Patients presenting with severe symptoms such as high fever, breathing difficulty, pneumonia, or coughing fits were taken to a negative pressure room to collect the samples.

No one had any idea what happened after the swabs were taken. Presumably, it was sent to a lab somewhere for analysis, and if it came up positive, the patient would hopefully be contacted and taken somewhere to be treated. However, Sharot had heard rumors, and those abounded that some of the city's hospitals were inundated, and so were the morgues and funeral homes. The rows upon rows of test subjects lining the hallways and wards requiring his and other's attention prevented Sharot from investigating the rumors.

The only thing they hadn't run out of was testing kits, protective gear, and hand sanitizing liquid. It seemed as if there was an unlimited supply.

The broad definition of an epidemic was the rapid spread of disease to a large number of people in a given population within a short period. The numbers required to qualify it as an epidemic varied from disease to disease, depending on the severity and the rate of spread. A few cases of a rare disease may be classified as an epidemic, while many cases of a common disease such as the common cold would not. For example, with meningococcal infections, an attack rate of more than fifteen cases per one hundred thousand people for two consecutive weeks was considered an epidemic.

It didn't require a genius to figure out that this virus, by any definition, would soon reach epidemic levels, if it had not already. At least it would have in Shanghai. Unless draconian quarantine and lockdown measures were introduced and enforced by the police and military, it was only a matter of time before it would spread throughout the country and then turn into a pandemic when it spilled over the borders into other countries.

It was after midnight when Dr. Sharot walked out of the hospital to go home and get some rest before he had to repeat it all in eight hours. Unless it was raining, he always used his bicycle to commute between home and work, about five kilometers each way.

When he got to the bicycle stand, he noticed something he hadn't seen for a very long time—a small strip of green duct tape wrapped around the left handle of his bicycle. Dr. Abiram Sharot was a *sayan*, and the green duct tape was a meeting request from his *katsa*. They had three pre-agreed meeting places, and the color of the duct tape determined at which one they were going to meet. Green meant the Mingbad café, not far from the hospital, and on the route of his daily commute. Sticking it on the left handle meant it was urgent. The restaurant was closed at that time of night; in other words, it was to be a breakfast meeting.

Chapter Twenty-Seven

EMERGING PICTURES

CIA Headquarters, Langley, Virginia

Day 13

Within twelve hours of the president's orders, with the help of the IT gurus and Chinese translators, Stacie's team had created their first search algorithms and started mining the NSA and CIA databases.

Information started to trickle in, and the first pictures began to emerge as they started getting hits matching their search criteria. Even so, as they expanded and fine-tuned their search parameters, it became clear that they were getting almost all the hits in the early data, three months to about eight weeks ago. Then the number of hits abruptly dropped off to a trickle.

Nevertheless, the information collected from intercepted emails, chat programs, blog posts, and such from the earlier data painted a picture. There was a virus problem in Shanghai. People were dying from it. Doctors didn't have a proper treatment for it. They were experimenting with antipyretic (antifever) medications, decongestants, and antibiotics, their standard treatment for influenza and pneumonia. But it was apparent, although this virus produced flu-like symptoms, it didn't respond to the conventional flu treatments. There were indications that certain medications, some of them readily available over the counter, exacerbated the problem, killing people much quicker than without treatment. And they hadn't yet figured out why.

Similarly, they had no idea how the virus interacted with other medications that patients were already taking. It became abundantly clear that finding the right treatment and medication was very much a hit-and-miss exercise. That's to say, the age-old practice of "Take two and call me in the morning" was in operation. If the patient was worse, take them off that medication and try another. If stable or better, that's a breakthrough, continue with it, and let the other doctors know.

The critical patients were placed on ventilators because they couldn't breathe on their own, but it quickly became evident that it was not a silver bullet. Some patients recovered because of it; others died because of it. And they didn't know how to predetermine who it would or would not help.

Some people were more at risk than others, such as the elderly and those with underlying medical conditions such as heart conditions, high blood pressure, diabetes, kidney conditions, and cancer. In other words, people with compromised immune systems.

But then, just as they thought they had it figured out, they found young, healthy people were also becoming severely ill, and in some cases, dying. According to Stacie's projections, extrapolated from the data, people between the ages of twenty and fifty-four had a thirty-eight percent chance of requiring hospitalization if infected.

An interesting snippet was discovered in an intercepted email from a physician to some of her colleagues, telling them she found noteworthy evidence that people in the A blood group were at significantly higher risk compared to those of the non-A blood groups; people with type-O blood being the lowest risk group.

Shanghai, China

Day 13

At eight a.m. the next day when Abiram walked into the Mingbad café, Joel Osche, his *katsa*, was already waiting for him with a humongous breakfast of pancakes, steamed stuffed buns, boiled eggs, and a pot of coffee.

"Shalom, my friend, how have you been?" Abiram said as he extended his hand and shook Osche's.

"Shalom to you too, Abiram. I'm well. But you look tired. Something the matter?"

Abiram shrugged. "Nothing but tiredness from too much work the last few weeks."

Osche smiled. "What happened to the hospital's work-life balance policy? What's keeping you *so* busy?"

Abiram looked around furtively.

"Don't worry; it's safe to talk. No one has followed you, and no one in here or outside is watching."

Abiram leaned slightly forward and lowered his voice.

"We've been inundated with patients presenting with the flu lately."

"The common flu. Really?"

Abiram said, "Of course it's not the flu. But we're not allowed to call it by any other name."

Osche said, "That's why I requested this meeting. We have heard that a very nasty virus may be killing people in large numbers in parts of the city. We've heard that some neighborhoods have been put into lockdown. No one can enter or exit, people have been ordered to stay in their homes, and the police are enforcing it. Furthermore, we've heard that the government is doing everything possible to keep everything under wraps. What do you know about this?"

"I heard the same rumors but have been too busy to look into them. What I can tell you is that at the hospital, we've been pushing swabs into people's noses twenty-four hours a day for six weeks. We're not allowed to treat anyone. We all had to sign pledges of secrecy, and those who were caught doing what I'm doing right now have disappeared.

"I can also tell you this; whoever calls this the common flu is an idiot, or a liar, or a joker. It's an insult to anyone with half a brain. After collecting what feels like thousands of samples over the past six weeks, I know the symptoms, all of them, from mild to severe. I've been practicing medicine for nearly forty years. I know what the flu looks like, and *this* is not it."

"Where do the specimens go after you've collected them?"

"I have no idea, and neither do any of my colleagues. We're not allowed to ask. We hand them over to government officials onsite. I'd say it's logical to expect they'd go to a lab for tests and subsequent treatment of the positive cases. But in the last few years, I've learned that it's not good practice to expect the government to always do things logically."

"Do you have any scientific information and data about the virus?"

"None. Zilch. We're not allowed to study the virus or collect data about it. I can only tell you about the symptoms I've been observing."

"Okay, tell me about them. I'm recording our conversation."

Abiram described the symptoms.

"We need samples. Would you be able to safely collect some and bring them out?"

Abiram thought about it for a few seconds and said, "Yes, it's possible."

"Without being caught?"

"That I can't guarantee, but it's highly unlikely. We're not searched when we report for duty nor when we leave. I guess they do not think anyone would want to smuggle lethal pathogens out of there."

"I take it you've got a computer at work, and it's connected to the hospital's network?"

"Yes."

Osche took the coffee pot and poured more coffee into Abiram's cup. When he was done and had replaced the pot in the spot where he got it, Abiram saw the tiniest flash drive he had ever seen on the table next to his coffee cup. He picked up his cup and the flash drive in one smooth action.

Osche said, "You'll have to shut your computer down, put that into the USB port, then start it up again. Wait for two minutes, then take it out and reboot your computer. And then you've got to destroy that drive. Crush it and flush the pieces down as many different drains and toilets as you can without raising suspicion."

"Will do."

"Don't worry; it's untraceable. No one will be able to trace it back to your computer."

Abiram nodded slightly. "Where do I drop the sample?"

"When you've got the samples ready, half turn the blinds in your office to your right as you face the window and leave them like that. When you go home at the end of your shift, a young man with a Yankee baseball cap will stop you outside and tell you he lost his wallet. He'll ask you for money to pay for the bus fare to get home and for food. Give him the money and your plastic lunchbox."

Abiram nodded, looked at his watch, and said, "I have to go. My shift starts in fifteen minutes. Thanks for breakfast. It was great seeing you again."

CIA Headquarters, Langley, Virginia

Day 13

At the six weeks mark, the information taps were turned off. Although bits and pieces were still dripping in after that date, it was mostly without context—no connection to other data.

Looking at the sharp drop, Stacie told her team, "That's when they deployed their oppressive censorship apparatus to block information about the virus from getting out."

Shafer, who was in the operations room at the time, said,

"And we know how adept the communist government has become at hiding unflattering or uncomfortable truths. We already know they severely restrict their internet—Facebook, Twitter, and YouTube are blocked—and online searches for even the most ordinary terms can come back empty."

The team expanded their search criteria and started looking for people mentioning anything related to the clampdown. It didn't take long to find snippets hinting that hundreds of Chinese citizens had been detained or punished by the communist party for spreading rumors.

Two of Stacie's team members, senior analysts on the China desk, used their fake credentials to log into their WeChat accounts. WeChat was a small Chinese internet chat application. They found that all threads talking about a virus had vanished.

Riana, one of the two analysts, said, "That's the work of their Cyberspace Administration. They use word and theme artificial intelligence technology to scrub social media platforms and remove any information they deem inappropriate."

"Let's have a quick look at YY," said Derrick, the other analyst. YY was the most prominent Chinese video-based streaming social network, with over three hundred million users.

A few minutes later, he and Riana looked up from their screens, and Riana announced, "Same story. They're using AI technology to identify and block 'offensive' speech in real-time."

"The result; only glowing praise for China gets sent into society and, by proxy, the world," Derrick said. "Censored content will include criticism of the government, rumors, and speculative information about the outbreak in Shanghai. And of course, any mention of the people who had been arrested or punished for spreading rumors."

Stacie produced a humorous interlude with her remark, "Obviously, there're no job opportunities for whistleblowers in communist China."

Another analyst who was fluent in Chinese said, "Look at the big screen. I found some official websites warning people that the Shanghai police would investigate and deal with illegal acts of fabricating, disseminating, spreading rumors, and disturbing social order. Look at this." He highlighted a paragraph on a website displaying on the big screen. He translated, "It is hoped that the majority of netizens will abide by relevant laws and regulations. Do not create rumors, believe rumors, or spread rumors, and jointly build a harmonious and clear cyberspace."

Shafer grinned. "I guess in China everyone knows that means shut up or say goodbye to your family as you get shipped off to an attitude adjustment camp, or as they like to call them, institutions of reeducation."

Over the past decade or so, China had invested billions into the development, acquisition, and deployment of the most sophisticated technology on the planet, enabling them to accumulate a massive body of information about its citizens. Their colossal surveillance apparatus helped them to exercise control over the one-point-four billion inhabitants of the country.

The latest facial recognition, artificial intelligence, and other digital technologies were integrated into its network of monitoring systems. It was estimated that the number of CCTV cameras was approaching three hundred million and expected to jump to five hundred sixty million within the next year. One camera for every four-point-one Chinese citizens. Globally, they had the dubious honor to have eight of the top ten most surveilled cities in the world within their borders.

Although the government wanted people to believe that Beijing's snooping on them was aimed at catching criminals, the truth was much more sinister. The surveillance tools were used to find the identities of people walking on the street, in addition to finding out who they were meeting with, and who wasn't a member of the Communist Party.

The most impertinent form of surveillance was the "social credit" system through which the ruling party tried to incentivize good behavior. People built up social credit by following the rules and good behavior, acting in a manner that pleased the authorities. All over the world, financial institutions used personal data to assess a person's credit-worthiness for a loan or credit card, but China's credit system applied to daily life as they looked at the person's record to find offenses such as jaywalking, walking a dog without a leash, how long someone played video games, etcetera.

Concepts such as human rights and privacy were not often debated, actually, not allowed to be discussed at all in the People's Republic of China.

Chapter Twenty-Eight

EXPORTER TO IMPORTER IN SIX WEEKS

Secured video conference

Day 14

Stacie's operations room had direct, secured video and audio links to Greg's team at CRC headquarters in Arizona as well as the *TOMATS* communications room, and she gave them regular progress updates.

Rex and the team on the *TOMATS* and the CRC team in Arizona were going through the information in Stacie's latest update when Rex had a lightbulb moment. "Greg, what will it take to find out if the Chinese government is stockpiling medical equipment, medicine, and such?"

Everyone's eyes had turned to Greg.

"Difficult to say until we try," Greg said. "I'm guessing it won't be easy to find information about the stuff that they manufacture in-country. If they're buying the stuff on the international markets, it might be much easier. What do you want us to look for?"

Rex shrugged and said, "I'm not sure what type of medical gear and drugs would be required to fight a viral epidemic. Things that come to mind are masks, gloves, overcoats, protective suits, oxygen masks, ventilators, aspirin, antibiotics, antiviral drugs, sanitizers . . ."

Brandt nodded slowly and said, "You're thinking they could be preparing themselves for a pandemic, making sure they're the only country still standing when it's all over?"

Rex nodded slowly and said, "I pray to God that I'm wrong."

Catia put her hand on Rex's arm and said, "God hears all prayers."

"Yes, but sometimes the answer is no."

Within fifteen minutes, they'd compiled a list of medical equipment and drugs, looked up the brand names of several of them, and Greg's team got busy.

Three hours later, they were back in conclave.

Greg and Rehka were sitting next to each other in CRC's operations room. Their faces were paperwhite. Brandt and McArdle's features radiated concern.

Brandt started. "Dalton, I don't know if the Almighty has spoken to you since our last meeting, but Greg and his team have their answer ready. It is as you expected. Unfortunately, you were not wrong. I'll let Greg and Rehka tell us what they've uncovered."

Greg took a large gulp of his coffee, cleared his throat, and said, "The executive summary is, they've vacuumed up most of the world's surplus PPE, personal protective equipment. Over the past six weeks, China, the largest manufacturer of PPE in the world, stopped exporting and started buying from other countries. They went from a net exporter of PPE to a large net importer in six weeks.

"They now own more facemasks, surgical gloves, goggles, and hand sanitizer than the rest of the world combined. Two billion masks . . . fifty cents apiece."

Rehka said, "But keep in mind, we've only scratched the surface. That's what we discovered in three hours. There will be much more, I'm sure. We haven't even looked at ventilators, oxygen masks, syringes, and drugs. If they're expecting trouble of the magnitude of having to use two billion masks, I expect they'd been stockpiling those items with the same vigor."

"That means the rest of the world would be defenseless when that virus hits them," Spencer said.

"Exactly," Brandt said.

"They bought masks for fifty cents; what do you reckon the price would be by the time the epidemic becomes a pandemic?" Marissa said.

"Maybe the same as what you'd be willing to pay for a glass of ice-cold water after two days in the desert without any," Rex said.

"Good analogy, Rex," McArdle said with a wry smile.

"I can already see it in my mind's eye," Josh said.

"What?" Brandt said.

"The title of the new international bestseller: How to profit from a virus pandemic in three easy steps. By Li Lingxin."

When the laughter ended, Catia said, "On a serious note, it's more than just a little worrisome that no one has, at least no one that we know of, noticed or questioned China's sudden need for mountains of PPE," Catia said.

"Well, that's about to change. I'll be on the wire to Richardson the moment we're done here," Brandt said.

Rex grinned, looked at everyone around the table on his side, and said, "I'm done. How about you?"

They all indicated they had nothing further to discuss.

"You've got our permission to call Richardson now," Rex said with a straight face.

Brandt flipped him the bird and severed the connection.

Chapter Twenty-Nine

NO SECOND TERM

Singapore

Day 14

Jethro has made one of Matz Enterprises' offices in Singapore available for the meeting between David and Dong. His security people had swept the room for bugs and confirmed it was safe. Jethro's staff assured they had refreshments and total privacy.

Although Brandt, Aderet, and the rest were supportive of David's idea to meet Dong Yan, Brandt and Aderet, who had both cut their teeth in the spy business during the Cold War, told him that defectors had to be treated with extreme caution.

A deceptive tactic used by spy agencies all over the world was to send one of their agents as a fake defector into the enemy camp. The Russians were exceptionally good at it. The defector would be a disinformation agent who could create havoc, for instance, telling his hosts that one or more of their own people had been spying for the KGB—or providing false information which the hosts would act upon. Spy agencies knew this and had protocols in place to root out fake defectors. But it was a long and tedious process that required months of interrogation, checking, and double-checking the veracity of the information provided by the defector.

"We don't have the luxury of time now," Brandt said. "My advice is that you tell him nothing about our operation. Let him do the talking, and be careful not to raise suspicions with your questions."

David heeded the advice and told Dong he wanted to meet with him to discuss his investment portfolio, given his new circumstances.

Dong seemed to accept it and said, "Yes, we have to look at that. My financial position has changed dramatically since those bastards that I thought were my friends, and I could trust them, seized seven billion dollars' worth of my assets—"

"Wow! Seven billion? I didn't know that."

"You wouldn't know. But you know how they operate. First, they tried to hide the fallout I had with Li Lingxin; I still can't believe that my lifelong friend betrayed me like that. When they couldn't bury it, they launched an expensive disinformation campaign against me—spending millions of dollars on a covert campaign to influence the Singapore government to repatriate me back to China.

"Not only that, they imprisoned my brother and sister, detained and interrogated some of my family members, and arrested one hundred and twenty of my employees."

"It sounds as if they're set on destroying you. I hope you don't mind me asking, but why have they turned against you like that?"

"It started when I told Lingxin that I felt it was time to start democratizing China, to move away from communism. At first, our discussions were amicable, but over time it became more and more heated until one day Lingxin accused me of playing into the hands of the Americans. He hates them. He feels the President of the United States has humiliated him. That's bullshit, of course. The thing is, China is losing the trade war with the USA, and in the process, Lingxin's image as one of the world's strongmen is withering.

"You see, after the 2008 global financial crisis, China became the key engine of world economic growth as other countries were licking their wounds and trying to recover. But since the President of America started to take them to task about the unfair trade practices and forced them to negotiate new trade agreements, their economy has been deteriorating rapidly. Their industrial output has dropped to the lowest levels since 2002, retail sales are slowing, and for the past year, their worldwide exports have dropped by one percent. Exports to the USA declined by sixteen percent.

"Lingxin is furious; he's on the warpath with America, specifically their president."

"May God forbid that there's ever a war between them. But I can't see how China could win a war with America. Although in a war, there are no winners and losers, there are only survivors; China would be utterly destroyed."

"It's not that kind of war that Lingxin has in mind; he's clever enough to know China would be decimated if it comes to that. No, his war is personal, with the President of America. And to that end, he had convinced the CCP to declare that this American president will not be allowed to have a second term."

"In other words, America's trade strategies are working, and for that reason, China wants a different American president?" David said.

"Precisely."

"How does Li Lingxin hope to achieve that? I mean, it's not as if he can tell the American voters to do as he wants or face punishment like he's doing in China?"

Dong shook his head. "He and his cronies worked out a plan to derail the president's reelection campaign. The plan is to use three, what Lingxin calls, weapons. I know some details about two of them; the third he kept from me, mentioning it only in vague terms.

"The first weapon is calling in the favors due to the CCP from political leaders and lobbyists in Washington whom they had been corrupting for many years, to use their influence to stop the president's reelection. And as you probably know, there is no shortage of those.

"The second weapon is the American mainstream news and social media. I probably don't have to tell you how hostile they already are toward the president. You can bet your bottom dollar that the media giants will be disinclined to come to the defense of the president when the Chinese Communist Party criticizes their mutual foe."

David nodded. "The enemy of my enemy is my friend."

"Exactly. The third weapon is what I don't know much about. The first two weapons Lingxin and his cohorts had been talking about for more than a year. The third weapon I only heard of about eight or so weeks ago. They seemed to be careful not to go into much detail about it whenever I was present. But what I've read between the lines while listening to their conversations was they're working on something that would weaken the American society and take advantage of it."

David felt a shiver running down his spine. "That sounds ominous, Yan. Any idea what it could be?"

Dong shrugged. "I can only speculate. I'm sure it won't be any kind of military action. I'm thinking it could be something on the financial front, manipulation of their currency, crashing the stock market, or commodity prices."

David only nodded. He was almost certain he knew what the third weapon was.

Dong said, "Well, now you know how I became public enemy number one in China. I dared to question the 'Führer's' wisdom about setting China on a collision course with the United States. My ideas that China could become the world leader by moving away from the oppressive and miserably failing communism practices to an open and democratic society, I might as well have been presented to the corpses in a graveyard. My ideas enraged them. They became suspicious of me and convinced Lingxin that with me, he was keeping awfully bad company. I think what finally sent them into a frenzy was when I told them the vast majority of the Chinese people, including the ninety million members of the CCP, want to see the disappearance of the Communist Party who, in reality, exist only to serve a hundred or so self-appointed elitists."

David laughed. "I can see how that could've upset them."

"And it did. The day after I said that, I got a message from a friend alerting me that they've issued orders to the MSS to pick me up for questioning. I've heard that I've missed the MSS officers and the inside of an MSS interrogation cell by only fifteen minutes."

"So, what you're saying is, the next US presidential election is not going to be for the American voters to decide between the Republican and Democrat nominees but a choice between dependence on China or American independence?"

"Couldn't have said it better myself."

Chapter Thirty

THE SAYANIM OF SHANGHAI

Shanghai, China

Day 14

Apart from Dr. Abiram Sharot, Aderet had two other *sayanim* in Shanghai. One was an international commercial lawyer, the other a pharmacist who owned a pharmacy.

The pharmacist was able to tell her *katsa* everything about the explosion in demand for flu medications, face masks, and sanitizer the last six to eight weeks. Her conversations with the throngs of clients lining up to buy those products pointed to one cause and one only. A new type of virus was out there infecting, afflicting, and killing people in ever-increasing numbers. The symptoms her clients told her about, and those she observed, left no doubt it was viral in origin. What she told her *katsa* just confirmed what Tao Meng's scouts discovered a few days ago and what Stacie's team discovered from the data they were analyzing.

She also told her *katsa* that one of the doctors who referred patients to her for the fulfillment of prescriptions had told her a few days earlier that a doctor who was among the first to sound the alarm about the new virus in Shanghai on WeChat, and five others who had participated in the chat group, disappeared and were reported dead a few days later.

However, the torrent of clients visiting her pharmacy to buy flu medication before had abruptly dropped to almost nothing a few weeks ago. The reason she said, was that the neighborhoods where the outbreak occurred had been cordoned off and people were in lockdown in their homes. The police were patrolling the areas, and offenders were punished harshly. The internet, cellphone network, and landlines in those areas were blocked completely.

The lawyer was a gold mine of information. He had unfettered access to international commerce data about imports and exports through the ports of not only Shanghai but most of China. He had many of Shanghai's and China's biggest import and export companies as clients.

With a few keystrokes on his computer's keyboard, he was able to give his *katsa* exact import and export figures for personal protection equipment that went through the ports of Shanghai and elsewhere in China for the past twelve months. With equal ease, he was able to extract the same information about ventilators, oxygen masks, drugs, and other medical-related items.

Brandt's mission team quickly analyzed that information, and it confirmed what they feared. China was stockpiling medical equipment and related items on a massive scale. As for the reasons, for now, it was safest to assume that China was preparing to deal with an unprecedented health crisis. But not only that, they were probably also expecting the health crisis to spill over their borders, in which case they'd be ideally placed to profit from selling medical merchandise to the affected countries and offer medical services if they had managed to get their problem under control by then.

It was ten a.m. after a twenty-four-hour shift when Dr. Abiram Sharot walked out the front door of ESPH to go home when he was stopped by a disheveled man in ragged clothes, unkempt hair and beard, and a red New York Yankees baseball cap pulled low over his face. The disgusting odor coming from the man reminded Sharot of the rubbish bins in the backstreets of the city.

"Please, sir, can you help me?"

The voice sounded very familiar, but he didn't recognize the face.

"Please sir, my wallet was stolen, I've got no money to pay for the bus to get home. Please, sir, will you please help me so I can get back home? Sir."

The man kept on rubbing his tummy, which Sharot thought was an indication that he was also ravenous.

Then two things struck Sharot: this was the man he was supposed to give the specimens to, and this man was his *katsa*, Joel Osche. He had a very hard time not laughing. While taking out his wallet, he whispered, "Joel, I had no idea you were such a good actor. You must consider the theater if this job doesn't work out for you. But you'll have to take a bath."

Osche made no reply; he only held his hands out for Sharot to put the money in it, which he did. Osche made a show of thanking him and an even bigger show when Sharot placed the plastic lunchbox packed with spring rolls and dumplings in his hands as well.

Four hours later, the specimens would be in Hong Kong.

Twenty-four hours after that, they would arrive in Washington, D.C., where it would be handed over to scientists of the U.S. Army Medical Research Institute of Infectious Diseases (USAMRIID) who would take it to their labs at Fort Detrick, Maryland, where the world's most dangerous pathogens were being studied.

Chapter Thirty-One

THE FUNCTIONAL EQUIVALENT OF WAR

White House, Washington, D.C.

Day 15

It was five thirty a.m., in the back of his official vehicle,
Howard Lawrence was taking small sips of piping-hot Star-
bucks coffee on his way to the White House for a meeting
with the president starting at six a.m. He was relieved that
the situation was not the same as it was four days ago when
he had to break the news to the president. However,
contrary to the president's hope that the virus problem
would go away quickly, the news got much worse as time
progressed. The president had been kept in the loop all the
way. He was a man who expected to be kept informed of
everything going on under his administration. It was impossible, he knew it. Lawrence had a convoluted theory that the
president employed some kind of reverse psychology by
acting as if he knew about everything that was going on,

while knowing it was impossible, but not ever saying so, which made everyone around him believe that he did know about everything that was happening.

Lawrence was thinking about the information collected by David Sarlin during his meeting with Dong Yan in Singapore. He had only received the translated transcript of the audio recording two hours ago.

It was early in the presidential election cycle, but it was never too early to start putting runs on the board. This president wanted what all presidents wanted, a second term. And the information in the transcript, if made public, would put a lot of runs on the board for him as he told the world how right he'd been about China all along. That his policies were working, and that's why the PRC was trying to get rid of him.

This morning's meeting was to discuss strategy. Present would be the President, Vice President, Director of National Intelligence (DNI), Lawrence's boss, the White House Trade Advisor, the White House Chief of Staff, the Chairman of the Joint Chiefs of Staff, the National Security Advisor, and the Homeland Security Advisor.

The meeting started on time. After the president welcomed everyone, the DNI reported that he and Lawrence had just received the news that the specimens containing the pathogen were en route to D.C. Seeing the apprehension on some faces, he said, "Don't worry, the container is secure; the virus cannot get out unless a human takes it out. The container is virtually indestructible, like the black box of an aircraft." That seemed to mollify them.

Lawrence had summarized the information in a Power-Point presentation. The first few slides were a review of the information he gave them two days ago. The rest of the slides were the information collected by Stacie's team and

Greg's team's hair-raising discovery about China's stockpiling of medical equipment and medicine. The final slide was a synopsis of the audio recording David made during his meeting with Dong Yan. Their names were not revealed in the abstract.

The president had one look at the final slide and said, "Now there's something the press needs to get their teeth into. It will at least keep their teeth out of my back for a few days."

The president's comment brought a smile to all the faces.

"If this guy can be trusted, is it likely that this third weapon he's talking about could be this virus?"

Everyone agreed; some only nodding and others saying so.

"Does anyone have any doubt that there's a virus problem in Shanghai, and their government is trying their best to hide it?"

There was no doubt.

"That brings us to the purpose of the meeting. What should we do about it? How prepared are we, and for that matter, how prepared are our allies if this virus hits our shores?"

The DNI started. "Mr. President, I'd like to start with your second question first. How prepared are we and our allies? To answer that, it's essential to understand the difference between our societies, China's and the Western world's, that is. In the democracies of the West, we don't have the same ability as the communist government of China to rapidly organize and unite our citizens behind a common goal. To a large degree, China is still a revolutionary society; they're a mobilized army, so to speak, ready to march at the drop of a hat. Western democracies are societies geared at functioning in peacetime. To mobilize them to head a major threat takes a lot of effort, money, and time. With the information we have, it seems the Chinese have at least a three-month head start on us; they're already in the process of mobilizing.

"I foresee if the virus is as lethal as we hear it is and it spreads to the rest of the world, that China would be ideally placed to emerge as the world's knight in shining armor. In the chaos that we and the rest of the world would be struggling to overcome, they'd be stepping forward to offer medical help and expertise. In the ensuing economic turmoil, they'll be offering their manufacturing services, lend out money, and present themselves as the financial haven and savior of the world. A repeat of their performance in the wake of the 2008 global financial crisis. However, this time it could be on a much larger scale."

"And I guess it's not too farfetched to think that they'd have the cure and vaccine by the time they dispatch the virus to the four corners of the globe?" the National Security Advisor surmised.

The DNI nodded. "No, not farfetched at all. But we don't have enough information to say with any degree of certainty that they have the intention of deliberately spreading the virus outside their borders. Not yet."

"Well, their deliberate efforts, including killing people, to cover it up doesn't exactly make them look innocent," the Chief of Staff said.

"Let's presume we're facing the worst-case scenario. What are the main things we should focus on right now?" the president asked.

The Trade Advisor responded, "Mr. President, over the past few days, I've been brainstorming what-if scenarios with some of my senior staff. We've come up with three main points.

"First, as the DNI said, China is better at organizing and mobilizing their society for a crisis than we are. If the virus pops its head out here in the next week or two, we'll be totally unprepared. As it spreads and the chaos increases, the world will quickly lose confidence in us as the most powerful nation on earth. We must take immediate steps to prevent that.

"Second. We have to look at what we can do to keep our economy going, no matter how severe the impact of the virus has on us. For every factory, plant, or business that we shut down, we would be creating an opportunity for China to step in and fill the void, expanding their market share, and replacing our products with theirs in the international marketplace.

"Third. In a worst-case scenario, due to the economic bedlam, many countries might experience widespread social and political upheaval and even collapse, which would create the ideal opportunity for China to come to their rescue by providing all kinds of aid while refashioning those countries in its own image.

"Mr. President, I think it would be wise for us to remember the words of Mao Tse Tung: 'Everything under heaven is in utter chaos, the situation is excellent.'"

The DNI said, "If this virus is indeed that third weapon we've heard about, then they'll have a plan to become the dominant world power while America is left in a debilitated position."

No one could find fault with the Trade Advisor or DNI's ideas.

The President said, "The bottom line is, we're not ready, not by a long shot. Now, although I don't like to dwell in the past, it is true that the past informs the present. Let's talk about how it got to this. How did we get into such a vulnerable position?"

The Trade Advisor spoke first. "Mr. President, for decades, the Chinese have been allowed to act with impunity when they contravened international laws. They've been stealing our intellectual property and trade secrets to the tune of $600 billion per year. American inventiveness had been a driving force in the international markets. We've been at the forefront of scientific and technological advances while the Chinese have been specializing in intellectual property piracy. They've built an entire economy on our innovations. And we've been unable to stop them or penalize them for their misconduct.

"Just think about their continued illicit production of the deadly opioid, fentanyl. They've promised to stop it. They lied and continued. If one American dies from this virus, it would be one too many; it would be tragic and heartbreaking. Just as tragic and heartbreaking as the deaths of every one of the forty-five thousand dying from opioid overdoses every year. You and presidents before you have openly confronted China about this and demanded that they change their policies about fentanyl production. Even so, it appears that they have not lived up to their promises.

"I've got one more comment, Mr. President if you'll bear with me?"

The President nodded.

"It's about our dependence on Chinese produced critical health care items such as pharmaceutical products, personal protective equipment, and other medical devices. After decades of outsourcing our technology and manufacturing jobs to countries such as China, we're now in an untenable position where eighty percent of the active pharmaceutical ingredients, known as basic components, that we need to manufacture our drugs, are made in China. Ditto for the overwhelming majority of all our medical supplies, including personal protective equipment.

"Sir, we even outsourced the production of all our penicillin to them in 2004."

The President nodded. "At the time, a lot of people applauded the move as clever and far-sighted, saving us money on generic drugs. It was a stupid move."

The vice president said, "Mr. President, it seems that the pragmatic action to take now would be to issue an executive order that would incentivize American companies to start producing medications and medical supplies locally immediately."

"We'll draft that order the moment this meeting is over," the President said.

The discussions continued for another half hour, and everyone agreed, this was the opportunity for the USA to reconsider the country's over-reliance on China. To stop ingratiating the Chinese government and put American workers first.

There was no dissent among them when the president said, "We have to get the American people to understand how important it is to buy American. We'll deregulate to make it easier for our manufacturers to start up. And we'll innovate to keep the prices down.

"This is our opportunity to explain to those who had been forever pushing for closer ties with China how wrong they were and the danger they've put us in by sending our manufacturing jobs offshore. It's been terrible for America."

To the speculation, if this virus were natural or manmade, the DNI replied, "The specimens will arrive tomorrow. It will take a few days to study and answer that question."

The meeting ended with a list of questions begging for answers. Manmade or not, did the virus enter the population of Shanghai naturally, such as jumping from an animal to a human, or was it released deliberately? What does President Li Lingxin know, when did he know it, and what did he do about it?

The Chairman of the Joint Chiefs of Staff left them with a chilling comment at the end of the meeting. "Mr. President, there are people who believe that our current world order can't be changed without another war on the scale of past world wars, and the likelihood of that happening is minuscule. But I think the proponents of that theory are missing the point that setting a pandemic in motion is the functional equivalent of war."

Chapter Thirty-Two

GAMBLING ON MACAO

Macao Special Administrative Region

Day 15 and 16

Macao was officially known as Macao Special Administrative Region of the People's Republic of China, an autonomous region on the south coast of China, across the Pearl River Delta from Hong Kong. They maintained separate governing and economic systems from those of mainland China. It was a Portuguese territory until 1999. The most densely populated region in the world, "Las Vegas of Asia," as some called it, had giant casinos and malls on the Cotai Strip, which joins the islands of Taipa and Coloane.

It was early Friday night when Jethro and his wife, Liu, met General Dai Min and his wife, Mei, in the foyer of The Venetian, the biggest casino in Macao. It boasted the world's largest casino floor, 34,931 square meters of gaming space, 640 gaming tables, and 1,760 slot machines.

Jethro had booked the general and his wife, as well as Liu and himself, into adjoining Royale Deluxe Suites. The seventy-square-meter suites decorated in elegant calm blue tones, creamy whites, gold accents, and marble baths were regarded as the best accommodation in Macao.

Over dinner, the ladies took the initiative to lay out the plans for the weekend. They would have a few after-dinner drinks and turn in early. The ladies needed to be rested to go out and paint the town red Saturday morning. Jethro and the general didn't care what the women did if they were permitted enough time to play eighteen holes of golf. Saturday night, they would have dinner together before hitting the casino's gaming tables.

Before they said goodnight to each other, Jethro slipped an envelope into the general's hand while Mrs. Dai's attention was focused on a story Liu was telling her. Jethro smiled. "Just a little something to help cover the cost of the paint."

The envelope disappeared into the inner pocket of the general's jacket. He smiled and said, "Thanks, the paint in this town can be expensive."

The next morning on the golf course, Jethro, who played off a ten handicap, told the general that he was a beginner.

"The same with me," the general said and extended his hand. "How about a little wager? Let's say three thousand US dollars?"

Three thousand to quench the wife's shopping thirst. Three thousand to deliberately lose a golf game. Plus food, drinks, accommodation, and gambling money. Trivial when you're trying to stop a virus from destroying the world.

"You're on. How can I turn down an opportunity to humiliate a general *and* take his money?"

They laughed and shook hands.

Ten minutes into the game, Jethro concluded that the general didn't lie about his beginner's status—he had no ball sense. Jethro's assessment of the general's golf skills was that it would probably take around three to five years, four hours a day, to get him to the beginner's handicap level, which was a twenty-four.

Fortunately, they were a twosome, and it was only Jethro who had to endure the fiasco. The general only got on the fairway when he crossed it to retrieve his ball from somewhere in the rough on the other side. That was beside the twenty or so times that the general missed the ball completely when he took a swing at it—a fresh-air shot, golfers, called it. Jethro had a hard time deliberately slicing and hooking his shots to appear even worse than the general. After five grueling hours, most of which was spent looking for missing balls, mercifully, the game was over. The general won by three points, Jethro coughed up the three thousand dollars, in cash, with a big smile and promised the general that he would not be so lucky the next time, while secretly hoping there would never be a next time.

The general's palms were both greased; his ego had been stroked, many times. All Jethro could do now was wait for the general to pick the moment to discuss business. It would not be good form for Jethro to initiate the conversation.

That night after dinner, when Madames Dai and Matz indicated they were ready to try their luck on the game tables, the general suggested the ladies go ahead and enjoy themselves, he wanted a bit of private time to talk business with Jethro.

The general watched the ladies walk away, reached into the inside pocket of his jacket, and retrieved a gold-plated cigar case filled with very expensive Cuban cigars. He offered one to Jethro, who politely declined. The general spent the next few minutes going through an elaborate ritual to light the cigar, took a puff, and while blowing the dense cloud of bluish smoke toward the ceiling, turned to Jethro and said, "Tell me about it. In my line of work, it's crucial to be able to recognize the signs of stress in people. That's my forte."

You could've fooled me. I thought the bribes are what got your attention.

Jethro smiled and said, "I didn't know it was *that* obvious. But thank you general, I appreciate very much that you are prepared to listen to me."

The general waved his hand in dismissal. "Don't mention it."

Jethro cleared his throat, feigning nervousness, and spun a story about Matz Enterprises' business interests in Shanghai and how some of the workers became ill and died. Jethro's concern was that he couldn't get any information about the causes of death for any of them. No doctor or coroner wanted to tell him. He said there were rumors that a very nasty virus was rampant in Shanghai. But he experienced the same problem trying to get accurate information; no one would confirm or deny it. It was obvious something untoward was going on, but the government blocked the information about it. Jethro said he was now worried about the future of his businesses in Shanghai.

Dai sat back, crossed his legs, and let out a long sigh in relief. "And there I was worrying that you had something dire on your mind. Jethro, you can relax. Yes, there is a virus causing illness and death in Shanghai. But it's not nearly as serious as the scientists initially thought. Their quick response assured that they got it under control quickly. It took them a few weeks to find the right combination of drugs to fight it efficiently. The virus is less harmful than the common flu."

Jethro nodded slowly, not in understanding or agreement, but because it was as he expected, the general was misinformed. It was not a surprise. General Dai was in charge of the People's Liberation Army Rocket Force, sixteen brigades of China's nuclear and conventional strategic missiles. It was a different arsenal of weapons of mass destruction than his colleague, General Yuan Lee, who oversaw China's biological warfare program. Yuan was one of the eighteen marshals, an ardent supporter of President Li Lingxin. General Lee would have been the one controlling the narrative about the Shanghai virus.

Dai continued, "The authorities in Shanghai ought to be congratulated for their rapid and competent actions. At the first signs of an outbreak, they immediately started quarantining people, enforced social distancing, and cordoned off the infected neighborhoods. Of course, they had to put a total blackout on electronic communications to avoid rumor-mongering and the onset of mass hysteria. There's absolutely nothing for you to be concerned about."

Jethro took a sip of his port while contemplating how to break the news to General Dai that he had been lied to. He had to be very careful not to offend the man.

Before Jethro could start, Dai said, "With that out of the way, let's finish up and go see what our ladies are up to. Maybe try our luck at blackjack."

It was not a suggestion; it was a command.

However, if Jethro obeyed, the whole weekend was a

waste of time and money. "General, is it possible that your sources could've been withholding information from you?"

Dai's face displayed a brief moment of irritation. "Not impossible but highly unlikely . . ." He paused, studied Jethro's face for a second or two, and said, "Is there something you know that I don't?"

"Unfortunately, General, that seems to be the case."

Dai raised his eyebrows and waited for Jethro to continue.

Jethro told him about the information provided by people in the streets of Shanghai. He told him about the disappearance of Benjamin Yatsir and his family. He told him about the MSS's attempt to kill Dora Frankel, the near killing of his sister, Tamara, the abduction of the three women, and the information given up by the gang leader, Tian Song-li. When Jethro ended with the information provided by Dr. Zheng Xuefeng, General Dai's face was distorted with rage. It was clear Dai had no idea what was going on in Shanghai. Jethro was disappointed. He had hoped that the general would know all about the virus and that a significant bribe would convince Dai to help them.

But it looked as if Dai was about to have a heart attack. His tone was soft and measured, "What's that moron doing?"

Jethro assumed the moron in question was General Yuan.

"He's going to start a war . . .," Dai whispered.

"Surely President Li wouldn't let General Yuan go that far, would he?" Jethro said.

"I'm talking about the president, Jethro, not that nincompoop Yuan."

"But there's no indication that the president knows . . ."

"Trust me, he knows. If that virus was engineered in a

lab in China, then Li knows. And don't be surprised if he has been orchestrating it himself. The man's a nutcase, a dimwit that had to apply several times to get membership of the CCP. How he got the support of the majority of the marshals has always been a mystery to me."

Dai seemed to have forgotten about sharing information with people who didn't have the right security clearances and told Jethro, "Our bioweapons program is operating under the Anti-Biological Warfare Unit. They are stationed in northern China and tasked to develop specialized equipment to counter any biological weapons threat against the soldiers of the PLA. But that unit also has a division that conducts research and development of bioweapons . . . . That's where this virus would've been engineered . . ."

"But how did it get to Shanghai?"

"The 'how' is easy. It's the 'why' that I'm worried about."

Jethro frowned. "Are you suggesting this could have been an experiment conducted on Chinese citizens in Shanghai?"

"I wouldn't put that beyond Li Lingxin. Release the virus to part of the population, keep it in check while developing a cure and a vaccine. But if your information is correct, the experiment has gone wrong."

"General, what will it take for you to work with us to stop this?"

"Who is us?"

"David Sarlin and me."

"And who else? CIA?"

Jethro nodded slowly. "The CIA, but we don't have direct contact with them. We're working through a private contractor organization employed by them."

After a protracted uneasy silence, to Jethro's surprise,

instead of exploding in anger about the audacity to expect him to collaborate with the CIA, General Dai said, "I need two days. There might be a way it can be done without ever revealing my involvement. I'll be in touch by no later than midday on Monday."

Their business discussion was over. Jethro was not entirely satisfied with the outcome; he had hoped that Dai would be the one to help them; now, like before, all he could do was to wait and see what the general's plan was.

None of them felt like gambling or drinking anymore. General Dai said he was going to cut the weekend short and fly back to Beijing very early the next morning instead of Monday morning as they had planned.

Chapter Thirty-Three

THE MARSHALS

Beijing, China

Day 17

By midday on Sunday, the seven dissident marshals were assembled in General Dai's study at his house in Beijing. When Dai called them to meet, they knew something important was in the cards. They'd never met like this. They were not worried about being watched or eavesdropped upon; not even the MSS would dare to do it, and Li, even if he knew about the meeting, would not be so stupid as to issue an order to spy on the marshals.

With growing fury, they listened in silence as Dai told them what Jethro told him the night before.

None of them cared for Yuan Lee. The man was an opportunist, a turncoat with no principles or moral compass. He had no patriotism for his country. His only patriotism was to himself and his career. When the internal struggle among the marshals was raging during Li Lingxin's rise to power, Yuan stayed on the sidelines, uncommitted until he knew which direction the wind was blowing and then added his support for Li. That's how he had made his way up the ladder his whole life. He supported whoever was in the lead. Whether that was the best person for the job or not was of no consequence to him. For Yuan, it was always about the betterment of his career. Loyalty was not part of his makeup.

General Wan Huang of the Air Force broke the silence that followed Dai Min's account. "Yuan Lee has not only deceived us; he also deceived the people of China and the world. He doesn't have the guts to do it on his own; he's following orders, and I'm sure we don't have to guess who that is."

They all nodded. No guessing was necessary — the president was behind it.

The seven had not given up their quest to get their own man into power when Li Lingxin became president. They'd been keeping a careful watch on the president's eleven supporters among their ranks. Two of them, on separate occasions, without knowing about the other, had made vague overtures to some members of the group of seven that they had come to regret their decision to support Li for president. But they were not prepared to abandon him without the guarantee that there would be enough absconders to bring about a bloodless palace revolution. They seemed to have been cut from the same cloth as their spineless colleague General Yuan Lee. Therefore, the seven couldn't make a move to topple Li from power until they had at least one more turncoat.

A few months ago, the group of seven got very excited when they discovered that Yuan had a sexual preference for underage boys. They were able to obtain a few video recordings of his flagrant acts and considered using it to blackmail him into changing sides.

But it was Dai Min who cautioned the group not to proceed in haste. "We all know Yuan's type of sexual promiscuity is a criminal offense; he ought to be prosecuted and shot. That's what would happen if he were an ordinary citizen, and Li wouldn't hesitate to let it be done to anyone of us if we ever did something like that. But Yuan, in his position as the president's ass-kisser-in-chief, would have the protection of the president and his supporting marshals. They would cover for him, and he would never be prosecuted."

"But he would be at their beck and call, and they'd drop him like a hot potato when they didn't need him anymore. So, his career ambitions would be destroyed," one of the seven said at the time.

"That may be so, but he would still be in his position, and Li would still be in power," Dai said. "I suggest we keep that information, collect more if possible, and wait for the right moment."

General Wan recalled their previous conversation and said, "I think this is that right moment we've been waiting for."

They all agreed and then launched into a discussion about how to approach the matter with Yuan. They wanted him out of their way. The next marshal in line in case of a vacancy was a fervent opponent of Li. With him and the two fence-sitters, they would have a ten-eight majority, and Li would be history.

Generals Dai Min and Wan Huang were tasked to have a meeting with Yuan.

Chapter Thirty-Four

WHAT DO YOU WANT?

Shanghai, China

Day 18

Yuan was working out of Shanghai for the week, no doubt overseeing the management of the crisis caused by the virus, which was created by his division.

The plan was to "persuade" Yuan to defect to America. As motivation to get him to cooperate with them rather than commit suicide, they had in mind to tell him that he would get a hero's welcome in the USA. He would be given a new identity and placed in the FBI's witness protection program. Dai was sure Jethro would not blink an eye to prop the offer up with a few million dollars. They had no idea whether any of those promises would come to fruition. They didn't care; Yuan lied to them. They were going to pay him back in kind.

They met over breakfast at the Waldorf Astoria hotel,

where Yuan stayed. It was the same hotel where Dai and Wan were staying as well.

Yuan acted as if he was delighted to see his colleagues, and they returned the gesture by pretending their delight to see him.

Shortly after they had filled their plates with food from the buffet and settled down to eat, General Wan asked Yuan about the virus outbreak in Shanghai.

Dai and Wan managed to keep their composure as they listened to the self-serving General Yuan lying to them for the next ten minutes.

Wan threw the first curveball. "So, what you're saying is that the stories we hear about many more deaths than what's being reported are just that, stories and rumors?"

They watched him closely as he replied, "Exactly that— vicious untruths, rumors by conspiracy theory enthusiasts. Everything is well and truly under control. I'm planning to issue the order to start lifting restrictions soon. In a few weeks, Shanghai will be back to normal."

Dai threw the next curveball. "Where did this virus originate from? Have the scientists been able to do a genetic sequence?"

"It comes from bats sold in the city's wet markets. It went from a pangolin to a bat to humans. It's a natural mutation. These wetmarkets, with its unregulated trade in exotic meats and the unchecked hygiene in them, are causing major health issues. At some stage, the government will have to step in and lay down the rules."

"Have you found patient zero?" Wan asked.

"Not yet. It's a long process to trace it back to the first person who was infected. There are so many connections branching out into an ever-increasing network of more connections. And to be honest with you, I'm not sure if it's even important anymore to find patient zero."

"So, the rumors about a lab-engineered virus is all bullshit?" Dai said.

"Absolutely."

"Do you know the company Zexian Biomed?" Dai asked and watched the blood draining from Yuan's face. Dai knew then that Jethro had not lied to him.

"I've heard of them, but I'm not sure what they do."

Dai decided it was time to pull the rug from under Yuan's feet and get to the point. "I'll tell you; they're working on a cure and vaccine for President Li's virus."

"Wha—what do you mean by President Li's virus? How . . . I mean . . . you can't say something like that. You'll get in trouble. I—"

"Well, Lee, then tell us who gave the orders to engineer this virus?" Wan said.

"There was no such order because it is not engineered. I told you where it comes from. Don't you believe me?"

"We'll get to that soon. Dr. Zheng Xuefeng says it comes from a lab. You know Dr. Zheng, don't you?"

"Yes, I do," Yuan said in an almost inaudible whisper.

"If you think Dr. Zheng is lying, why don't we visit Zexian Biomed and talk to the scientists? Then after that, we go to your office to pull all the research data from all the labs you ordered to find a cure and vaccine. Then we also go to your office and look at all the data I'm sure you've been collecting."

Yuan made no reply. His eyes were darting between Wan and Dai.

Dai continued, "I take it you've got all that data, and it will tell us everything we're wondering about, such as if this virus is natural or not, numbers infected, rate of spread, gestation period, symptoms, treatments, mortality rates, etcetera. Right?"

"What do you want?"

"We just told you," Wan said.

"I can't give it to you."

"Says who?"

"The president."

"Why?"

"Ask him."

"Lee, don't be a fool. You're lying for him. Do you think he'd do the same for you? Who do you think will take the fall if the truth comes out? You know the truth always finds its way out into the open."

No reply

Wan said, "Okay, then have a look at this." He placed his cellphone on the table in front of Yuan and started the video showing Yuan with one of his conquests.

Yuan's lips were dry, and he wiped at the sweat from his eyebrows with his napkin. His eyes were wide in shock and fear. "How . . . where . . . I . . ."

"What do you think, in the light of our discussion so far, would happen if we leak these videos to the president?"

"You've ruined me. What do you want?"

"Yuan, you'll have to learn how to listen to people. We told you many times what we want. We want the truth. Oh, and by the way, we didn't ruin you, you ruined yourself. We're just pointing it out to you," Dai said.

"What do you want me to do?"

"You're going to defect."

"De . . . wha— defect. Where to?"

"We're still negotiating on your behalf. But don't worry, we're sure they will take you if you cooperate. And we're sure you'll like the place. You'll live in the lap of luxury for the rest of your life."

"When?"

"We would've preferred right now," Wan said, "but it's not good manners to turn up at someone's house who invited you for dinner empty-handed. So, what you'll need to do is collect and copy every bit of information you have and give it to us so we can assess it and use it in our negotiations with your new host country."

"I have no choices, do I?"

"Oh no, you have. There are two. One ends well, the other not so much. We'll leave it to you to figure out which one you prefer," Wan said.

"Okay, we don't have much time," Dai said. "You better get going; we need a copy of the information before midday. And Yuan, as you have seen, we know much more than you think. Don't leave anything out. This is a test to see how honest you are. We need to know that because your new country would want to know if you can be trusted. If you're painfully honest and do exactly as you're told from now on, you don't have a thing to worry about; you'll be set for life."

Yuan remained silent as he collected his belongings to leave.

"Eleven thirty, in the foyer, Lee. Please don't be late," Dai said as Yuan stood to leave.

"I won't."

Shanghai, China

Day 18

When Yuan had left, General Dai made a call to Jethro and told him in cryptic terms he was right about what was happening in Shanghai, and that information was forthcoming soon.

Finishing the call, he turned to Wan and said, "Let's hope Yuan doesn't go and commit suicide."

Wan shook his head. "He doesn't have the guts to do that. Besides, he has this mysterious new locale where he is going to live in luxury to look forward to. Although, if I were him, I'd seriously consider changing my sexual habits. In America, he's not going to get the same protection from his political buddies as he would get here. But don't worry, he'll be here by eleven-thirty. In the meantime, you and I must go buy General Yuan a little present."

Wan was right. It was 11:20 a.m. when General Yuan Lee walked into the foyer of the Waldorf Astoria hotel.

They took him to Dai's room, which had been swept for bugs and safe to have their next meeting.

Yuan handed them two one terabyte external hard drives and explained that the first one contained all the information that his office had been collecting from clinics, hospitals, and healthcare workers. The second contained the research conducted by various labs across the country. "The information on those disks is damning. It will destroy me and the president and many others. If you don't get me out of China, I've just signed my own death warrant."

Dai started his laptop and made sure it was not connected to the internet or any network router. He plugged the hard drives into the laptop one after the other, opening them, and quickly scanned the various files and folders with Wan looking over his shoulder. He opened a few files to see what was inside and assured that the contents of both drives were not corrupt.

"So far so good," Dai said as he unplugged the device and shut down his laptop. "Now, the next step is for you to book a meeting with the president to give him an update of the progress you and your team have made with fighting the epidemic here in Shanghai."

Yuan looked crestfallen. "I thought this is what you wanted. I deliver it, and you get me out."

Dai looked at Wan and said, "I can't remember saying that. Can you?"

Wan shook his head.

"Yuan, relax. We will keep our word and get you out. But there are a few more things to take care of before you can go."

Yuan stared at him for a while and said, "Such as?"

"One thing at a time," Dai said. "Now, phone the president's office and set up a meeting. Tell them you're planning a trip to Beijing and would like to use the opportunity to give the president an in-person update."

Yuan retrieved his cellphone, started it up, and made the call to the president's secretary. Two minutes later, he had a one-hour slot booked for Wednesday morning at ten.

"Excellent," said Wan when the call ended. "Now, switch off your phone and pay close attention."

Yuan did as he was told.

"You're going to give the president an update. You're not going to tell him what he wants to hear, as you always do. You're going to tell him the truth. The virus has reached epidemic proportions. You're struggling to contain it. There is no cure or vaccine for it yet. The real numbers are much, much higher than what is reported in the media. The information blackout is the only thing that's working fairly well, but you're worried that at the current rate of spread, it's going to become more and more difficult to keep the blackout working effectively."

Yuan only nodded.

"That is the truth, is it not, Yuan?" Dai said.

"Yes, it is."

"Okay, you're going to record your conversation with the president—"

"They'll never allow me to take a recording device into a meeting with him. Security scans and searches every person that enters the president's office. I won't be allowed to take my cellphone or even a pen in. I just can't see how—"

"Relax. It's going to be okay."

"I still don't think it's a good idea even to try it."

"Yuan, your future now depends on it. You've compromised yourself beyond reprieve. Your choices, if you haven't figured it out already, are either you get charged with treason and get a bullet in the back of the head, the traitor's death. Or you get a life of luxury in a very nice country. I suggest you make it work. The recording of that meeting is crucial to get the nod from your new country. We spoke to them while you were away, and that's what they told us. No recording, no deal." Of course, that was a lie, but Yuan had no way of knowing.

"What's your decision?"

"I'll work it out."

"Excellent," Wan said. "Now, the third step. We want you to tell us everything. Start right at the beginning and tell us, in minute detail, when it all started, who ordered it, who met with whom, when, and where. What had been said and what had been done. Tell it all; don't leave anything out."

Yuan must have realized that this was the point of no return. As soon as he gave them that information, he would give away any leverage he still had. Even if he didn't have the meeting with the president or he got caught in the act of recording the meeting, Dai and Wan would have all the information they needed to cause irreparable damage to the reputation of the president and all the others who were involved in this conspiracy.

Nonetheless, he started talking.

It took Yuan all of three hours to spill it all.

What he told them left the two generals shocked and horrified. President Li Lingxin was steering the world to another World War, and he was foolish enough to think that China would come out of it victorious.

By four p.m., the hard drives and the recordings of the breakfast meeting and that afternoon's meeting were on their way to Hong Kong onboard one of Jethro's jets.

Chapter Thirty-Five

SO CRAZY IT'S ACTUALLY GOING TO WORK

Aboard the TOMATS, Matz Island, Hong Kong

Day 18

Shortly after seven p.m., Jethro's jet with its precious cargo landed on Matz Island. The hard drives and flash drives with the audio recordings were handed to Rex immediately, and the letter addressed to Jethro was given to him.

Minutes later, Catia and Marissa were ready to upload the information to the CRC and CIA secured servers. By their calculations, to transfer the information on the external hard drives would take four to five hours. They first transferred the two audio files, which took only a few minutes, and then kicked off the big data transfer job. While CRC and Langley were waiting for the other data to arrive, they had close to four hours of listening to keep them busy. Transcripts had to be made and translated.

Three days before, USAMRIID scientists had taken

delivery of the specimens collected by Dr. Abiram Sharot in Shanghai. They were hard at work studying the virus and its genome. The early findings were that it was indeed a manmade pathogen. But they were cautioned that, due to the potential international upheaval it could cause, their final report had to one hundred percent accurate. There was no room for error.

The information in those recordings made by Generals Dai and Wan confirmed what the USAMRIID scientists suspected. However, they would not be given the recordings or any of the data until they had reached their own independent conclusions. On the other hand, for the president, this information would be invaluable. Hearing it firsthand from the mouth of the man who commanded the engineers who created the virus would be a powerful weapon in his hand when the inevitable confrontation with President Li Lingxin took place.

Around the table in the *TOMATS*'s comms room were Rex, Catia, Josh, Marissa, Spencer, Jethro, and David, as well as Tamara. She had recovered enough to start fulfilling her duties as co-CEO of Matz Enterprises again. It was her first visit to the *TOMATS*, and the first time she met Spencer. On the big screen were the faces of John Brandt and Chris McArdle from CRC headquarters and Yaron Aderet from Tel Aviv. Digger got his jerky treats from Catia when everyone poured their drinks and snacks and took up his usual place in the corner of the room, settling in for a nap.

Catia introduced Tamara to the people she didn't know, and Brandt started the meeting. "The information is coming in thick and fast now. That's good. Jethro, I want to congratulate you and David for the information you've been able to collect over the last few days. Without that information, especially that which came out of Shanghai today, we would no doubt still be spinning our wheels."

Jethro and David nodded their acknowledgment for Brandt's compliment.

Brandt continued, "Yaron, it would be much appreciated if you could thank your *katsas* and *sayanim* on behalf of us for the sterling job they did. Especially whoever it was that got those specimens out of Shanghai."

"Will do," Aderet said.

"So, all that remains to be said now is, mission accomplished. Thank you all for a job well done. As much as I hate the idea, there's nothing we can do about it; we're now at the mercy of the politicians to save the world. Damn, I hate to even think about that."

Jethro cleared his throat and said, "John, there is one small matter that would require our attention before we end the mission."

"We're listening."

"General Dai wrote me a letter that was delivered with the information pack earlier. I've got it here. The guy who gave them that information on the hard drives and in the audio files is General Yuan Lee. He's in charge of China's biological weapons program; it's all in the files. The thing is that Dai had convinced Yuan to defect to America. The information on the hard drives and audio files, according to Dai, is beyond reproach. Dai feels with delivering that he would have established his credentials. He's going to bring one more stash of information with him. If he can pull it off, it'll be the motherlode. But then he must be sure that he'll be able to escape from China and will be offered residence and protection in the USA.

"In summary, we need to get assurances that America will take him, and we need to get him safely out of China."

"Getting him an invitation to come and live in America I can't do, but I know people who know those who can. Getting him out of China is more up my, CRC's, alley. But before we go into that, what is it that he thinks could be more valuable than what he already gave us?" Brandt said.

"He's scheduled to have a meeting with Li Lingxin the day after tomorrow to update him in person about the situation in Shanghai . . . He plans to record the meeting."

There was a long silence before Rex said, "Now that would most assuredly be the motherlode . . ., if he can pull it off."

"Okay, I withdraw my mission accomplished statement of earlier, but my gratitude for the work of those who I mentioned still stands."

When the laughter ended, Brandt continued, "Let's work on the premise that the American authorities would grant this guy asylum, then it's our job to get him out. Jethro, you seem to know more than anyone else here about him. Tell us what you know."

"All I know is that he is based in Shanghai at the moment. His meeting with the president is Wednesday morning at ten in Beijing. I'll have to ask General Dai to provide details. If you could tell me what you want, I'll handle the rest."

Rex, Catia, Josh, and Marissa started listing what they wanted to know; photos, videos, home and work address, phone numbers, email, social media accounts, work, and after-work routines, family, friends, and associates. "That would be a good start," Josh said.

"Height, weight, and measurements," Rex said, and everyone shifted their eyes to him.

"Shouldn't you perhaps wait until he's in the States before you go clothes shopping, Rex?" Marissa asked.

Catia smiled and said, "Rex, you have that look on your face. Tell us."

"What look would that be?"

"The I-have-an-idea look."

"Oh, that one. It's probably because I have an idea."

"Let's have it," Brandt said.

He told them, and when he finished, he found them all staring at him as if he had just arrived from a different galaxy.

"Rex, my dear friend," Josh said, "the stress of this job has finally caught up and gotten the better of you. You are a couple of sandwiches short of a picnic. But don't worry, my friend, there are shrinks that will be able to help you."

Marissa shook her head, "You need help, Rex. Professional help. Those voices in your head are not real. Don't listen to them."

Spencer was wondering, out loud, if it was maybe time to turn one of the rooms on the *TOMATS* into a brig.

McArdle only shook his head as if he felt sorry for Rex, the best agent they ever had, losing his mind.

Catia only smiled. She knew Rex's plan sounded crazy, but it would work.

Something must have stirred Digger. He got up from the corner, walked over to Rex, stared at him for a while, then looked at everyone else as if he wanted to say, "Stop harassing my alpha; there's nothing wrong with him." He turned around, went back to his corner, sighed, closed his eyes, and went back to sleep.

Some of them thought Rex was crazy when he took Digger and Josh with him and made a HALO (high altitude low opening) parachute jump onto the back of a moving cargo ship in the middle of the night to save John Brandt from his kidnappers a few years ago.

It was very likely that memory that made Brandt remain quiet until everyone had their say. "Dalton, I've never heard anything as crazy as that. I'm wondering if I should get Rick Longland in to give you a psych check."

Rex said nothing; he had a big grin on his face.

Brandt continued, "But here's the thing—that plan is so crazy it's actually going to work."

Silence descended. Then, as if on cue, they all started talking, looked at each other, and suddenly stopped. All at the same time, they looked at each other and Rex again.

Rex said, "That's what I like about working with you. You're always so insightful and sensitive to each other's feelings. I can't tell you how much I appreciate having your unanimous support. Now let's get the wheels rolling. There's a meeting in Beijing in two days. We've got a lot of preparations to make."

Jethro, David, and Tamara glanced at each other, shaking their heads. Not in disagreement but in amazement.

Jethro said, "You still want that information about Yuan Lee?"

"Absolutely," Rex and Josh said in chorus.

Chapter Thirty-Six

LESS THAN TWO WEEKS AWAY

Langley, Virginia | Washington, D.C.

Day 19

Within minutes of receiving the audio files from Hong Kong, Stacie had reorganized her team, calling in the IT people and more Chinese-English translators. The IT gurus used what she thought of as wizardry to run the audio files through a language-voice translation system that produced an English version. Then they used another program, which she was more familiar with, to convert the speech to text. Within half an hour, they had an English version in audio and writing in their hands. They explained to her that the output would not be a hundred percent accurate until humans went through it and corrected errors. However, what she had in her hands now was about eighty percent accurate, giving them a reasonably good idea of what was said.

For the data on the hard drives, the IT people used a similar program to translate the contents of the files before handing it off to the translation team to improve the accuracy.

An hour after receiving the audio files, Howard Lawrence, Martin Richardson, Bryan Shafer, and Stacie Barrett were in a meeting room looking at the machine translation on the big screen. Soon they were troubled in the extreme. All information collected before this pointed to a sinister plot, but they had no idea just how menacing it was and how high up in the Chinese government it went. What they were reading on the screen, answered all of their speculations, and left them with a sense of shock.

Director Lawrence called the DNI and asked him to come over. He walked into the meeting room half an hour later.

Lawrence started with a quick summary of where and how the information was collected, then a summary of the bottom line of the contents of the document on the screen. "It is as we feared. The virus was engineered in a lab. The President of China knows all about it. They are planning to release it to the world within the next ten to fourteen days."

The DNI let out a long, noisy breath. "My God, we're on the brink of war, and we don't even know it . . ." He took his cellphone out and dialed the president's direct line.

Ten minutes later, Lawrence and Richardson were with the DNI in his official vehicle speeding across town to the White House. By the time they arrived, the first members of the National Security Council were filing into the Situation Room. They didn't know it yet, but the room was going to be their home for the next forty-eight hours.

It took them not much more than an hour to see the horrific picture. The virus was engineered and weaponized in a lab in the north of China by the scientists of their Bioweapons Program under the auspices of the President of China. The epidemic in Shanghai was deliberately caused as an experiment to test the virus's capabilities and to develop a cure and vaccine.

The epidemic in Shanghai was on the verge of spinning out of control. Nonetheless, they were planning to release it to the world within the next ten to fourteen days by putting infected people on planes and cruise ships to destinations across the globe. By the time they reached their destinations, hordes of people would be infected without knowing it and would spread it from there. By the time a travel ban was imposed on China, it would be too late. Every country in the world would have the virus on the rampage inside their borders.

With growing apprehension, they read about Li Lingxin's virus task force made up of scientists, economists, strategists, and other experts who had developed a comprehensive plan. They had carefully considered and prepared themselves for the world's reaction to a virus pandemic. And although it pained the NSC members to admit it, Li's virus taskforce was spot-on with their anticipation that in the first stage, panic would erupt among the citizenry, and traditional and social media would help it spread.

Not only did the members agree with the taskforce's predictions about the chaos that would break out, but they could also not deny the predictions about how the world's democracies would handle it all. The taskforce foretold, correctly in the opinion of the NSC members, that in stage two, the politicians would launch into vicious debates about who was responsible. Why didn't the leaders act earlier? Why didn't they know earlier? Opposition parties would not let the opportunity pass to recruit voters because none of this would have happened on their watch.

In stage three, they prophesied that by the time national emergencies were officially declared, the health systems would be overwhelmed, and people would be sent away from hospitals, clinics, and healthcare facilities for lack of capacity to treat them. People, especially the old and infirm, would be dying in droves. Doctors and nurses would be overworked while having to make terrible decisions about who qualified for treatment and who should be left to die.

By stage four, pervasive panic would reign among the citizenry, the flames of which would be stoked by traditional and social media, further proliferated by rumors and speculation that would cause mass hysteria, uncertainty, and indescribable emotional stress. Politicians would be pointing fingers at each other for lack of action or overreach or ignorance or incompetence. Whatever measures would be implemented would quickly be declared as either not enough or too little too late. They would circle the political party wagons, and it would be political football, not a health crisis.

The president was shaking his head in disgust. "It's scary to see that these guys know us better than we know ourselves. Let's look at the rest."

Li's advisors expected that the reaction would be to isolate and quarantine people in an attempt to slow down the rate of infections, which would slow down the rate of spread and flatten the curve of projected infections to manageable levels, which would ease the burden on the healthcare systems. But that would bring their economies to a halt. Businesses would be forced to cease operations and send their staff home. With no income but overhead still running, people would lose their jobs, and businesses would go into bankruptcy. People would deplete their savings, stock markets would crash, unemployment would rise to unprecedented levels, and civil unrest would be lurking on the horizon as people became more desperate to feed their families and stay alive.

Governments would print money to foot the stimulus and rescue packages, and a global economic collapse would be a foregone conclusion.

The Secretary of the Treasury nodded slowly. "And by the time we're ready to open the economy with what is left, China would be in the driver's seat of the world's economic and military might."

There was very little doubt in the minds of the members about the veracity of the Secretary of the Treasury's statement. That was China's ultimate goal.

According to Yuan's report, the release of the virus in Shanghai was an experiment authorized by Li Lingxin. It was a test run on real people, their own citizens no less, to learn all about the virus, how to combat it, and find a cure and vaccine before releasing it to the world.

According to Yuan, President Li's words were, "Then the world will come to us, and we'll save them."

But it was as Jeff Bezos, CEO of Amazon, said, "Any plan won't survive its first encounter with reality. The reality will always be different. It will never be the plan." The Shanghai strain was on the verge of uncontrollability. Instead of throwing everything they had at it to stop it, Li Lingxin's advisors told him not to back off. They told him it was a great opportunity that presented itself. Now, when the world started blaming China, they could say, wait a minute, we're suffering just as much as you. Therefore, they encouraged him to let it go and start preparing for the global release, which, according to Yuan, was less than two weeks away.

Chapter Thirty-Seven

THE PRESIDENT IS ON THE LINE FOR YOU

Washington, D.C. | Hong Kong

Day 19

The President called a half-hour refreshment break during which experts were summoned to the White House. When the meeting resumed, they were all there and called upon to advise, to project, to guesstimate, to draw graphs, to use the China data to make extrapolations, to look deep into their crystal balls and predict best and worst-case scenarios.

Military leaders were given instructions to draw up military response plans ranging from bombing China and their virus into oblivion to threatening them into submission.

Potential responses were formulated, and then they had to answer the question of when the right time was to act. Of course, the overarching principle was that prevention was better than cure. That, however, did not negate the fact that the timing of the action was crucial.

Whatever the response was going to be, it would be preceded by a call from the President of the United States to the President of China to put him on the spot. A few of the attendees, although they agreed with the approach, felt strongly that the president had to wait for the outcome of the meeting Yuan Lee was scheduled to have with President Li Lingxin in about eighteen hours. They were hoping that Yuan would be able to make a recording and that it would contain enough damning evidence in Li's own voice to give the president the upper hand and have Li in a position from which he would not be able to wiggle himself out of with lies and denials.

While the NSC was wrestling with the issues in D.C., eight thousand miles away on the *TOMATS* in Hong Kong, Rex and his team, enforced by a CIA specialist a few hours before, were making their final preparations for the mission to move General Yuan Lee out of China in one of the most daring covert operations ever authorized by the CIA. If it worked out as Rex and the team planned it, the Chinese would only discover their general had defected when he appeared on American TV to tell the world what President Li Lingxin and his cronies had been up to. But pulling it off was going to be an exercise in precision where seconds could mean the difference between success or failure.

During one of the breaks, the President asked the White House Chief of Staff to get him the team leader of the mission team that was going to get this general and his recording out of China on the line. "I want to tell him how important this mission is and wish him all the best."

The team was in mission mode, and Digger had picked up on it. Rex and Josh were joking with each other as they always did when they were ready to go into action, but in truth, they were as tense as piano wires. Catia and Marissa had seen them in that state of mind enough times to know that no outside interference or interruption would be appreciated.

When Rex's phone rang, he didn't answer it. He probably didn't even hear it. A few seconds later, it started ringing again. Catia picked the phone up and saw it was from John Brandt. She answered and told Brandt to tell her whatever it was he wanted to say to Rex, and she would tell him—at the appropriate moment.

He told her, she gasped and said, "No, it's better you tell him that yourself."

Rex wasn't even aware of the conversation going on until Catia said, "Rex, John has something important to tell you."

He held out his hand for the phone without looking away from the map he was studying on the computer screen. "Be brief and be gone," he told Brandt.

"Dalton, the president wants to talk to you."

"Take his number. I'll call him back."

"Dalton, does your arrogance have any limits? It's the President of the United States of America who wants to talk to you."

"Oh, him? I don't have time to talk to him either."

"Who the hell did you think I was talking about?"

"Li Lingxin, wanting to discuss the conditions of China's surrender."

"Bloody hell, you jackass! Turn your chair and look at the TV screen. He's already there."

Rex and Josh swiveled their chairs to face the TV. Lo and behold, there was the President of the United States smiling and waving at them. Rex immediately knew the president would have heard every word of the conversation he had with Brandt.

Rex swallowed hard, decided to keep the pose, waved, and said, "Hi Mr. President, thanks for popping in, but we're really very busy over here. My team is leaving in two hours. Give me your number, and I'll call you as soon as we're in the air."

By now, the president was shaking with laughter. "No worries. Here's my personal number." He gave the number. "Have a safe trip. Get that guy out of there. No pressure, but the world will be in grave danger if you don't. May God bless you and your team. Oh, and call me on that number when the mission is over."

"Thank you, Mr. President. I will."

The screen went blank, but somehow the microphone must have remained hot, and everyone on the call, including the president, heard Rex mumble, "I'll do better than that. The team and I'll come over for a cup of coffee one afternoon. You're the guy who lives in that big white house on 1600 Pennsylvania, right?"

The president replied. "Yep, that's the one. And you're welcome. It'll be my honor."

Rex almost fell out of his chair when he heard the president's voice.

The president was still laughing when the call ended. "Now there's a man with a pair of tungsten balls. That's the kind of American that'll make our enemies shake in their boots."

Brandt had no love lost for politicians and mandarins, but Dalton almost caused him a heart attack. He knew Richardson was on the call as well as the Director of the CIA, the DNI, and a host of other big names.

Richardson's call came through ten minutes later. "John, off the record, that was one of the best shows I've ever attended. On the record, you'll have to reprimand and discipline Dalton. Tell him he will find his ass in the brig unless he apologizes to the president in writing. Oh, and while I have you on the line, on the record, here are the names of people who were on the call." Richardson read the names. "They ordered me to convey their utter dismay about Dalton's behavior. Off the record, they want me to let you know that your agent had brightened up their miserable day."

Rex, Josh, Marissa, Catia, and Digger were oblivious to the storm that erupted over Rex's head eight thousand miles away. They barely smiled while watching Rex tell the President of the United States to get off the phone.

Spencer was speechless. He had to take a stiff shot of Jack Daniels before he could see any humor in the event.

The CIA specialist, who had just arrived from a twenty-one-hour flight, and who was too jetlagged even to recognize the president onscreen, put down her arsenal of supplies. She had no sense of humor after that grueling flight only to be told, "Sorry, no rest for you. We've got a mission to plan and a general that has to get to America in a hurry."

Chapter Thirty-Eight

REPORTING TO THE PRESIDENT

Beijing, China

Day 20

Zhongnanhai, literally translated as "Central and Southern Seas" was a former imperial garden in the Imperial City of Beijing. It was next to the Forbidden City and was the central headquarters for the Communist Party of China and the State Council, the central government of China. Zhongnanhai housed the office of the General Secretary of the Communist Party of China, also known as the paramount leader, or more common, the President of the People's Republic of China. The word Zhongnanhai was used in the same sense that the world used the term White House when referring to the U.S. executive branch.

General Yuan Lee had one final look at himself in the mirror. He was in full military dress uniform, complete with rank, insignia, medals, and ribbons. All of it testified that he was a general in the Chinese military. But the man inside the uniform was not a soldier at heart; he was a scientist, a microbiologist. Although, sometimes, he did think of himself as a soldier, a different kind, the kind who fought wars with invisible weapons. At five-foot-ten, he was one inch taller than the average height of a Beijing urban male. He was in good physical shape for someone of fifty-five. He dusted some imaginary fluff off his tunic, drew a deep breath, and let it out slowly to calm himself.

He was a nervous wreck, and the more he told himself it would be his undoing if he let any of it show in the meeting, the tenser he became. Unfortunately, the human body was not created with an on-off switch for nervousness. He had been in the presence of the president many times. For more than two years, he had been reporting progress on the virus project and the Shanghai experiment personally to the president at least once a month. Lately, he had been reporting almost daily, but that was over the phone or video conference most of the time.

The engineering of the weaponized virus was the president's pet project, and the president had always treated him well, which put Yuan at ease in his presence. Today, however, he would be facing the president as a traitor. Although, the president would not be aware of his betrayal unless he'd been set up in an elaborately wicked scheme by Generals Dai and Wan to get him out of the marshals' group. He had tried to convince himself that was not the case but couldn't shake the feeling that it was a distinct possibility.

He had taken a Valium, a sedative and anti-anxiety drug. It felt as if it helped. Within half an hour, the fluttering of butterflies in his stomach had decreased, nausea had subsided, and so had the excessive shaking of his hands.

He looked at his new watch; it was ten minutes before the meeting would start—time to make his way to the reception desk.

He arrived at the reception desk of the president's office at precisely 9:53 a.m., seven minutes early, in conformance to military etiquette.

He gave his name, posed for the security cameras on the walls, showed his ID, handed over his cellphone, and walked through the full-body scanner while another security officer scanned his briefcase. Exiting the body scanner, he was told to stand with his legs spread and arms raised and was scanned again with a handheld scanner. The security officer gave him the nod, and he proceeded to the next guard who would escort him to the president's office.

No one looked at or mentioned his new watch. The one he got from his colleagues, Generals Dai and Wan. Not even the body scanner had an issue with his watch. The battery was fully charged and would record for a little over two hours.

When Yuan entered the opulent office of President Li, he was relieved to find the president in a good mood. A talkative mood, it seemed.

"Glad to see you, General. Please have a seat."

The president spent a few minutes on the usual pleasantries before he got to the purpose of the meeting, the purpose the president thought it was. "Tell me what's going on in Shanghai. The numbers are not coming down."

"No, Mr. President, they're not. Though, I'm not overly concerned about that. We can bring the numbers down at any time we want, with stricter quarantine measures. However, as you know, at this stage, it's not in our best interest to do so."

"Yes, yes, of course. We have to show the world that we

haven't been spared and that we're also struggling and suffering. Although, to be honest, I would've felt so much better if we had a cure or a vaccine, preferably both, before we go to market." He laughed at his own joke.

Yuan followed suit; it was considered bad form not to laugh at the jokes your superiors made.

"How long before we have one of those, a cure or vaccine?"

"Mr. President, a complete cure is very difficult to say. Cures are often discovered by accident. We have made significant progress in testing various drug cocktails that help to shorten the duration of the symptoms in some patients. The problem is it doesn't work all the time for all the patients. Only when we have that do we have a cure.

"On the other hand, when it comes to vaccines, we know how to develop them. The practice of immunization goes back hundreds of years. Our ancestors drank snake venom to confer immunity to snakebite and smeared cowpox over open cuts in their skin to confer immunity to smallpox. The west developed their first vaccine, the one for smallpox, in 1798. Louis Pasteur developed vaccines in the late 1800s and early 1900s that are still in use today. The development is not difficult nor too complicated, but it takes time. I would say we're looking at twelve to eighteen months."

The president nodded. He had heard it before. "What are the current projections for the number of infections and mortalities in Shanghai?"

Yuan retrieved the stack of documents he had prepared out of his briefcase, placed it in front of the president on his desk, and walked him through the data and projections.

"Ten thousand deaths out of four-hundred and fifty thousand infected in a city of twenty-four million. That's not bad. Sacrificing only ten thousand, albeit our own people, to put China on the world throne is insignificant compared to the benefits China and its people stand to gain. Imagine what the cost in lives would have been if we had to resort to conventional warfare to achieve it."

The president was too self-centered and shortsighted to spare a moment's thought for the millions of people who would die in other parts of the world in this virus war of his. Yuan didn't care either. He had his own life to worry about.

"I've decided to commence deployment on Friday," the president said.

"Two days from now?"

"Yes. At precisely midday Friday, Beijing time, the first virus couriers will leave our shores." The president smiled.

Out of courtesy, Yuan also smiled.

"Come Monday morning, wherever in the world you are, this virus will be with you in the same country. You'll have nowhere to run and nowhere to hide. But don't worry, China will rush to your side to aid you. You'll see, we commies are not as bad as your politicians have been telling you all your life."

Yuan remained quiet; the president had a habit of getting a bit melodramatic at times. But Yuan did wonder where on the planet he would be, come Monday. He still had no idea which country he was going to, that is, if he were alive on Monday. America? Taiwan? Europe? America was his first choice. He thought it would be bad karma to put prison or a cemetery on that list.

Yuan was relieved that the president had made no remarks about his nervousness. The valium must have helped to make it unnoticeable even though he still felt nervous as if the effect of it was wearing off quickly.

But Yuan's assessment was wrong. The president had noticed, he just didn't mention it.

When Yuan's report came to an end, the president thanked him, stood, shook his hand, and wished him a safe trip back to Shanghai. Yuan saluted and left.

A few minutes after Yuan had left his office, the president called his Chief of Staff in. "I want you to put surveillance on General Yuan. He was uncharacteristically nervous during our meeting. Of course, there could be many reasons, all of them innocent. I want you to find out if they are."

When Yuan got outside, he let out a long, noisy breath in relief. Then he heard someone call out his name, turned to see who it was, and saw General Wan approaching him. Wan was smiling and waved as if they hadn't seen each other in a long time.

They shook hands, and General Wan invited him for tea and something to eat at a nearby restaurant before his next meeting.

Shortly after they were seated and had placed their orders, Wan took a watch out of the side pocket of his tunic and placed it on the table. It was identical to the one on his arm, Yuan took the watch off his arm, placed it on the table, and put the new one on. When he was done, the old watch had disappeared into General Wan's tunic pocket.

Their tea was served with shrimp dumplings and steamed buns, but Yuan, still too nauseous to eat anything, only sipped on his green tea. Wan told Yuan to cancel his booking on the commercial flight and join him on the military passenger jet for the trip to Shanghai later that afternoon.

Yuan accepted. He had no choice. He had handed over his last bargaining chip when he handed over the watch with the recording on it to General Wan. Wan and Dai now had everything they wanted; they didn't need him anymore. The Americans would have said, "he was toast."

What Yuan had no way of knowing was that the seven dissident marshals had the very same thoughts. The moment they had the recording, Yuan was of no use to them. They would have what they needed to get their crown prince in as the new president of the PRC. However, after some brainstorming between them, they reached an agreement that it was much better if they let America handle the issue for them. If the Americans were not successful, they still had what they needed to sink Li Lingxin's ship. Letting the Americans do it was much less messy, and they, the seven marshals, would not feature anywhere in it.

To keep up the pretense, Yuan attended two more meetings before he was picked up by Wan's driver, who took him to the jet where he found only General Wan on board.

On the way, Wan explained in detail how things were going to go down from the moment he was back in his hotel room at the Waldorf Astoria hotel in Shanghai.

The driver of General Wan's official vehicle dropped Yuan off at the hotel at six thirty p.m. and drove his remaining passenger, General Wan, to the Marriott hotel where he was booked in for the night. Yuan went straight to his room, ordered room service, took a shower, put on jeans and a T-shirt, and waited.

Chapter Thirty-Nine

HOW DID THEY DO IT?

Shanghai, China

In the aftermath of General Yuan Lee's defection, it took a team of China's top investigators the better part of ten days to collect the information and attempt to reconstruct the chain of events only to end with no idea of how it could have happened. Even so, their timeline of the events would prove to be accurate.

It started on Wednesday morning at the Shanghai Waldorf Astoria while General Yuan Lee was in Beijing to meet with President Li Lingxin. It was 10:03 a.m., according to the note made in the register by the desk clerk on duty. However, the clock on the CCTV cameras said it was 10:05 a.m. when an old couple with a big black service dog arrived in a taxi from Shanghai Pudong International Airport after their flight from Hong Kong that morning and checked in for two nights. Studying the images on the CCTV in the aftermath, they saw the man was slightly bent over, walking with the aid of a cane. The woman had her right arm hooked into the left arm of her companion and the leash of their big black dog in her left hand. They quickly identified the dog as a Dutch Shepherd. Their Italian passports said they were Rowan and Catherine Donnelly, and their photos on the copies of their passports made by the desk clerk matched the images on the CCTV footage and gave their ages as sixty-five for the man and sixty-one for the woman. The copies of the dog's papers were scrutinized and found to be in order.

For the discrepancy in the time of arrival that the desk clerk noted and the CCTV clock, he was detained and interrogated thoroughly. Ten hours later, the investigators were satisfied that the desk clerk's watch was two minutes behind the clock on the security cameras. During the interrogation, he did, however, recall that the old man wore earpieces and seemed to be hard of hearing, which could have been the reason the woman did all the talking, in English. The desk clerk was set free.

At 12:13 p.m. on the same day, according to the note in the register made by another desk clerk who was then on duty, the time was confirmed by the CCTV cameras, a flamboyant American couple arrived in a taxi from Shanghai Pudong International Airport after their flight from Hong Kong and checked in for one night. Studying the footage from the CCTV cameras, the leather boots, jeans, large shiny belt buckles, and Stetson hats told the investigators that the American tourists were from Texas. The woman had blonde, shoulder-length hair and sported large sunglasses. The boisterous man had black hair, and he was wearing wraparound sunglasses. Their passports said they were Joshua Crawford, forty-two, and Marissa Elizabeth Crawford, thirty-seven, American citizens, and their passport photos also matched their faces on the CCTV footage.

The desk clerk who handled the Crawfords' check in was spared a trip to the MSS interrogation cells.

At six p.m. on the same day, another American citizen arrived in a taxi from Shanghai Pudong International Airport after her flight from Beijing, where she had attended a meeting earlier in the day at the American embassy after her flight from Hong Kong early in the morning. She checked in for an overnight stay, after which she would return to the USA. She was a little overweight, brown hair, and of average height. Very friendly, although she could not speak a single word of Chinese. She carried a diplomatic passport, which said her name was Yasmin Burke, forty-one, and her passport photo also matched her face on the CCTV footage.

The desk clerk who handled her check-in was also spared a trip to the MSS holding cells and an interrogation.

At six thirty p.m. on the same day, General Yuan Lee arrived after his meeting in Beijing with President Li Lingxin in an official vehicle. He walked through the foyer, nodded a greeting to the desk staff, and proceeded to his room from where he ordered a room service dinner shortly after.

The lady who took the General's order on the phone that night, as well as the chef who prepared his dinner, and the server who delivered it to his room, were promptly taken into custody and interrogated for close to twelve hours before the investigators were satisfied that the lady on the switchboard took the general's order over the phone and passed it onto the kitchen staff. They were also satisfied that the chef received the order, prepared the food, placed it on the trolley, and told the server to deliver it to the general's room, which he did. There were no other messages passed between them or between any of them and the general.

At exactly 10:02 p.m., according to the clock on the CCTV cameras, the Italian couple and their dog appeared at the front desk. The clerk recalled under interrogation that the old couple looked distressed. The woman had explained that they had received bad news from home. Her husband's brother had been in a car accident and was in a critical condition. They had to cancel the rest of their stay and get to the airport to catch a flight to Vancouver, Canada, and from there directly to Rome. Yes, it was going to be a very long trip but still the shortest possible time in which they could get to Rome. No, they didn't ask for a refund for the unused time. They had a taxi waiting for them when they walked out of the hotel. They had waved to the desk clerk before they got into the cab. The old man was in the front passenger seat and the woman in the back with the dog.

The taxi driver was tracked down and taken into custody. After a lengthy interrogation, the investigators were satisfied that on the night in question, the driver got a call from his base to pick up two old people and a service dog from the Shanghai Waldorf Astoria and deliver them to the international departures terminal at Shanghai Pudong International Airport. No, they didn't talk much on the way there, his English was poor, and they spoke no Putonghua, the city's standard language, also known as Mandarin. Yes, he dropped them off at the airport, they paid him in cash, and he left. No, he didn't see them enter the building; he assumed they did.

On Thursday morning at precisely six thirty a.m., General Yuan, in full-dress uniform, sat down for his breakfast in the hotel's dining room as he had been doing every morning for the past two months since he took up residence there. According to the entries made on the computer by the dining room manager, the general had his usual breakfast of tea, shrimp dumplings, steamed buns, and corn fritters. The computer records also showed that the general swiped his room card as he had been doing every morning. The CCTV cameras showed that the general walked through the lobby at 7:20 a.m., nodded at the desk staff, and entered his official vehicle waiting to transport him to his office. No one had noticed that the general had grown one inch taller overnight and had lost about two pounds.

At nine fifteen a.m., the Crawfords sat down for their breakfast, and they checked out at 10:32 a.m. and got into a waiting taxi. The taxi driver was tracked down and questioned until the investigators were satisfied that on the morning in question, the driver received a call from his base to pick up the American couple from the Shanghai Waldorf Astoria and deliver them to the international departures terminal at Shanghai Pudong International Airport from where they were going to fly back home. They talked a bit on the way to the airport, but it was all about how they loved Hong Kong and how much they were looking forward to getting back to the USA. Yes, he dropped them off at the airport, they paid him in cash, and he left. No, he didn't see them enter the building but assumed they did.

At nine forty-five a.m., Yasmin Burke, the American woman with a diplomatic passport, sat down for breakfast. She checked out at 10:47 a.m. and caught a taxi to Shanghai Pudong International Airport, where she would board a flight directly to Los Angeles, California. Her taxi driver gave the investigators an account very similar to what they'd heard from all the other taxi drivers they had questioned.

With the wisdom of hindsight, the chief investigator

would later point out that the first sign that something was amiss came on Friday at ten a.m. That was when the chambermaid had entered General Yuan's room and found his bed had not been slept in since she had made his bed and cleaned his room the morning before. Her failure to report it earned her six grueling hours in the MSS interrogation cells. She had a hard time convincing the investigators that it didn't raise her suspicions at all because the General could have been working through the night. He could have been visiting friends or, as a single man, he could've found company and spent the night. No, it never happened before, but there is always a first time.

Questioning the general's aide de camp revealed that the general told him over the phone late afternoon on Wednesday that he was going to be out of town for the next two days as he had been summoned to Hong Kong for important meetings. According to the aide, the general said he would be back in the office on Monday morning. No, there was nothing untoward about that, the general was a busy man and often had to change his schedule to attend to urgent matters all over the country. Yes, that included Hong Kong. No, the general didn't tell him who he was meeting in Hong Kong; if the general wanted him to know, he would've told him.

The chief of the MSS was livid as he paced back and forth in front of the wide-eyed team of investigators. "The Americans made fools of us! We look like idiots! Morons! And you're supposed to be our best. The top investigators in the country, and you can't tell me how they snatched one of our most senior generals, a traitor to be sure, from right under our noses.

"He didn't decide to defect on the spur of the moment, that we know now. He had been planning it for a while. He had help, and that help is staring at you from the informa-tion you've collected. It's right in front of your eyes, but you're too stupid to see it! How did they do it? I want answers! I want them in the next twenty-four hours. Get out! Go, and do your job!"

The team scurried out of the room and assembled in another room. The lead investigator suggested they start again and review each bit of information they had. He agreed with the chief; they had the answer in their hands—they only had to find it.

It took them a few hours to sift through the information and ended up with the six suspects: the Italian couple with their dog, the Texas couple, and the American woman with a diplomatic passport. Two of the investigators were assigned to check if those people did board planes indeed for the destinations mentioned in the computer records when they checked out of the hotel. It took half an hour to get confirmation from the airlines, the airport's CCTV cameras, and customs, and again CCTV camera footage showing them board their flights. No discrepancies there. Even General Yuan's trip to Hong Kong on a military passenger jet was verified. They didn't check if the Italian couple and their dog got a connecting flight from Vancouver to Rome. If they did, they would have found their first discrepancy.

Next, they considered the roles each of the six could have played. For the dog, they were unable to come up with an explanation of what his role could have been. The five humans did it. But how? Out of desperation, they called in their facial recognition experts and told them to analyze each of the five faces. Change their faces, make them younger and older. Change their hair color. Then try and match each change with what they had in their vast databases. A study of the CCTV camera footage, collected from the moment they entered the country until they had left, told them nothing more. Hours later, they admitted defeat.

The lead investigator was sitting with his hands in his hair; he looked as if he was ready to start pulling it out. He looked up at the leader of the facial recognition team and said, "I want you to try one more thing. It might be crazy, but then this whole case has been crazy all along. I want you to take the CCTV footage of the Italian couple checking in at the hotel and compare it with the footage when they checked out. I want you to compare the gait of the old man arriving with the gait of the old man leaving. Then do it for all of them."

The team lead nodded and went to work. Twenty minutes later, he declared with certainty, "The old man with the woman and the dog arriving is not the same old man that left with the woman and the dog that night."

A protracted silence descended upon the room as they stared at each other in disbelief, and the realization dawned on them. The old man who had been at the side of the woman, accompanied by the big black Dutch Shepherd service dog, at 10:02 P.M. on that Wednesday night at the front desk of the Shanghai Waldorf Astoria was General Yuan Lee, the traitor, and defector. That then meant the man who sat down for breakfast at precisely six thirty a.m. on Thursday and who walked through the lobby at precisely 7:20 a.m. was an imposter. The best imposter anyone of them had ever seen except for those seen in Tom Cruise's *Mission Impossible* movies. That was their conclusion; the Americans had used one or more disguising experts to disguise the two men. It was so expertly done not even their much-acclaimed facial recognition technology was able to pick it up. It was only the different gaits of the two men that gave it away.

Which one of the Texas couple or the woman with the diplomatic passport was the disguising expert they could only guess. Maybe it was all of them. Perhaps the Texas couple . . . They decided to stop speculating and report to the chief of the MSS.

What they would never know, and it didn't matter that they didn't know, was that the disguising expert was the woman with a diplomatic passport. Everyone else, including the dog, were there for purposes of deception and backup if it were required.

It was only much later that the lead investigator, who was still troubled by how the Americans got the better of them, would come across an article that described how brilliant the CIA disguising experts were. According to this article, one morning during the presidency of George H.W. Bush, the CIA's chief of disguise entered the White House wearing a mask that was an exact replica of the face of a female colleague of hers. She sat in the intelligence briefing close to the president for the duration. When the meeting was over, she removed the disguise and surprised the president with the fact that he had been in the presence of an impersonator without an inkling of an idea.

After reading that, the lead investigator knew how it was possible that a Caucasian person could be made to look Asian and vice versa in such a manner that no human or computer program could spot it. Not without a deliberate effort at a very close range, and even then, it would not be easy.

Chapter Forty

Shanghai, China | Hong Kong

Day 21

By 9:00 a.m. Thursday, when Rex boarded the military passenger plane for the three-hour flight to Hong Kong, the British Airways Boeing Airbus was already eight hours into its fourteen and a half-hour flight to Vancouver. Onboard was Catia disguised as an old Italian woman, Digger was in his disguise as a service dog, and General Yuan Lee was disguised as an old, near-deaf Italian man and husband of the woman he was with.

Rex was in the full-dress uniform of a general of the People's Liberation Army, and the nameplate on his chest said his name was Yuan Lee.

The plane had seating for twenty, and Rex was glad to see only ten of the seats were occupied. He had two seats for himself. As soon as the plane reached cruising altitude, an air hostess served them with drinks and snacks. When Rex opened the small packet of peanuts, he was not surprised to find peanuts nor the tiny thumb drive inside. On that thumb drive was one of the most critical pieces of intelligence that a courier had ever carried in the history of humankind. The race against time was on. The lives of millions of unsuspecting, innocent people across the globe were at stake. Putting that information in the hands of the President of the United States in time was vital to ensure their survival.

However, before any of that could happen, it was necessary to find out if the thumb drive contained a verifiably authentic audio recording of the meeting between Yuan and Li Lingxin in Beijing the day before.

Apart from the authenticity of the recording, a lot of things still had to fall in place before John Brandt would be able to put his "Mission Accomplished" stamp on it. Besides General Yuan, who had to get to Washington, D.C. safely, Catia and Digger, Josh and Marissa, and the CIA disguising expert, Yasmin Burke, all had to get to D.C. safely as well. Rex had to get the information on the thumb drive verified in Hong Kong and then make his way to D.C. via Australia and Los Angeles. And most important of all, the final step, the president had to put the fear of God into President Li Lingxin and sway him to cease and desist from his diabolical plans.

Unable to contact Catia or anyone else to get status updates, Rex couldn't help but worry a little about her and Digger and everyone else who had been involved in the escape of General Yuan the past twenty-four hours. Yet Rex's face revealed only impassiveness, and his body language showed no tension.

On arrival at the Shek Kong Airfield, home to the Hong

Kong Garrison air force units of the People's Liberation Army, the first thing Rex did when he was out of the plane and outside earshot of anyone was to take his satphone out and call John Brandt. He was relieved to hear that the Chinese were still oblivious about their general. Brandt also told him that the CIA had been keeping track of the three planes carrying his team and General Yuan, and all aircraft were on course and schedule as per plan.

Ending the call, he noticed a driver with a military vehicle was waiting for him. The driver approached and saluted, and Rex returned the salute. The driver relieved him of his grip bag, which he carried to the car and placed in the trunk. He held the back door open for Rex to get in. Half an hour later, they pulled up in front of the JW Marriott Hotel, where the driver retrieved Rex's bag from the trunk and handed it to the waiting porter. The driver saluted, Rex returned the salute, and the driver left.

Rex checked in at the front desk for a two-day stay and went to his room. There he took the uniform off, removed his disguise, and placed it in the grip bag from which he had taken his jeans, T-shirt, and sneakers. He wiped the room clean of his fingerprints and took the elevator down to the parking area in the basement. He found the Mercedes in the parking bay where Jethro told him it would be and the key below the left front mudguard. It took him less than fifteen minutes to get to the ferry terminal, where two of Ramesh Ojha's men were waiting for him to take him across to Matz Island.

On approaching Matz Island, Rex looked at the empty space in the marina where the *TOMATS* had been lying at anchor for the past fourteen days. Spencer had lifted anchor early in the morning the day before. Rex glanced at his watch and made a quick calculation; the TOMATS would by now be about four hundred fifty nautical miles away, more than one-third of the way to Singapore.

In Jethro's study, Rex plugged the thumb drive into Jethro's secured laptop computer and started the audio recording on it. The conversation between General Yuan and Li Lingxin was in Mandarin, of which Rex only understood a few words. Mandarin and Cantonese speakers were able to understand each other with minimal difficulty when they used the written form of the languages, but the two languages were distinct when spoken. Jethro, Tamara, and David were in the study, all fluent in both Mandarin and Cantonese. They listened to the recording of the meeting and told Rex that they could not confirm or deny that the voice of General Yuan was authentic because they had never heard him talk before. Nonetheless, they had no doubt whatsoever that the second voice on that recording was none other than the President of China.

As a first step in the verification process, their word was good enough for Rex. He immediately called John Brandt and told him that the audio file was in the process of being transferred to the CRC's secured servers from where Greg had to transfer it to the CIA servers because Rex didn't have access to them. The file transfer was complete before the call ended. Within minutes, the CIA's technicians with the world's most sophisticated voice analysis software would run a comparison of the voices on the recording to the voices of Li Lingxin and Yuan Lee in their databases and deliver a verdict.

While waiting for the CIA to deliver the verdict, they talked about the contents of that recording. It was two p.m. in Hong Kong and Beijing—twenty-two hours to H-hour, the time when the virus would be set free upon the unsuspecting citizens of every country across the globe. H-hour was the military term for the time of day at which an attack, landing, or other military operation was scheduled to begin.

Half an hour after the call to Brandt, Rex's satphone rang, and Brandt told him, "Both voices are a hundred percent match. Now, get your ass out of there."

Rex was forty minutes into his flight onboard Jethro's Gulfstream G550 private jet speeding at 705 kilometers per hour towards Brisbane, Australia, 6,930 kilometers away, when the machine transcription and translation of the audio recording were brought up on the big screen in the Situation Room in D.C. The human translated and transcribed versions would arrive two hours later.

A little over an hour into the flight, Rex called John Brandt again and said, "John, can you do me one big favor, please?"

"Just say the word."

"I don't know how you're going to do it, but I know you have the contacts to make it happen. Contact that British Airways Boeing with my wife on it and tell her I'm fine and that I love her."

"Consider it done. I'll let Josh and Marissa know as well but leave out the I love you part." Brandt chuckled.

"Thanks, John, I appreciate it. I'm going to eat then sleep."

"Have a safe trip. See you in D.C."

Chapter Forty-One

20 HOURS TO WAR

Situation Room, White House, Washington, D.C.

Day 21

In the Situation Room, the atmosphere was somber before the arrival of the transcript, and it got worse after. By the President of China's own words, the world was twenty hours away from the outbreak of a biological world war.

The president had kept the USA's allies informed from the day the NSC had received the tranche of information from Hong Kong that Jethro got from Generals Dai and Wan. He was ready to notify the Secretary-General of the United Nations. The US ambassador to the UN had all the information she needed; she was in her office in the UN building in New York, waiting for the president's orders.

By the time they had read the meeting transcript, Yuan Lee's flight was two and a half hours out of Vancouver. From there, it would be another five and a half hours by commercial passenger plane to D.C. on a direct flight without the time it would take to get off the British Airways plane, go through customs, and check in for the flight to D.C.

"We need to get Yuan here much quicker," the president said as he looked at the Chairman of the Joint Chiefs of Staff.

The General shook his head and said, "I've already thought about a fighter jet, Mr. President. By my calculations, with a Gulfstream or similar jet, we can get him here in a little over three hours. I suggest we make arrangements with the Canadians to get him off the plane immediately after landing and put him on such a jet."

The president looked at the vice president and said, "Can you make it so?"

"On my way, Mr. President," the vice president said and left the room.

They didn't have to spell it out. If all the chips fell in the right place at the right time, General Yuan would be walking into the White House no sooner than six hours from now—thirteen hours before H-hour.

They had set the cutoff point at ten hours before H-hour. If General Yuan Lee were not in the White House, standing next to the president at that time, the president would make the call to President Li Lingxin without him. The Secretary-General of the UN would be informed after the call irrespective of whether the president was successful in persuading the Chinese president to back off or not; the world deserved to know what this maniac had in mind for them.

If General Yuan arrived within the next six hours, as planned, they had three hours to talk to him and prepare him for what was about to happen.

Chapter Forty-Two

FROM SHANGHAI TO D.C.

Various transcontinental flights

Day 21

Catia, Digger, and Yuan had no trouble during their check in at Shanghai Pudong International Airport. The English lady at the British Airways check-in counter fell in love with Digger immediately. It was so much easier to travel with Digger on airplanes since Catia and Rex had discovered that service dogs were allowed to travel with their owners in the passenger cabin and didn't have to be checked into the cargo area. The customs officers were equally enamored by Digger and waved them through after only a cursory check of their passports and travel documents. Catia had been watching Digger closely, and she became convinced that he knew what was going on and used all his charms to pave the way for them.

The plane was packed, which made it impossible for

Catia and Yuan—whose English, although Chinese accented, was perfect—to have any confidential discussions. It didn't matter much; they were both drained of energy by the stress and lack of sleep over the past few days. Although Digger was quiet and well-behaved, Catia could see he was not entirely himself. It was the longest time he had been separated from Rex since they became partners on that fateful night of the ambush in Afghanistan when his handler, Trevor Madigan, was killed. She wished she had a way of telling Digger how long it would be before he would see Rex again, and most of all, say to him that his alpha was going to be okay.

It was stressful for her to be unable to get in touch with Rex to find out how he was doing, and she knew it was the same for Rex. For them, it was also going to be the longest separation since they had been married. She resisted all thought that it was possible Rex didn't make it out of China. Likewise, as she stared out the window, she fought against the fear that a squadron of Chinese military jets might appear and force them to land. Fortunately, those fears receded with each passing hour they were in the air.

An hour before landing in Vancouver, one of the air hostesses brought Catia a sealed envelope, which she said was from the captain. She opened it and started smiling, and soon a few tears of joy rolled over her cheeks. Yuan was asleep. She bent down to Digger and whispered in his ear, "Digger, Rex is safe and on his way to Brisbane. He sends his love."

Digger looked at her, smiled, and licked the tears from her face, which, of course, made a mess of the makeup that the disguise expert had put on her with so much attention. But Catia didn't care.

Josh and Marissa were on an American Airlines plane to

Los Angeles with a connecting flight to D.C. They had a sixteen-hour flight ahead of them to get to Los Angeles, where they had a layover of three hours before they would board for a five-hour flight to D.C. Even though they didn't have Digger to bedazzle airport staff and custom officers, their check in and boarding was as uneventful as Catia's. They were bone-tired, but the space and comfort of the seats in first class assured that they could sleep most of the way without waking up with pains and aches every few minutes as it would have been if they were in the cramped space of the economy class.

They were relieved when they got a message from the captain that Rex was safe.

Yasmin Burke, the CIA disguising specialist, was on a Delta Air Lines flight to Los Angeles, from where she would get a connecting flight to D.C. She was in economy class. It didn't matter to her; she was asleep before the plane took off from Shanghai. Over the past forty-eight hours, she had already flown from D.C to Hong Kong, then to Beijing, then to Shanghai. She had only seen the inside of her eyelids for about six hours, which was between the time the night before when she turned a Chinese general into an old Italian man and very early this morning when she had turned a black-ops specialist into a Chinese general.

Rex's flight to Brisbane International Airport, Australia, was ten hours. Digger was born and bred and trained at a military airbase about an hour west of the city. For the past few years, since tracking him down, Rex had maintained contact with the trainer of the dog handlers at the base, Mitch Roberts. He was the handler of Digger's father, Duco, and also trained Digger for a few months when he was a puppy before the late Trevor Madigan became his handler. When Rex had tracked Mitch down and contacted him via video conference, Digger was beside himself with joy to see him, and Mitch couldn't stop the tears. Up till that moment, Mitch believed Digger had also died in that ambush with Trevor Madigan. At the time, Rex had promised Mitch a visit from him and Digger, but so far, that hadn't happened. And it was not going to happen now. Rex smiled as the thought crossed his mind that it would probably not be a good idea to tell Digger that he had been to his place of birth without him.

Rex reclined his chair, placed the pillow under his head, and with thoughts of Catia, Digger, and the rest of his team somewhere in a plane above an ocean on their way to the USA, he closed his eyes and fell asleep within seconds. He was going to be the last one of the team to arrive in D.C. at around H+11.

None of the team members on their way to D.C. were haunted by viruses in their sleep. They were too tired to dream.

Situation Room, White House, Washington, D.C.

Day 21, H-18

In the Situation Room, the members of the NSC and the president had their plan in place; there was nothing else they could do but wait for the arrival of General Yuan, reviewing all the information and their plans again to make sure they hadn't missed anything.

Once they had done that, they started on a timeline that would demonstrate what President Li Lingxin knew, when he knew it, and what he did about it. That was going to be a powerful tool in the president's hands during the call with President Li.

No one bothered to write a script for the president. They knew he wouldn't follow it, and he told them so. They did, however, create talking points for him, and with that, he was happy.

At precisely H-13, a very tired and very nervous General Yuan, accompanied by a stunning Italian woman who had a big black Dutch Shepherd on a leash, was escorted into the Oval Office.

Chapter Forty-Three

SEVEN THINGS

Oval Office, White House, Washington, D.C.

Day 22, H-13

A very relieved president welcomed Yuan, Catia, and Digger. They got a handshake, and Digger, probably not realizing what a momentous occasion it was to meet the leader of the free world and the expectation to behave well in his presence, insisted on his usual paw-shake. The president was a dog-lover; he laughed and shook Digger's extended paw. The president asked them to please make themselves comfortable on the famous brown couches and offered them something to drink before getting down to the matter at hand.

The General declined the offer to have a translator present.

For the next two and a half hours, the president, the DNI, and Howard Lawrence stepped Yuan through a summary of all the data they had collected, not only that which Yuan had supplied but all the others as well as the results of the tests and analysis by USAMRIID scientists confirming that the virus was manmade.

Yuan cooperated without objection, hesitation, or deceit. He indicated that he had no problem appearing with the president on the planned video call to the President of China and national TV afterward if it was deemed necessary.

In return, he was told that he would get permanent residence in the USA, a new identity, and placed under the FBI's witness protection program after his debrief, which was made clear to him was not going to be an easy or speedy process, but he would be kept safe at all times. He would receive a monthly allowance, which would be negotiated after he had been debriefed. He wouldn't be rich but would receive enough to live comfortably for the rest of his life.

Half an hour before the call to Beijing, Yuan was taken away and given a chance to shave and shower and put on the dark suit, white shirt, and red tie supplied to him.

Beijing, China / Washington, D.C.

Day 22, H-10

Washington, D.C. was twelve hours behind Beijing. The call was placed at two a.m., Friday, Beijing time, which was two p.m., Thursday, D.C. time. It took more than ten minutes before the faces of President Li Lingxin and his vice president appeared on the screen.

POTUS was on the warpath; this was not the time for diplomacy, at which he was not good in any event, even at the best of times. He didn't start with a greeting or any pleasantries. "Mr. President, I'm not going to apologize for the time of this call. There's not enough time for niceties and quibbling. Here's what's on my mind. You're about to start a biological world war. I'm not asking you to stop it; I'm telling you to stop it right now."

Li gulped and looked at his vice president, who did his best to avoid looking at his president. Li started speaking in Mandarin although he was fluent in English, and on every previous occasion, he had met with POTUS, they spoke English.

Clearly, he was playing for time to order his thoughts and formulate a response.

"I have no idea what you're talking about, and I don't like your tone. It's also a ridiculous and totally unfounded accusation."

"Mr. President, I told you at the outset, this is not a courtesy call. I'll lay it out for you once, and once only. Two years ago, you ordered your scientists to develop a weaponized virus. You've placed General Yuan Lee in charge of the project, and he reported to you directly—"

"That's a lie! Where did you get that false information?"

"I'm not finished. You have also ordered the establishment of an advisory committee to work out a plan of how and when and where to release this virus. They, your advisors, have created a four-stage plan of how China was going to become the world's superpower. I use the word because we will not allow you to carry out your plans."

"Is that a threat?"

"No, not at all, it's a promise, and we intend to fulfill it."

"Are you threatening me with war? Is that why the Secretary of Defense and the Chairman of the Joint Chiefs of Staff are sitting next to you?

"No, *you* are the one threatening us and the rest of the world with war. I have my Secretary of Defense and the Chairman of the Joint Chiefs of Staff next to me so that they can tell you that we will defend the United States of America and its allies with every means available to us. And please note, defense includes all and any preventative actions necessary to stop your virus from reaching our shores."

"To be honest, I am now very much inclined to believe the rumors that you are mentally incapable of the office you're holding," Li Lingxin said. "If you attack us, it will be the Armageddon your Christian bible talks about. And you can't win it."

POTUS grinned and shook his head. "I've heard the rumors about my insanity, so don't listen to me. But your advisory committee told you war with us you cannot win. I've got a copy of their report to you right here." POTUS held a stack of papers up for Li to see. "They told you there would be casualties on both sides, but China will cease to exist. I tend to agree with your advisors. Maybe you should heed their advice too."

"Enough! You've got no evidence to prove what you're saying. You sound like a madman. You're fabricating lies to use as an excuse to start a war with my country. I've had enough. This conversation is being recorded; I am going to release it to the media so that the world can see how insane you are. It's insulting. I am about to end this very unpleasant call."

"I'd welcome that because I am going to then release

every bit of information about your virus that I have. In fact, I've got my press release ready. All I must do is push a button, and it will become public in less than thirty seconds right across the world.

"And just so you know, I have all the information. I know all about your experiment in Shanghai. I also know you're deliberately not doing anything to get it completely under control so that you can also play the victim card when your virus kills innocent people across the planet. I know your experts are projecting ten thousand deaths in Shanghai, and I know you said, let me see, here are your words verbatim, 'Ten thousand deaths out of four-hundred and fifty thousand infected in a city of twenty-four million. That's not bad. Sacrificing only ten thousand, albeit our own people, to put China on the world throne is insignificant compared to the benefits China and its people stand to gain.' Your own words, Mr. President."

"I never said anything like that! Who told you I said such a thing?"

"I'll tell you in a minute. Let me tell you a little more about what I know. You've got two thousand people infected and ready to board planes and ships to go and infect the world. Your virus couriers, as you call them. You're planning to start sending them at midday your time. By your own words, 'Yes. At precisely midday Friday, Beijing time, the first virus couriers will leave our shores.' And here's more of your own words on that topic, 'Come Monday morning, wherever in the world you are, this virus will be with you in the same country. You'll have nowhere to run and nowhere to hide. But don't worry, China will rush to your side to aid you. You'll see. We commies are not as bad as your politicians have been telling you all your life.'"

263

"Ridiculous! Outrageous fabrications! I never said anything like that. Who told you that?"

"You did, Mr. President."

"What? Have you lost your mind?"

"No, I don't think so. Listen to this and decide for yourself."

The next moment, the voice of President Li Lingxin, talking to General Yuan during their meeting two days before, came over the speakers, loud and clear.

Li was pale as a ghost. His anger had been replaced by panic.

"Where did you . . .?"

"This man brought it to us."

General Yuan Lee appeared on the screen.

Li's hands started shaking. He ran his tongue over his lips, took a sip of water, and jumped out of his chair. Pointing his shaking finger at Yuan, he started shouting, "Traitor! Traitor! Traitor!" louder and louder. "I'll kill you! I'll kill you for this with my own hands. Traitor!"

The Chinese vice president was next to him and tried to calm him down. Li threw a clumsy punch at him, missed, and plonked down in his chair, elbows on the table and his face in his hands. The international sign of despair.

The President of China stayed in that position for nearly two minutes. In fact, the clock on the recorder would later show that it was precisely one minute and forty-eight seconds without making a single sound.

Scientists say that the human brain processes around seventy thousand thoughts per day, about fifty per minute. During that one minute and forty-eight seconds, President Li's brain probably processed a lot more than one hundred.

When he finally looked up, the audience was looking at

the face of a defeated man—a man with his head on the chopping block.

"What do you want?" he finally whispered.

POTUS nodded and said, "Seven things. It's being emailed to you as we speak so that there are no misunderstandings afterward."

Li Lingxin only nodded.

"One. You keep those virus couriers in China. We want their names, location, photos, and fingerprints within the next two hours.

"Two. You immediately issue an executive order to assign more resources to combat and get control of the epidemic in Shanghai. To save time, we've taken the liberty to draw up the executive order for you. It's in your email. Print it out, sign it, and tell your officials to make it happen.

"Three. You sign the executive order we've sent you to immediately authorize our scientists and doctors and workers to enter China and help your people in Shanghai. Any attempt to block our people to do their work will not be tolerated. Your people will share every bit of research about this virus with our people.

"Four. You'll issue a travel ban on your own country by executive order immediately. The ban will stay in force until *we* have agreed that the Shanghai epidemic is over. No one leaves China unless it's essential. The executive order is in your email. Print it, sign it, and tell your officials to make it so.

"Five. In your email, you'll find the list of names of the people who we deem not fit for service in the government of China because they were all involved in this virus project of yours. Their employment will be ended immediately.

"Six. If they're alive, Benjamin Yatsir and his family will be released immediately. The release order is in your email.

Print it, sign it, and tell your officials to execute it. If they're not alive, you will provide a detailed written explanation about who killed them, how, when, where, and why.

"Seven. When all of the aforementioned actions have been completed, you will sign your own resignation. It's in your email. Print it, sign it, and hand it to the National Congress."

President Li Lingxin had barely moved an eyelid while listening to the first six demands stated by POTUS. Hearing the seventh condition, he had moved slightly in his chair and closed his eyes for a while before nodding almost imperceptibly. The Vice President of China sat through it all in the pose of a Buddha statue with his hands in his lap, his mouth shut, and his eyes closed. His name was on the list of people who had to be fired.

"Questions?" POTUS asked.

Both shook their heads.

"Good. I suggest you get to work right now. We're expecting the signed copies of the executive orders and other documents within the hour."

The screen went dark, and the call ended.

In Washington, D.C., the waiting had begun.

In Beijing, an hour later, President Li Lingxin had signed the last executive order and had been staring at his letter of resignation for almost ten minutes when there was a knock on the door. It was his aide telling him that there were ten marshals in the reception area, demanding to see him immediately.

Epilogue

When Rex arrived in D.C., his entire mission team, which included Yasmin Burke, was there to meet him. Digger was unstoppable, he dragged Catia across the floor, as she tried to hold him back with the leash. When they were a few paces away from Rex, she let go of the leash. Digger took two, three steps and jumped. He landed on Rex's chest, which threw Rex onto his back. He was laughing as Digger whined and licked his face. "I missed you too, boy. I'm so glad to see you. Hey, thanks for taking good care of Catia."

Some of the bystanders were horrified, thinking this big black dog was attacking the man on the floor and was busy ripping his face apart. A few of them, however, saw there was no blood and soon realized what they were looking at was a big black dog that was thrilled to see his master. It took a few minutes before order returned, and Rex was able to get Digger off him and get to his feet to take Catia into his arms and kiss her before greeting the rest of the welcoming party.

Josh had the use of a ten-seat van into which they all piled for the trip to the White House.

Rex smiled when he said to Catia, "I've been told that you've become a kind of celebrity at the White House the last day or so. Care to tell me about it?"

Catia laughed. "Yeah, well, I don't know about the celebrity thing, but I did meet a guy there yesterday morning who looked kind of important to me. He had his own office, a strange, oval-shaped room. I had two cups of the worst coffee imaginable with him and a few others, which I guess were also kind of important but less so than the guy whose office we were in."

By now, everyone was screaming with laughter. But Catia kept her feigned ignorance.

"This guy with the odd-shaped office, what did he look like?"

"I can't remember. I was too tired to take notice of that."

"Can you remember what the others called him?"

"Yep, *that* I can remember. It's the weirdest name I ever heard. His first name is Mister and his surname President. Have you ever . . ." was as far as she got before she succumbed to laughter herself.

"Hey, I saw on the news China got themselves a new president?"

"Yeah, they did. I hope he's going to be less of a jerk than the previous guy," Josh said.

"I'd hope so too," Rex said. "I had enough of Chinese communist maniacs to last me a lifetime."

As they got closer to the White House, Rex asked how it came about that they got invited to meet with the president.

Josh told him, "The moment Li Lingxin resigned, the president stated his desire, and I quote his exact words, 'to meet with that arrogant son of a bitch who led the mission to get Yuan Lee out of China. So that,' and this is still his exact words, 'I can personally see to it that his ass gets thrown into the stockade for insubordination.'"

"I see. Well, I must admit I'm guilty as charged. I can only hope they serve Italian food in prison."

Catia laughed and said, "Don't worry; I've tried to smooth things over for you. He might let you get away with it this time."

Ten minutes later, they arrived at the main gate, where they went through the first of many security checks. It took another half hour before the chief of staff led them past the Secret Service agents into the Oval Office.

The president was a jovial man who enjoyed a good joke. Howard Lawrence, Martin Richardson, the White House Chief of Staff, the Chairman of the Joint Chiefs of Staff, and the Director of National Intelligence were present and to the surprise of them all, John Brandt as well. The moment Rex walked into the Oval Office with the rest of the team, before he got to shake hands with the president, Brandt grabbed his arm and said, "Behave yourself Dalton, or I'll have you shot."

Rex promised.

The president shook his head when the team told them how they managed to pull Yuan out of Shanghai so stealthily that Li Lingxin only became aware that his blue-eyed general had defected when he saw his face on the screen during the video call halfway across the globe.

It was with great relief that they received the news from the president that Benjamin Yatsir and his family were alive and had been released hours before and would be arriving in Hong Kong soon.

Half an hour later, it was time to go; the president's next

meeting was about to start. He had a good chuckle when Brandt wanted to know if Rex was allowed to leave with them instead of being led away in handcuffs.

It was only when they were in Brandt's private plane on the way to CRC headquarters in Arizona that Brandt told them what a hard time they had to persuade the president to keep this meeting a low-key affair and not to invite the media.

It was Howard Lawrence who told him, "Mr. President, they are a covert operations team. They don't want to be known; that's what they do. They definitely don't want media attention at all. I strongly suggest you help them keep it that way. You never know when you're going to need them again for a job of the kind they just did for you, and America, and the world."

A FREE Novella from JC Ryan

vinci-books.com/no-doubt-free

Even paradise has shadows…

When a beautiful woman is found stabbed to death on the tranquil island of Olib, police quickly blame her boyfriend. But, Digger, a big black Dutch Shepherd, a trained military dog, and his alpha, Rex Dalton, a former black ops specialist, know the police were mistaken.

Fact and Fiction

Visitors to Hong Kong would not find Matz Island, nor would they find Sarlin Tower in West Kowloon or anywhere else, or the Matz Enterprises building in the financial district. Likewise, a search of the records of the company registrar's offices for HK Securities or Matz Enterprises would come up empty.

My sincerest apologies to the management of Shanghai Waldorf Astoria for abducting a fictitious general of the PLA from their hotel without their permission and the same apology goes to the management of the Shanghai Pudong International Airport for running an unauthorized fictitious covert operation at their airport.

Researchers would search in vain for data about a virus epidemic in Shanghai during the period covered in this book.

All the characters in the story come from my imagination. As I have said in the foreword, any likeness to actual people, alive or dead, businesses, companies, events, or places is entirely coincidental.

The parts in the book about the history of the Jews of Hong Kong and Shanghai are, to the best of my knowledge, correct.

About China's status as the second most powerful economic and military power in the world, there is no doubt. Neither could there be much doubt about China's expansionism. Nor about how reliant many countries around the globe have become on the products of China's manufacturing industry, which not only include electronics, technology, and clothing products but also pharmaceutical and medical products, and many, many others.

About China's intellectual property piracy costing its victims billions of dollars in lost revenue, there can also be little doubt. In this regard, China has been behaving like a third-world country for decades, with impunity.

China's illicit production and trade in fentanyl and the indescribable suffering its causing is a fact. And so is their refusal to stop manufacturing it despite repeated requests from the USA and other countries to do so. The number of Americans dying from opioid overdoses in 2018 was more than forty-five thousand, many of them from the very deadly synthetic opioid, fentanyl.

Many international security experts agree that China is the biggest threat to world peace and stability.

Much of the contents of the discussions taking place at the White House, described in this book, come from the headlines of the news over the past few months of the proliferating COVID-19 pandemic.

The COVID-19 pandemic has touched the lives of everyone; it has forced us to make changes and rethink what's important. Maybe it is also time for the world's democracies to rethink their relationship with China?

vinci-books.com/delphi-technique

Assassinations, conspiracies, and a mastermind's plot. Can Rex Dalton save Europe from chaos?

A shocking assassination unfolds before Rex Dalton, Catia and Digger's eyes in Greece. Soon they are plunged into a CIA operation to stop a delusional genius from unleashing chaos across Europe in his quest to restore a fallen empire.

Turn the page for a free preview…

The Delphi Technique: Chapter One

A BRUSH PASS

Rhodes City, Rhodes Island, Greece

Day 1

It was Digger's curiosity that inadvertently hauled Rex Dalton and his wife, Catia, out of their Greek Island holiday back into the world of covert operations.

Usually, when the Daltons, both history enthusiasts, went exploring, they preferred to do it on their own, avoiding organized excursions where they had to adhere to strict timelines, predetermined routes, and often unknowledgeable guides. However, this morning after breakfast, when they visited their hotel's information desk to collect information about the Palace of the Grand Master, the lady, speaking perfect Italian, changed their minds. "The guide today is Liza, the most knowledgeable and friendliest you'd encounter anywhere on this island. She'll show you every nook and cranny of that palace, and she won't rush through it. She also speaks five languages: Italian, Greek, English, French, and German."

On the bus on the way from their hotel to the palace, Liza, a petite, good-looking, middle-aged, friendly woman with dark brown hair, told the group, "Rhodes Island is the largest of the Dodecanese islands of Greece." She spoke perfect English with a strong pronunciation of the r, characteristic of the Irish brogue. "Although Dodecanese means twelve islands, there are one hundred and eight islands; only twenty-six are inhabited.

"Rhodes city is the historical capital of the Dodecanese islands. It was once the home of one of the Seven Wonders of the Ancient World, the Colossus of Rhodes. It was a bronze and iron statue, thirty-two meters, about one-hundred and five feet tall. It was erected in honor of the sun god, Helios, for helping them fend off the ruler of Cyprus, who besieged Rhodes in 305 BC.

"It's believed that Rhode Island, in the United States, was named after this island."

She only had to use three of her five languages; English, Italian, and Greek, to inform her audience of twenty-one, excluding Digger. He was seated between Rex and Catia, staring at Liza as if he understood every word she was saying, irrespective of what language she spoke.

When they arrived at the palace, Liza handed out a set of wireless earphones to each member of the group. Then tested that they could all hear her before leading them to the entrance of the Gothic-style building where she stopped to give them a quick overview.

"The Palace of the Grand Master is also known as the Kastello. It was the ancient bastion of the Knights of Rhodes. That's the name given to the Knights Hospitaller, a medieval Catholic military order, after they occupied the Island of Rhodes and established their headquarters here.

"The original palace was constructed in the late 7th century as a Byzantine fortress. After the Knights Hospitaller came to Rhodes in 1309, they converted the fortress into their administrative center and the palace of their Grand Master. The palace was damaged in the earthquake of 1481 and repaired soon afterward, and that's the palace you see here today.

"Italy occupied the island since 1912 and repurposed the palace into this ersatz medieval style. Since the Italians rebuilt it, it served as a holiday residence for the Italian king, Victor Emmanuel III. In 1937, Benito Mussolini, the Fascist dictator from Italy, whose name can still be seen on the large plaque there at the entrance, transformed it into a summer residence for his high-ranking military officers and himself. After the war, it was converted into a museum."

Rex, Catia, and Digger were standing at the back of the semicircle of tourists listening intently to Liza when Rex became aware that Digger wasn't paying attention to Liza anymore.

Digger had a 'Service Dog' sticker attached to his harness. Rex had the necessary paperwork to back it up. But the big black Dutch Shepherd wasn't a service dog. It was the ruse Rex had used ever since inheriting the dog from his friend, Trevor Madigan, a former SAS operative from Australia, who'd been killed in an ambush in Afghanistan in 2014. Digger, an Australian military dog, had been his companion since Trevor asked Rex to take care of him with his dying breath. Rex, mortally scared of dogs since he'd been attacked by one as a small child, had agreed.

And since Rex was a man of his word, he and Digger worked through their issues, and they'd become inseparable mates. Digger had acknowledged him as the alpha in their pack and accepted Catia into the pack from the moment he met her. Digger was Rex's 'best man' at their wedding; he brought the wedding rings in on a dainty white satin cushion balanced on his nose.

Although Rex never learned to give Digger proper commands, like military dog handlers do, over the years, working as a team on many missions, they had developed a unique communications system. Some of Rex's colleagues believed that the two indeed spoke a language that only they understood. However, the truth was, it was always Rex who had learned to be very attentive to Digger's behavior as he was doing now.

Digger had gotten up from where he was sitting between him and Catia and moved forward a few paces. He was staring raptly at someone or something to Catia's left. His ears were pitched forward, and his nose was wiggling a little. Rex could see he wasn't alerting to danger, but something must have stirred his senses and curiosity.

Rex followed the line of Digger's gaze, and about four paces away he found the object of interest; a man, about five foot ten, dressed in faded black Levi's jeans and matching Levi's jacket, dark blue t-shirt, and black sneakers. The olive-skinned man, by Rex's estimates, in his late forties, had a smooth-shaven face, dark hair, prominent cheekbones, and dark-brown eyes, lending him an air of intellect. The man carried a small black nylon shoulder bag, about six by twelve inches, hanging off his right shoulder. Although at first glance, his posture suggested he was relaxed, it was his head moving slowly from side to side, his darting eyes, and the biting of his lower lip that were telltales of anxiety.

Rex was a highly-skilled former black operations operator with, among many other specialist aptitudes, exceptional spycraft skills. He removed his earphones, put his arm around Catia, pulled her close to him, and whispered in her ear, "The man to your left with the black shoulder bag. He's on edge about something."

"How do you—," she started, turned her head slowly, and looked at the man. After a few seconds, she nodded. Catia was a former Mossad agent, skilled in street craft, surveillance, counter-surveillance, hand-to-hand combat, and use of weapons. "What's making him nervous? He's not behaving like he's a fanatic about to launch an attack," Catia whispered.

"No, he's not aggressive. Digger would've warned us. I think he's looking for someone."

"Questions?" Liza asked in three different languages.

A few paces ahead of the Daltons was an old man with a black fedora hat and full-face silver beard, hornbill glasses with thick lenses, in a wheelchair pushed by a young woman with dark hair in her mid-thirties, dressed in dark slacks, sneakers, and sunglasses. Probably his daughter or his caretaker. The old man asked a question which Rex couldn't hear.

But Liza's reply he heard. "Yes, that's correct. Archaeologists found evidence that this was the exact spot where the ancient temple of the Sun-god Helios once stood and, in all likelihood, this is also the spot where the Colossus of Rhodes stood."

The old man asked another inaudible question. Liza replied, "Yes, in 1522, the island became part of the Ottoman Empire, and they used it as a command center."

The old man smiled and thanked her.

"Any other questions?" Liza asked. When there were none, she said, "Please follow me."

The group followed her through the arched entrance and ended in the quad. Other groups varying in number from fifteen to twenty-five were already inside.

While Rex and Catia surreptitiously kept Digger's man in sight, they saw him opening the shoulder bag. They were ready to spring into action if a knife, gun, or bomb trigger came out of the bag—but he only retrieved a pair of sunglasses and a light-blue bucket hat with London printed in black on the front and donned them. He moved the black nylon shoulder bag to his left shoulder.

"Ahh… signaling someone," Rex muttered.

"Ten o'clock. The blond man with the Roma cap," Catia whispered.

Rex spotted a Caucasian male among a group leaving the palace heading toward them. He was in his mid to late forties, blond hair, about six feet tall, blue jeans, black t-shirt, and blue denim jacket. On his head was a black baseball cap with Roma embroidered in gold on the front. A black nylon shoulder bag identical to London's was draped over his left shoulder.

They saw London making eye contact with Roma, and the very slight, almost imperceptible, nod from Roma.

Roma and London were a few seconds and about ten to twelve steps away from making what was known in the lexicon of covert operators as a 'brush pass.' A technique typically used in a crowded public area, where operatives pass information to each other. In a properly executed brush pass, they won't even stop walking; at most, they'd bump into one another. A common method of exchanging the information was for both to carry identical objects, such as a newspaper, briefcase, magazine, or, as in this case, black nylon shoulder bags, containing the information.

Then they saw Roma come to a sudden stop and twist

around. A tall woman with a shock of shoulder-length raven-black hair, large sunglasses, dressed in dark blue jeans with a white blouse and zipped up jean jacket, bumped into him. She apologized, took a step to the side, and kept on walking straight toward London, who stood about five paces away from Rex and Catia.

Roma had turned back to start walking again, but he took only one step, grabbed his heart with both hands, and dropped to his knees without making a sound, then slowly tipped forward on his face.

In different languages, people had started screaming, "Heart attack!" "Is there a doctor here?" "Get an ambulance!"

By now, the tall woman was next to London. She stopped and turned to look back at Roma, then slowly turned sideways, looked at London, and said something to him. He turned to face her looking surprised, raised his sunglasses, and smiled. The woman put her arms around his neck, and he put his arms around her in an embrace.

Digger started growling, and that was when Rex saw the stiletto in her right hand. Rex pulled the quick-release string on Digger's leash and started toward London and the woman, but he was too late. The stiletto had plunged into London's heart.

London screamed and dropped to his knees; his hand clasped over his chest.

The woman tried to rip the shoulder bag off London's shoulder, but couldn't get it off; his arm was inside the loop of the strap. The woman saw Rex and Digger coming, turned, and ran toward the exit, the stiletto still in her hand.

London toppled forward onto the gray tiles of the court-yard floor.

"Digger, follow! Don't attack! Catia, help him," he pointed to London. "I'm going after the woman."

As Rex set out after the woman, she was already more than fifteen paces away. Mass hysteria erupted as people started yelling, "Terrorists!" "Attack!" "Hide!"

Digger was about three yards behind her, barking and yelping. Rex was worried that the woman, no doubt a professional killer, would hurt Digger with that stiletto if he came too close to her. But Digger must've understood the command not to attack as he kept his distance.

As she exited the palace gate at full speed, she turned left and headed for the nearby copse of trees.

Rex was closing in on her quickly. He was about seven yards away from her when she stopped and turned to face him and Digger with the stiletto in her left hand, swinging it in a wide defensive arc in front of her.

Rex didn't slow down. Digger had stopped out of her reach but kept on growling and snarling.

With her right hand, she reached inside her denim jacket.

A gun!

Rex raced past Digger.

When the woman's right hand reappeared, there was a .22 Beretta pistol in it, and she was about to turn it on Rex. He was three steps away from her; he had the momentum, he leaped into the air and kicked her in the solar plexus with both feet. The force of the kick body-slammed her into the tree behind her with a grunting thud. Her sunglasses and the stiletto were gone. She had light-gray eyes, the eeriest, most lifeless eyes he'd ever seen. *Contact lenses.* She was shocked and bewildered and looked as if she was going to lose consciousness. The gun was still in her right hand, which was crossed over her breasts.

Digger was next to him.

"Stand down, Digger!" Rex got up and took a step forward to disarm her. He was reaching for the gun when her hand twisted slightly, pointing the gun up at her face, and she pulled the trigger. The bullet went through the bottom of her chin, straight through her mouth into her brain. Her body fell sideways.

"Damn!"

Rex didn't touch her or the gun. Below her mane of black hair, he noticed a patch of blonde hair—she'd been wearing a wig. He took his satellite phone out and snapped a few photos. Then he removed the wig and took a few more.

He looked around; there was no one outside who could've seen what just happened. He wasn't sure if that was necessarily a good thing. He'd have to tell the police what happened, and a corroborating eyewitness would've been very helpful. Even so, the absence of onlookers gave him the opportunity to search the body for identification quickly. But the search confirmed Rex's suspicion that the woman was a professional when it only produced two hundred euros in cash, which he left in the jacket pocket where he found it, and an iPhone which was switched off.

He had a decision to make; take the phone or leave it? *Why would you want to do that? What are you going to do with the phone? This is not your case. Yes, but she killed at least one person and was about to kill me.* His thoughts were interrupted by Digger's yelp—a sign that he was distressed. He patted Digger's back, "Don't worry, it's over, buddy, you can relax now." He clipped the leash on. He stood, looked at the phone, which he still had in his hand, and shoved it into a side pocket of his cargo pants. "Let's go and check on Catia."

When they arrived back in the courtyard, Digger snarled and growled a path through the crowd for him and Rex, sat down next to Catia, and started nosing her while making soft whining noises to comfort her.

Catia was sitting on the ground. London's upper body was resting on her lap. Her hands and face and clothes were covered in his blood. He was dead. She put her arm around Digger's neck and whispered, "Thanks, Digger. I'm okay."

Rex moved London's body off her lap and laid him gently on the tile floor. Then he stood and pulled Catia up into an embrace and whispered, "It's over. The police should be here soon."

"Thank you. I'm okay now." She looked in the direction where Roma had gone down. Another crowd had gathered there. "Let's see if we can help."

It didn't take long to find out that Roma was dead. There was no blood.

"A massive heart attack, I suspect," said a paramedic from England.

Rex and Catia agreed but didn't tell him what they thought caused it.

Three people dead in less than three minutes was more than enough to ruin everyone's day, if not their entire holiday. Within minutes the palace had been shut down. No one could come in or go out. The police were on their way.

All but a few had their cellphones out, taking photos and videos, making calls and sending text messages. Rex and Catia made no calls and sent no text messages. Still, as inconspicuously as possible, under the pretext of typing messages, they both took photos of Roma and London and tried to capture as many of the other faces in the courtyard as they could on video.

"Let's find a quiet place," Catia said after a few minutes. "I have to tell you something."

With all the people still milling around in anguish and uncertainty, many of the benches beneath the arcades of the quad were empty. As they made their way to an empty bench, they passed within two paces of the old man in the wheelchair and his minder. The old man was staring quietly and impassively at them as they passed. Rex couldn't help but wonder what was going through the old man's mind, he must have been in shock. The woman with him nodded at them but didn't say anything.

They picked an isolated bench and sat down with Digger between them. Catia noticed Digger's intent stare at the old man and the woman who were now about fifteen yards away. She reached out and scratched Digger's back, "Don't worry, Digger, they'll be okay now." She turned to Rex. "It never ceases to amaze me how sensitive he is to people's emotions."

"It's mindboggling isn't it," Rex said.

"Okay," Catia said, "here's what I want to tell you. In the few seconds, while the man I tried to help was still conscious, he asked me to take a USB flash drive out of his shoulder bag and give it to the CIA man..."

"CIA man?"

"Yes, apparently the blond man with the Roma cap was CIA. I didn't want to rummage through his bag in full view of everyone, so I just shoved his bag into mine. I hope in the turmoil no one noticed."

Grab your copy...
vinci-books.com/delphi-technique

About the Author

JC Ryan is a bestselling author renowned for his intricate espionage, archaeological thrillers, and conspiracy mysteries. With over 30 acclaimed novels, including the popular Rex Dalton K9 Thrillers, Rossler Foundation Mysteries, and Carter Devereux Mystery Thrillers, Ryan has captivated readers around the globe.

Drawing from his diverse professional background—as a military officer, lawyer, and IT manager—Ryan creates compelling narratives that skillfully blend historical accuracy with thrilling adventure. He is celebrated as a master storyteller, known for crafting riveting plots, meticulous historical details, and engaging, multidimensional characters. Ryan's meticulous research lends authenticity and depth to each story, immersing readers in richly constructed worlds filled with intrigue, suspense, and adventure.

Fans of David Baldacci, Lee Child's Jack Reacher, Tom Clancy's Jack Ryan, Nelson DeMille's John Corey, Vince Flynn's Mitch Rapp, Mark Greaney's Gray Man, Gregg Hurwitz's Orphan X, Robert Ludlum's Jason Bourne, Daniel Silva's Gabriel Allon, Brad Taylor's Pike Logan, Brad Thor's Scot Harvath, James Rollins' Sigma Force, Steve Berry's Cotton Malone, and Dan Brown's Robert Langdon will find JC Ryan's novels equally compelling and unforgettable.

When not writing, Ryan enjoys spending time with his college sweetheart, whom he married in 1978. They are proud parents of two daughters, have two sons-in-law, and are grandparents to two grandchildren.